Deliverance

James Dickey

BLOOMSBURY

Series editors: Maxim Jakubowski and Adrian Wootton

This paperback edition first published in 2005

The moral right of the author has been asserted

Bloomsbury Publishing Plc, 36 Soho Square, London, W1D 3QY

A CIP catalogue record is available from the British Library

ISBN 0 7475 7869 9
9780747578697

10 9 8 7 6 5 4 3 2 1

All papers used by Bloomsbury Publishing are natural,
recyclable products made from wood grown in
well-managed forests. The manufacturing processes
conform to the environmental regulations of the
country of origin.

Typeset by Hewer Text Ltd, Edinburgh
Printed and bound in Great Britain by
CPI Antony Rowe, Chippenham and Eastbourne

www.bloomsbury.com

*Il existe à base de la vie humaine
un principe d'insuffisance.*

GEORGES BATAILLE

*The pride of thine heart hath deceived thee,
thou that dwellest in the clefts of the rock,
whose habitation is high; that saith in his heart,
Who shall bring me down to the ground?*

OBADIAH VERSE 3

Before

I T UNROLLED slowly, forced to show its colors, curling and snapping back whenever one of us turned loose. The whole land was very tense until we put our four steins on its corners and laid the river out to run for us through the mountains 150 miles north. Lewis' hand took a pencil and marked out a small strong X in a place where some of the green bled away and the paper changed with high ground, and began to work downstream, northeast to southwest through the printed woods. I watched the hand rather than the location, for it seemed to have power over the terrain, and when it stopped for Lewis' voice to explain something, it was as though all streams everywhere quit running, hanging silently where they were to let the point be made. The pencil turned over and pretended to sketch in with the eraser an area that must have been around fifty miles long, through which the river hooked and cramped.

'When they take another survey and rework this map,' Lewis said, 'all this in here will be blue. The dam at Aintry has already been started, and when it's finished next spring the river will back up fast. This whole valley will be under water. But right now it's wild. And I *mean* wild; it looks like something up in Alaska. We really ought to go up there before the real estate people get hold of it and make it over into one of their heavens.'

I leaned forward and concentrated down into the invisible shape he had drawn, trying to see the changes that would come, the nighttime rising of dammed water bringing a new lake up with its choice lots, its marinas and beer cans, and also trying to visualize the land as Lewis said it was at that moment, unvisited and free. I breathed in and out once, consciously; my body, particularly the back and arms, felt ready for something like this. I looked around the bar and then back into the map, picking up the river where we would enter it. A little way to the southwest the paper blanched.

'Does this mean it's higher here?' I asked.

'Yes,' Lewis said, looking quickly at me to see if I saw he was being tolerant.

Ah, he's going to turn this into something, I thought. A lesson. A moral. A life principle. A Way.

'It must run through a gorge or something' was all he said though. 'But we can get through that in a day, easy. And the water should be good, in that part especially.'

I didn't have much idea what good meant in the way of river water, but for it to seem good to Lewis it would have to meet some very definite standards. The way he went about things was strictly his own; that was mainly what he liked about doing them. He liked particularly to take some extremely specialized and difficult form of sport – usually one he could do by himself – and evolve a personal approach to it which he could then expound. I had been through this with him in flycasting, in archery and weight lifting and spelunking, in all of which he had developed complete mystiques. Now it was canoeing. I settled back and came out of the map.

Bobby Trippe was there, across from me. He had smooth thin hair and a high pink complexion. I knew him least well of the others at the table, but I liked him a good deal, even so. He was pleasantly cynical and gave me the impression that he shared some kind of understanding with me that neither of us was to take Lewis too seriously.

'They tell me that this is the kind of thing that gets hold of middle-class householders every once in a while,' Bobby said. 'But most of them just lie down till the feeling passes.'

'And when most of them lie down they're at Woodlawn before they think about getting up,' Lewis said.

'It's the old idea that you're going to get yourself in shape, one of these days. Just like you were when you were on the B-team in high school and had to do all those wind sprints. Some few people may jog, once in a while. But who runs sprints? Who goes down rivers?'

'Well, you've got a chance to go down one,' Lewis said. 'The chance is coming up this weekend, if you can get Friday off. Either Ed and I will go, or we all four can go. But you have to let me know right now, so I can get the other canoe.'

I liked Lewis; I could feel myself getting caught up again in his capricious and tenacious enthusiasms that had already taken me bow-hunting and varmint-calling with him, and down into a small, miserably cold cave where there was one dead, crystalline frog. Lewis was the only man I knew who could do with his life exactly what he wanted to. He talked continuously of resettling in New Zealand or South Africa or Uruguay, but he had to be near the rental property he had inherited, and I didn't much think he would ever leave. But in his mind he was always leaving, always going somewhere, always doing something else. These techniques and mystiques had built up in him something that impressed me a good deal, even so. He was not only self-determined; he was determined. He was one of the best tournament archers in the state and, even at the age of thirty-eight or -nine, one of the strongest men I had ever shaken hands with. He lifted weights and shot arrows every day in a special kind of alternating rhythm and as a result was so steady that he could easily hold a sixty-pound bow at full draw for twenty seconds. I once saw him kill a quail with an aluminum target arrow at forty yards, the arrow diving into the back feathers at the last possible instant.

So I usually went with him whenever he asked me. I had a bow that he helped me pick out, and a few tags and odds of secondhand equipment, and it was enjoyable walking in the woods with Lewis, when the weather was good, as it usually is in our part of the South in hunting season. Because it took place in such pleasant country, and because of Lewis, I liked field archery – with its faint promise of one day killing a deer – better than golf. But it was really Lewis. He was the only man I knew determined to get something out of life who had both the means and the will to do it, and it interested me to see how, as an experiment, this turned out.

I was not much on theories, myself. But I had a good feeling about this trip. After so much shooting at paper images of deer, it was exciting to think of encountering a real one.

'How, exactly, do we get to the river in the first place?' Drew Ballinger asked.

'There's a little nothing town up here, just past the high ground,' Lewis said, 'name of Oree. We can put in there and come out in Aintry a couple of days later. If we get on the water late Friday, we can be back here the middle of Sunday afternoon, maybe in time for the last half of the pro game on TV.'

'There's one thing that bothers me,' Drew said. 'We don't really know what we're getting into. There's not one of us knows a damned thing about the woods, or about rivers. The last boat I was in was my father-in-law's Chris-Craft, up on Lake Bodie. I can't even row a boat straight, much less paddle my own or anybody else's canoe. What business have I got up there in those mountains?'

'Listen,' Lewis said, knocking on the air with his foreknuckle, 'you'll be in more danger on the four-lane going home tonight than you'd ever be on the river. Somebody might jump the divider. Who knows?'

'I mean,' Bobby said, 'the whole thing does seem kind of crazy.'

'All right,' Lewis said. 'Let me demonstrate. What are you going to be doing this afternoon?'

'Well,' Bobby thought a minute. 'Most likely I'll see a couple of new people about mutual funds. I have to draw up some papers and get them notarized.'

'How about you, Drew?'

'See some more route salesmen. We're making a cooler count to figure out who's doing what, and where we're falling short. We're trying to find ways to up the cold-bottle sales, the same as always. Sometimes they're up, sometimes they're down. Right now they're down.'

'Ed?'

'Oh,' I said. 'Take some photographs for Kits Textile Mills. Kitt'n Britches. Cute girl in our britches stroking her pussy. A real cat, you understand.'

'Too bad,' Lewis said, and grinned, although talk about sex was never something he seemed to enjoy. He had made his point without saying anything about the afternoon. He looked around the suburban bar and brought his hand under his chin, waiting for the other two to decide.

I thought that they probably wouldn't go. They were day-to-day happy enough; they were not bored in the way Lewis and I were bored, and Bobby, particularly, seemed to enjoy the life he was in. He came, I believe, from some other part of the South, maybe Louisiana, and since he had been around – since I had known him, anyway – had seemed to do well. He was very social and would not have been displeased if someone had called him a born salesman. He liked people, he said, and most of them liked him – some genuinely and some merely because he was a bachelor and a good dinner or party guest. He was always around. Everyplace I went I saw him, or caught a glimpse of him going by or leaving. If I was at a driving range or supermarket I would be sure to see him; when I thought beforehand I would see him, I would, and, if I didn't, I'd also see him. He was a pleasant surface human being, though I had heard him blow up at a party once and hadn't forgotten it. I still don't know what the cause was, but his face changed in a dreadful way, like the rage of a weak king. But that was only once.

Drew Ballinger was a straightforward quiet fellow. He was devoted to his family, particularly to his little boy Pope, who had some kind of risen hornlike blood blister on his forehead that his eyebrow grew out of and around in a way to make you realize the true horrors of biology. He worked as a sales supervisor for a big soft-drink company and he believed in it and the things it said it stood for with his very soul. He kept a copy of the company history on his living room coffee table at home, and the only time I ever saw him get mad was over a rival and newer company's sales claims having to do with its drink's weight-reducing properties. 'Goddamned liars,' he had said. 'They've got just as many calories as we have, and we can prove it.'

But Lewis and I were different, and were different from each other. I had nothing like his drive, or his obsessions. Lewis wanted to be immortal. He had everything that life could give, and he couldn't make it work. And he couldn't bear to give it up or see age take it away from him, either, because in the meantime he might be able to find what it was he wanted, the thing that must be there, and that must be subject to the will. He was the kind of man who tries by any means – weight lifting, diet, exercise, self-help manuals from taxidermy to modern art – to hold on to his body and mind and improve them, to rise above time. And yet he was also the first to take a chance, as though the burden of his own laborious immortality were too heavy to bear, and he wanted to get out of it by means of an accident, or what would appear to others to be an accident. A year or two before, he had stumbled and crawled for three miles to get out of the woods and back to his car and then driven it home using a stick to work the gas because his right ankle was so painfully broken. I visited him in the hospital mainly because he had asked me to go to the woods with him and I hadn't been able to go, and I asked him how he felt. 'It's luxury,' he said. 'For a while I don't have to lift weights, or work out on the bag.'

I glanced over at him. He had a face like a hawk, but it was a special kind of hawk. Instead of the front of his head seeming to be made from top to bottom, his looked like it had been palm-molded into a long-nosed shape from the sides. He was clay red and sandy haired, with a whitish patch back up toward the crown of his head, where the other hair was darker.

'Well well,' he said. 'What about it?'

I was very glad I was going. While I thought about Drew and his cooler count, I began to see my own afternoon. The studio lights came on without my wanting them to, and I heard the crackle of newspapers under my feet. I saw what the model would probably look like, though I had seen only a photograph of her, standing in the second row of a nearby small town beauty contest and ringed by

7

the red pencil of Thad Emerson, my partner. He had gotten together with her by means of the newspaper and the chamber of commerce and taken her up to Kitts Mills, where they'd liked her. The agency Kitts used had also liked her well enough, though to the account man she hadn't seemed 'quite professional,' and now we were going to use her. She would be the half-conventionally-beautiful focus of a thousand decisions and compromises that would eventually end up in a small-circulation trade magazine, looking much like the other ads in it. I saw what she would be and what we would do with her, and the layouts I would mess with for hours, and the endless hassles with the agency, the billing, the paraphernalia of bookkeeping and the rest of it, and I was glad I was going with Lewis. In a curious connection between my time with Lewis and my ordinary time, I looked down at the map again, but now as though it were a layout.

It was certainly not much from the standpoint of design. The high ground, in tan and an even paler tone of brown, meandered in and out of various shades and shapes of green, and there was nothing to call you or stop you on one place or the other. Yet the eye could not leave the whole; there was a harmony of some kind. Maybe, I thought, it's because this tries to show what exists. And also because it represents something that is going to change, for good. There, near my left hand, a new color, a blue, would seep upward into the paper, and I tried to move my mind there and nowhere else and imagine a single detail that, if I didn't see it that weekend, I never would; tried to make out a deer's eye in the leaves, tried to pick up a single stone. The world is easily lost.

'I'll go,' Drew said, 'if I can bring a Martin along.'

'Sure, bring it,' Lewis said. 'It would be kind of good to hear, way off up in there.'

Without having any talent, as he would be the first to tell you, Drew played mighty well, through sheer devotion. He had been at it with guitar and banjo – mostly guitar – for twelve years, and went in for all the really hard finger-picking stuff; Reverend Gary Davis, Dave Van Ronk, Merle Travis, Doc Watson.

'I've got a stove-in reconditioned Martin I picked up from some school kid,' Drew said. 'Don't worry, I wouldn't bring my number one.'

'OK, fellow primitives,' Bobby said. 'But I insist on some creature comforts. Namely liquor.'

'Bring all you like,' Lewis said. 'In fact, the sensation of going down white water about half-drunk is not to be missed.'

'You taking your bow, Lewis?' I asked.

'You know it,' he said. 'And if one of us stabs a deer we can eat the meat and pack the hide and the head out, and I'll cure the hide and mount the head.'

'Atomic-survival stuff, eh?' Bobby said.

'The best kind.'

It sounded fine to me, though I knew it would be poaching, this early in the fall. But I also knew Lewis would do what he said; these were some of the other things he had learned.

Waitresses in sheer net tights and corsages kept staring down into the map. It was time to go. Lewis took off the weight of two steins and the map leapt shut.

'Can you get your car, Drew?' Lewis asked, as we stood up together.

'Sure,' he said. 'One of 'em's mine, and my boy's not old enough to drive it.'

'Ed and I'll meet you-all early Friday, around six-thirty, where Will's Ferry Road runs into the four-lane, at the big new Will's Plaza Shopping Center. I'll call Sam Steinhauser this evening and see what shape his canoe's in. Most of the other stuff I've got. Wear tennis shoes. Bring liquor and an open mind.'

We went.

I was walking in the sun and thinking. I was a little late, but it didn't matter. Thad and I ran a no-sweat shop, as Thad once said in a phrase that he was happy to see get around town and get back to us in a short time. We had had the studio about ten years, having bought it from the fellow – now about seventy – who'd founded it, and who was now realizing a lifelong ambition of making drawings of tourists in Cuernavaca. It was, in a way, a pleasure to work at Emerson-Gentry, at least compared to the way things were in the other studios around town. Thad had developed into a reasonably good businessman, and I was better than adequate, when I worked at it, as a graphics consultant and director. The studio was full of gray affable men who had tried it in New York and come back South to live and die. They were competent, though we demanded no very high standard from them, and when they weren't working at layouts and paste-ups they would sit tilted back from the drawing board with their hands behind their heads, gazing at whatever same thing was there. Now and then we also had boys just out of art school – or, rarely, engineering school – who would have an amazingly good design idea about once out of six months and the rest of the time come up with nothing but trying-for-it absurdities. None of these worked for us for very long; they either used us for the purpose of getting some experience and then moved on to better jobs, or they drifted through us back out into the world and tried something else. During the time Thad and I had had the shop, we had also hired a small number of people who believed themselves real artists and were willing to do what they openly considered hackwork in order to do their own work in the evenings and on weekends and holidays. These were the saddest of all: sadder than the ex-bomber copilot now drawing-in sacks of fertilizer; sadder than the young design school graduate who sees that he must leave the business, because he can't move up in it. One was a middle-aged local fellow who hung Utrillo prints in his cubicle and tried to keep up the appearance of being in a kind of temporary position or way station that would remember him after he left. But he never would have left, if we had kept him on. When we let him out, he went to another studio for a while and then just disappeared. I never saw anyone so passionately interested in art. Unlike Lewis, he had only one interest, and he believed he had the talent to become more than a local artist; for local artists and Sunday painters he had nothing but contempt and refused to go to any of their shows. He was always talking about applying Braque's collage techniques to the layouts we were getting ready for fertilizer trade books and wood-pulp processing plants, and it was a great relief to me not to have to listen to any of that anymore.

For we had grooved, modestly, as a studio. I knew it and was glad of it; I had no wish to surpass our limitations, or to provide a home for geniuses on their way to the Whitney or to suicide. I knew that our luck was good and would probably hold; that our success was due mainly to the lack of graphic sophistication in the area. What we had, we could handle, and we were in a general business situation that provided for everybody pretty well, even those shading down toward incompetence, so long as they were earnest and on time. The larger agencies in the city and the local branches of the really big New York and Chicago agencies didn't give us much work. We made a halfhearted pitch for some of it, but when they were not enthusiastic we – or at least Thad and I

– were happy to take up where we had been. The agencies we liked and understood best were those which were most like us – those that were not pressing, that were taking care of their people. We worked on small local accounts – banks, jewelry stores, supermarkets, radio stations, bakeries, textile mills. We would ride with these.

Going under a heavy shade tree, I felt the beer come up, not into my throat but into my eyes. The day sparkled painfully, seeming to shake on some kind of axis, and through this a leaf fell, touched with unusual color at the edges. It was the first time I had realized that autumn was close. I began to climb the last hill.

I was halfway up when I noticed how many women there were around me. Since I had passed the Gulf station on the corner I hadn't seen another man anywhere. I began to look for one in the cars going by, but for the few more minutes it took to get to the building, I didn't see a one. The women were almost all secretaries and file clerks, young and semi-young and middle-aged, and their hair styles, piled and shellacked and swirled and horned, and almost every one stiff, filled me with desolation. I kept looking for a decent ass and spotted one in a beige skirt, but when the girl turned her barren, gum-chewing face toward me, it was all over. I suddenly felt like George Holley, my old Braque man, must have felt when he worked for us, saying to himself in any way he could, day after day, I am with you but not of you. But I knew better. I was of them, sure enough, as they stretched out of sight before me up the hill and into the building. And I was right in one of the lines that ceremoniously divided around a modern fountain full of dimes and pennies.

The door swung and a little beehived girl ducked under my arm into the cold air. The lunch hour exhaled from several women and me with a long low sound as we revolved in the door. Muzak entered the elevator and we rose on 'Vienna Blood,' played with lots of strings. Between the beginning and end of one chorus my stomach fell like a stone. I let out my belt a notch and the beer settled as I wiped my forehead on the inner part of my jacket sleeve. At the sixth floor there were only two female survivors and myself; the others worked in the larger, open bay offices on the lower floors – insurance companies. I walked down the clean, walled-in corridor to the horse-headed glass of our studio. The only good thing Holley had done for us was to turn one of Braque's birds into a Pegasus. It flew delicately aside and around me as I went in.

'Any calls?'

'Not any awfully interesting ones, Mr. Gentry. Shadow-Row Shell Homes would like to see the comps next week. You had a request for a job interview from a young lady who wouldn't give her name, says she'll call back. And the model is here for Kitts.'

'Thank you very much,' I said to Peg Wyman, who had been with us the whole time and showed it. 'I'll go on back.'

I went down the office hallway taking my coat off pinch by pinch. It was the first time I had thought to notice that the hall was inside a larger hall, part of the length of the building and the floor. It was a very tasteful place, though. Thad and I had really nice offices with tensor lights all over the place, and the longer-lasting or more highly paid art directors had small offices or at least cubicles. The rest of the studio was a large open bay with drawing boards, and I watched for a minute the gray and bald heads in their places, the shiny black ones, the curly ones and lank ones returning. I may not have had everything to do with this – with creating this – I said to myself in a silent voice that was different from my usual silent voice, but I have had something to do with it. Never before had I had such a powerful sense of being in a place I had created. Alton Rogers would not be sitting there, dreaming of flying the Hump in the old days. If it weren't for me, George Holley's cubicle would still be full of Utrillo. The arrangement of heads and fingers and glasses would not be like it is, at this moment, if it were not for me. These people would probably be working for somebody else, but they would not be here. They are in some way my captives; their lives – part of some, most of some – are being spent here.

But then so was mine. I was not really thinking about their being my prisoners, but of being my own. I went into the office and hung up my coat, and for a second put one hand down on my drawing board, as though posing for a house ad: Vice-President Gentry makes important decision. It would be one of those poses that aspires to show you that such decisions by middle-aged responsible men are an important factor in maintaining the economy and the morale of the whole Western world. This could have been true, so far as I was able to tell. Probably in some ways it was.

There were piles of roughs, among which sat my wife and my little boy, Dean. There were stacks of copy, approved and tentative, from agencies, and I made a note to remind Thad that certain of the less inventive outfits were pressing us into service as agency art departments, which neither of us liked at all. And I called Jack Waskow, the photographer, to see if he was ready for me. He wasn't, quite, and I sat down to see if there was anything I could do right quick, anything I could get out of the way.

Before I made a move, though, I sat for maybe twenty seconds, failing to feel my heart beat, though at that moment I wanted to. The feeling of the inconsequence of whatever I would do, of anything I would pick up or think about or turn to see was at that moment being set in the very bone marrow. How does one get through this? I asked myself. By doing something that is at hand to be done was the best answer I could give; that and not saying anything about the feeling to anyone. It was the old mortal, helpless, time-terrified human feeling, just the same. I had had a touch or two before, though it was more likely to come with my family, for I could find ways to keep busy at the studio, or at least to seem busy, which was harder, in some cases, than doing real work. But I was really frightened, this time. It had me for sure, and I knew that if I managed to get up, through the enormous weight of lassitude, I would still move to the water cooler, or speak to Jack Waskow or Thad, with a sense of being someone else, some poor fool who lives as unobserved and impotent as a ghost, going through the only motions it has.

I picked up a rough I had done of the Kitts' ad. If there was one thing I felt a reasonable certainty about, it was my ability to get the elements of a layout into some kind of harmonious relationship. I didn't as a rule like too traditional, cheap Boraxy ads, with screaming typeforms and an obvious and chillingly commercial use of sex, nor did I like the overly 'creative' kind of ad, with some farfetched or gimmicked-up formula or calculated craziness. I liked harmoniousness and a situation where the elements didn't fight with each other or overwhelm each other. I had won a couple of modest awards for art direction around town, where admittedly the competition was not of the first class, and they were hanging in the office. I took a close look at the Kitts' layout, which was for a line of artificial silk women's underwear called Kitt'n Britches. It showed a girl in nothing but panties with her back to the camera looking over her shoulder. As we had planned it, a kitten's head was to appear under her chin as she held it, and I was a little worried that, with a photograph large enough to show the britches, the cat's head might be too small. We could crop in, of course; we didn't actually need to show the girl's *feet*, as the account man had said, but I kind of wanted to. I like feet, for one thing, and a whole being in a photograph is in an odd way more effective, a lot of times, than someone who has been cut up with scissors. We had gone back and forth with the agency about this, and with the Kitts' sales manager, an incredible countrified jerk who had originally had the idea of using a real girl in a situation like the one in the Coppertone ad, where the Scotty is pulling the little girl's bathing suit down off her bare behind. 'If we did it with a cat,' he said, 'it would also show that the pants won't run or tear.' The agency and I had managed to talk him out of this, explaining that a reputable trade book wouldn't run it, and we couldn't find a decent-looking girl who would pose for it, either. He agreed with us, finally, but he still wanted more obvious sex in the ad than I did, and had told me when we broke up that 'Whoever we get should really fill out those panties.'

I fiddled with the elements of the rough, bringing the girl forward and moving her back, until I thought I had what was a good compromise, with the type centering around the girl's hips. Who will she be? I wondered. Whose body will try to fill out these lines I've put down? I went in to look at the studio.

Thad was there, moving things and people around with his expert, interior-decorator's formality and fussiness. The model was sitting in a camp chair, shading her eyes against the lights. She was in a checked black-and-white robe that – at least to me – had something unexpectedly carnivallike about it, and she looked nothing like a carnival girl, thank God. Around her the room seemed to swarm and tremble with men, though there were actually only five of us, including the lighting technician. Thad's secretary, a mean-mouthed little woman named Wilma, came in with the kitten we'd got from the SPCA, holding it in the crook

16

of an arm as though she were going to be photographed herself. Max Fraley, one of the paste-up men, went to get a saucer of milk for it. I sat on the edge of a table and undid my tie. Inside the bright hardship of the lights was a peculiar blue, wholly painful, unmistakably man-made, unblinkable thing that I hated. It reminded me of prisons and interrogations, and that thought jumped straight at me. That was one side of it, all right, and the other was pornography. I thought of those films you see at fraternity parties and in officers' clubs where you realize with terror that when the girl drops the towel the camera is not going to drop with it discreetly, as in old Hollywood films, following the bare feet until they hide behind a screen, but is going to stay and when the towel falls, move in; that it is going to destroy someone's womanhood by raping her secrecy; that there is going to be nothing left.

Thad asked the girl to stand up. Her feet were strongtoed and healthy and a little tomboyish; I would have bet money that she came from a farm. She had a fine, open, gray-eyed face with a few freckles. She was somebody I didn't mind looking in the eyes. And straight into them, too, so that if she'd permit it, the look would go deep. I did this, because on the spur of the moment I wanted to. There was a peculiar spot, a kind of tan slice, in her left eye, and it hit me with, I knew right away, strong powers; it was not only recallable, but would come back of itself. One hand, also strong and quiet, was holding the throat of her robe closed, and she put her head back – very far back, almost like an acrobat – and and shook her hair so that it hung free of her neck. All at once two more secretaries materialized like nurses or prison matrons, all revolving around the model. Thad had her stand in the chalk marks from around which we had cleared the newspapers. Her feet gripped the cold cork floor. She held out her arms, and Wilma slipped off her robe. She had soft long

17

legs, not as muscular as I would have thought, with those feet, but very shapely and harmonious, though it struck me that they were not firm enough to last for long. Her bare back had a helpless, undeveloped look about it, and this seemed to me more womanly and endearing than anything else about her except her eye. She filled the Kitt'n Britches well enough, but there was nothing especially provocative about the way she did it; she might have been someone's sister, and that was not at all the effect we wanted. Not knowing exactly how I wanted to change the pose, or if it could be changed, I stepped over and touched her.

She turned and looked into my face at close range, and the gold-glowing mote fastened on me; it was more gold than any real gold could possibly be; it was alive, and it saw me. Standing this close, she changed completely; she looked like someone who had come to womanhood in less than a minute. Her hands were folded across her breasts in a way that managed to give the effect of casualness, and Max was not quite sure of how to hand her the cat. She took it with one hand, and in doing so, protecting herself with the other, she simply took her left breast in her hand, and the sight of that went through me, a deep and complex male thrill, as if something had touched me in the prostate. She fixed her feet in the marks, wavering for a moment throwing light off her shoulders, the filaments of the bulbs spitting and buzzing about her, and then seemed to settle.

We got what Thad thought might be some good stuff, though he really didn't believe, he said, that the girl was good enough to use again. I went back to the office and did something I hadn't done since the early days of the studio. I brainstormed with myself for the rest of the afternoon. Nothing much came of it, but my mind was jumping quickly from one thing to another, and the associations were very good ones. I left a sheaf of roughs

18

with Thad and told him I needed Friday off to do some work around the house. He didn't argue with me. We had made it as it was; we had made it.

September 14th

THERE WAS something about me that usually kept me from dreaming, or maybe kept me from remembering what I had dreamed; I was either awake or dead, and I always came back slowly. I had the feeling that if it were perfectly quiet, if I could hear nothing, I would never wake up. Something in the world had to pull me back, for every night I went down deep, and if I had any sensation during sleep, it was of going deeper and deeper, trying to reach a point, a line or border.

This time the wind woke me, and I dragged upward and tried, with the instinct of survival, to get clear of where I had been, one more time. I was used to hearing Martha's breath bring me back, for she breathed heavily, but this time it was the wind. First the wind by itself and then the wind ringing a little set of metal figures on strings that Martha had put out on the patio – bronze figures of birds surrounding an owl which, because of a long wind vane attached to him, moved when the air moved and touched the others, making a chiming sound something like the one made by the Chinese glass windbells that everybody used to have in the thirties, when I was growing up. It was a small, inconstant sound, a lovely sound, I always thought, and as I came up from the sleep-dark to the real dark of the room, I had an idea that it might evoke something, and I lay with the room becoming actual around me, in the dark, beside my wife, in a body.

I reached for Martha, as I always did, and her head stirred under the towel she wore at night. I held her shoulder lightly, and it was then I remembered I was going with Lewis. The routine I was used to pulled at me, but something in me rose daringly above it, full of fear and feeling weak and incompetent but excited. I took Martha in my arms to see if she would try to get away and back to sleep, or come to me for warmth, and then go back.

She was a thin girl whom I had married fifteen years before; she had been working as a surgical nurse. The fact that she might or might not be pretty did not occur to me at all, though friends, without great enthusiasm or conviction, used to tell me she was. But the question of beauty, beyond certain very obvious considerations, never really interested me in women; what I looked for and felt for was the spark, the absolutely personal connection, and when I found a genuine form of it, small but steady, I had married it. There was nothing to regret about this, and I didn't regret it. She was a good wife and a good companion, a little tough, but with a toughness that got things done. She was genuinely proud of my being vice-president of a company, and she insisted on believing that I had talent as an artist, though I had none. I was a mechanic of the graphic arts, and when I could get the problem to appear mechanical to me, and not the result of inspiration, I could do something with it. On this principle I had done a few big collage-things for the living room, made from torn-up posters, movie magazines, sports headlines and the like. And that, as far as art was concerned, was it. Remembering these, I thought that it might be that Martha cared for them not so much because I had done them, but because they represented some side of me she didn't know. But it was a wrong faith on her part, and, though I never told her how I felt, I never encouraged it. I drew on her, and she slid to me.

'What time is it?' she said.

'Six,' I said, looking at the frail hands of the clock by the bed as they pulsed and glowed. 'Lewis is coming by at a little before six-thirty.'

'What do you have to do to get ready?' she asked.

'Not much. Just throw on my old nylon flying suit and put on some tennis shoes. And, when Lewis comes, load up the back of his car with my stuff. There isn't much, but I've got it all ready. I piled it out in the living room after you went to bed.'

'Do you *really* want to go, baby?'

'It's not something I'm dying to do,' I said. 'And I won't die if I don't do it. But the studio is really bugging me. I had a terrible time yesterday, until I got down to doing some work. It seemed like everything just went right by me, nothing mattered at all. I couldn't have cared less about anything or anybody. If going up in the woods with Lewis does something about that feeling, I'm for it.'

'Is it my fault?'

'Lord, no,' I said, but it partly was, just as it's any woman's fault who represents normalcy.

'I wish you didn't have to go off like this. I mean, didn't *want* to. I wish there was something I could do.'

'There is.'

'Have we got time?'

'We'll make time. There's nothing Lewis has to offer that matters all that much. He can wait. I don't feel like I can.'

We lay entangled like lovers.

'Lie on your back,' she said.

She had great hands; they knew me. There was something about the residue of the nursing in her that turned me on: the practical approach to sex, the very deliberate and frank actions that give pleasure to people. The blood in me fell and began to

23

rise in the dark, moving with her hands and the slight cracking of the lubricant. Martha put a pillow in the middle of the bed, threw back the covers with a windy motion and turned facedown on the pillow. I knelt and entered her, and her buttocks rose and fell. 'Oh,' she said. 'Oh yes.'

It was the heat of another person around me, the moving heat, that brought the image up. The girl from the studio threw back her hair and clasped her breast, and in the center of Martha's heaving and expertly working back, the gold eye shone, not with the practicality of sex, so necessary to its survival, but the promise of it that promised other things, another life, deliverance.

I went to the bathroom and stood with my eyes closed and flowed. When my bladder was empty I pulled a robe around me, looking in the side-lighted mirror, which shone far up into the thinnest of my hair, unerringly finding the part of it that was receding the most rapidly and shadowed the underpart of my eyes in a way that made me know that they would never again be as they had been. Aging with me was going to come on fast. And yet I had good shoulders, and my hips and belly were heavy but solid. The hair was thick on my chest and across the top of my back, like an oxbow, and in the light some of it glowed a soft gray, like monkey fur.

If I had had my choice of looking like any man, or combination of men or earth, or in history, I would not have known how to make it. I suppose I got some of this attitude from Lewis, who exercised incessantly but only had two or three suits for each season. Clothes were not a mystique with him, but his body was. 'It's what you can make it do,' he would say, 'and what it'll do for you when you don't even know what's needed. It's that conditioning and reconditioning that's going to save you.' 'Save me?' I asked Lewis. 'Save me from what? Or *for* what?'

And yet Lewis approved of me at least enough to associate with me; I was probably his best friend. He had taught me how to shoot a bow, and I was fairly good. Lewis said I was unusually steady, and I could hold on a point almost as well as he could. My trouble was in judging distances, and Lewis didn't believe that archery with a sight, that is, archery that was not purely instinctive, was really archery. On a field round I scored consistently in the 160's for fourteen targets. Lewis was around 230, and had gone as high as 250. It was a real pleasure to watch him shoot, and to see the care that he took with his equipment, which he made himself, strings and all.

In the living room it was half-lit dark. The moon was gone from the floor and windows. I stood looking at one of the few dawns I had seen in the last ten years, and Martha came softly into the room in a frilled gown and continued on past me into the kitchen. She paused at the door.

'Have you seen Dean anywhere?' she asked.

'What do you mean? Isn't he in his room?'

My equipment, piled on the floor and dark as solid shade, laughed like Dean, and he rose up from behind it. He had a big Bowie knife in his hand, in the case.

It was odd. It was as though he both knew what the knife was and didn't know at all, and as he waved it around and threatened me with it – with the greatest love – I was caught in the same curious dance as he, knowing what the knife would do and not believing it for a minute. Finally I took it away from him and pitched it down where he had got it, in the dark of the rest of the stuff. It was only then that I felt the chill of the room, and realized that the air was cold as it came from the floor, up from the pile carpet, and that under the robe I was naked.

On top of the air mattress and sleeping bag and thin nylon rope lay the knife and my bow and four arrows. The rope I had bought on impulse at an army surplus store, mainly because Lewis had once told me that you should 'never be in the woods without rope.' I picked the bow up off it, enjoying the cold, smooth feel of the recurves. It was a good one; better, probably, than I deserved. It was not one of the standard makes – a Drake, for example, or a Ben Pearson or a Howatt or a Bear – but was homemade from what seemed to be a kind of composite design that ended up by looking and shooting like none of these. The handle section was heavy, and it actually looked like an experimental bow. I had come to like the weight and depth of the handle, though, and wouldn't have felt comfortable with anything smaller. Lewis had got it for me secondhand from a former state champion who'd made it, and who shot the same kind of bow, and he kept telling me of advantages which began, as I remember, by seeming completely psychological, but gradually came to seem real ones. There was, in fact, very little hand shock on release. The arrow went off very smoothly, and quietly, too. It had nothing like the snap or kick of Lewis' bows. The initial tip speed was nothing extra; the first time I shot it I thought it was terribly slow until I checked my point of aim and found that the bow was point-blank at sixty-five yards. When the string was released, the bow seemed to hesitate, and then the limbs gained speed at a terrific rate, and the arrow left the string with the feel of being not so much shot as catapulted. The trajectory was as flat as any bow I'd ever seen, and the left-right problem was not nearly so pronounced as it was in Lewis' bows. Now, as I held it and looked at it, with its white Gordon-Glas inner and outer faces, it seemed exactly the bow I ought to have. I depended on it and believed in it, though the laminations were beginning to tire a little, letting a few fiber glass splinters half-rise from the edges of the upper limb. I had a new string, too. Unlike Lewis, I used a peep sight in the string, and there I had something really good. Martha and I had separated the Dacron strands, put snap fasteners between them, and Martha had wrapped the separated halves with orange thread. It was a very handsome bowstring, and I enjoyed using it. When the bow was at full draw, the peep sight came naturally back to the eye and the target came to rest within it, trembling with the effort of the body to keep still. The effect of framing the target was a big advantage, at least to me, for it isolated what was being shot at, and brought it into an oddly intimate relation with the archer. Nothing outside the orange frame existed, and what was inside it was there in a terribly vital and consequential way; it was as though the target were being created by the eye that watched it.

The arrows were not so good, though they would do. They were aluminum, for I shot aluminum target arrows, and I knew from experience that arrows of this spine and length – twenty-nine inches – would shoot accurately out of my bow. They were in a bow quiver taped to the bow, for I wanted to be able to carry everything in one hand, and I had no back quiver anyway. They looked deadly, with their two-bladed Howard Hill broadheads and long yellow helical fletches. I had tried to camouflage them with black and green house paint, making random slashes up and down the shafts, and I had sharpened the heads on one of my neighbors' emery wheel. That was one thing I had done well, for they were nearly as sharp as new razor blades. They would shave hair, and I had also put on them, with a file, a slight burring roughness, very good for deep cutting, so said the archery magazines. I felt the edge of one of them with a thumb, and then drew back into the light of the hall to see if I had cut myself.

I hadn't, and I went back to the bedroom, got twenty dollars from my wallet, then walked back out through the living room to the kitchen, where Martha was moving barefooted back and forth in front of the stove, her glasses winking, and stared out into the backyard. I had my tennis shoes in my hand and sat down on the floor to put them on, still looking out behind the house. The trees there seemed perfectly wild, free objects that only by accident occurred in a domestic setting, and for some reason or other I felt strangely moved. Dean came up behind me and pulled at the leg-back of my flying suit. I picked him up, still looking out at where I lived. Usually children are bored with that sort of thing, not understanding how someone can look where nothing is moving. This time, though, Dean was as quiet as I was, observing what existed. I kissed him and he held me close around the neck. He was not ordinarily an affectionate child, and his acting this way made me nervous. Martha also came up, her face warm from the upcast heat of the stove. I got up, and we stood like a family group.

'Do you know where you're going?' she said.

'Not exactly. Lewis does. Somewhere up in the northeast part of the state, where he's been fishing. If everything goes off OK, we ought to be back late Sunday.'

'Why wouldn't it go off OK?'

'It will, but you can't predict. Listen, if I thought there was anything dangerous about it, I wouldn't go. Believe me, I wouldn't. It's just a chance to get out a little. And they say the mountains are really beautiful this time of year. I'll get some pictures, come to think of it.'

I went back to the bedroom once again and picked up a Rolleiflex that belonged to the studio. I also got another bowstring and put it in the leg pocket of my outfit. When I came back, Lewis had driven in. I put one arm around Martha as around a buddy, and then changed and held her with both hands, locking them, while Dean went around behind her and tried to get them loose. I opened the door, and by that time

Lewis was already out of the station wagon, coming and coming at us. His long wolfish face was flushed, and he was grinning. He grinned continually, but other people never got the grin directly, but always just sidelong parts of it, so that there was always an evasive, confident and secret craziness in his look; it was the face of a born enthusiast. He had on an Australian bush hat with a leather chin strap, and I could not help feeling that the occasion was a good one. I picked up the bow and the camera and went out with him to the car.

It was full of gear: two pup tents, ground sheets, two bows, a box of arrows, life preservers, a fly rod, groceries. He was a fanatic on preparedness – it was the carry-over from this part of him that had made me get the rope that was now looped at my side, when I knew I'd never use it, and the flying suit as well, because 'nylon dries out quick' – and yet he'd take off up some logging road that hadn't been used in fifteen years, bashing over logs and jumping gullies with no regard for himself, for the car or for whomever was with him. I hoped there wouldn't be much of that, for standing there in the light-shift of early morning, I felt genuinely close to him. He had the appearance of always leaping to meet something, of going forward with joy and anticipation. I was tired of dragging; I felt a great deal lighter and more muscular when I was around Lewis.

Now he was hauling my gear out to the car and stowing it up. The rear window filled with equipment, almost all of it different shades of green. Before he put it in, Lewis turned my bow over in his hands.

'You're losing glass,' he said, thumbing the edge of the upper limb.

'It'll hold up, I think. It's been like it is for a good long time.'

'You know,' Lewis said, 'I like this bow. You stand holding

it after you turn loose the string, thinking, what the hell. And then you look yonder and the arrow's sticking in the target.'

'You get used to it,' I said. 'It's very relaxed.'

'Now you see it, and now,' Lewis broke off. 'And now and now.'

'Let's go ahead,' I said. 'The sun's coming up. We can eat on the road. Up north the water's running.'

He spread his thin face crookedly. 'You sound like me,' he said.

'How about that,' I said, and went back one last time and got a bag of clothes I'd thrown together: a sweat shirt and a couple of T-shirts and a pair of long johns for sleeping.

We turned and waved good-bye to Martha and Dean, who were drawing together in the door. Martha's glasses were orange in the rising sun. I got in and clashed the car door. The bows and the woods equipment were heavy behind us, and the canoe clamped us down. We were not – or at least I was not – what we were before. If we had had an accident and had to be identified by what we carried and wore, we might have been engineers or trappers or surveyors or the advance commandos of some invading force. I knew I had to live up to the equipment or the trip would be as sad a joke as everything else.

I thought of where I might be that night, and of the snakes that would be out in the unseasonable warmth, and of being among the twigs and insects of remote places in the woods, and I was tempted – I must say I was – to back out, get sick, make some sort of excuse. I listened for the phone to ring, thinking of what I might say to the paper boy or my insurance agent, or whoever it might be, so that I could get out of the car, make a believable excuse to Lewis and take off my costume. What I really wanted was to go back in the house for a little sleep before driving to work. Or maybe, since I had the day off, to go out and play nine holes of golf. But the gear was in the car, and Lewis looked near me with his longest smile, showing plainly that I was of the chosen, that he was getting me out of the rut for a while or, as he put it, 'breaking the pattern.'

'Here we go,' he said, 'out of the sleep of mild people, into the wild rippling water.'

With the canoe beaked over us, we slid down the driveway, turned left and picked up speed, then turned left again and cruised. I propped up a foot and waited for the last of the downhill, and when we leveled out we were at the shopping center. Drew's Oldsmobile was parked about fifty yards this side of the four-lane. An old wooden canoe, something that looked like it belonged on a lake instead of a river, was webbed onto the top of the car with a lot of frayed rope; it had an army blanket under it to keep it from scratching the car.

Lewis gunned past the Olds and up the ramp onto the freeway. As we went past, I gave the others the Churchill V-sign, and Bobby replied with the classic single-finger. I faced ahead and stretched out on the seat and watched the rest of the light come.

It came, steadying on my right arm stronger and stronger, lifting up past the Texaco and Shell stations and the hamburger and beer drive-ins that were going to fly and shuttle on the highway for the next twenty miles. I had no particular relation to any of these; they were sealed from me and slid by on the other side of a current of cellophane. But I had been here, somewhere; my stomach stirred and I knew it. Moving up at us on the right was a long line of white concrete poles, a red-and-white drive-in whose galvanized tin roof made the sun flutter and hang and angle, and my half-shut eyes singled out one pole from the rest, magnifying it like a hawk's.

I had leaned there, Christmas before last. I had leaned and leaned, until the leaning turned into a spinning round and round

31

the pole, and then I had come to a slow stop and vomited, spilling half-solids first and then color after color of powerful liquids, all from an office Christmas party. As I remembered, Thad had thought that driving me out for a last beer might help sober me up, but he was more horrified than any stranger when he saw what shape I was in. A lot of times when drunk I've felt things that seemed to share the drunkenness with me – friendly tables and sofas and even trees – but the pole in that drive-in was thing-cold, set in all that concrete, in the southern winter. It had no movement and I couldn't give it mine, drunk as I was, spinning among the disgusted people in overcoats in their cars, their faces going blue and red with neon – that tired, never-dying color-changing – and something colder than the metal in my hand touched the very bottom of my stomach, the blood heaved, and I held to the pole and let it come. I could hear the cars near me starting, and I tried with every muscle to bring up my stomach. I might also have hit my head a couple of times against the pole, for there were some lumps on my forehead, over one eye. Now as we passed I swiveled to look at the post, half expecting to see something special about it: the ground around it bleached, maybe, or some other indication that I had taken a stand there. There was nothing of that sort, of course, but an inhuman coldness touched me, my stomach clenched, and we were past. The highway shrank to two lanes, and we were in the country.

The change was not gradual; you could have stopped the car and got out at the exact point where suburbia ended and the red-neck South began. I would like to have done that, to see what the sense of it would be. There was a motel, then a weed field, and then on both sides Clabber Girl came out of hiding, leaping onto the sides of barns, 666 and Black Draught began to swirl, and Jesus began to save. We hummed along, borne with the inverted canoe on a long tide of patent medicines and religious billboards. From such a trip you would think that the South did nothing but dose itself and sing gospel songs; you would think that the bowels of the southerner were forever clamped shut; that he could not open and let natural process flow through him, but needed one purgative after another in order to make it to church.

We stopped in a little town named Seluca and had breakfast at a restaurant called the Busy Bee. It was great, I thought, a big meal with grits and eggs and lots of butter and biscuits and preserves. My gut heaved and rubbed against the slick nylon I was wearing and the sun, as I got back into the car, drained from my face down into some central part. I barely remember Lewis starting the car, but I do remember thinking of Martha and Dean just as I drifted out, recalling that they were mine, that I was always welcome in that house.

I was dead, and riding, which is a special kind of sleep not like any other, and I heard Lewis saying something that strove in and out of my consciousness. Later in the trip I asked him to repeat it.

'. . . and was there in the Grass Mountain National Game Management Area; gone up after trout. That's not too far from where we're headed, either. Bad roads in there, but my God Almighty, the little part of the river I've seen would knock your eyes out. The last time I was near there I asked a couple of rangers about it, but none of them knew anything. They said they hadn't been up in there, and the way they said "in there" made it sound like a place that's not easy to get to. Probably it isn't, but that's what makes it good. From what I saw, the river is rough but not too rough just south of Oree. But what's on down from that, I don't have any idea. What we'll do first is to find a place to put in. Oree is on kind of a bluff, and most likely we'll have to get on the other side of it to put in. We might want to get some more supplies in Oree first, though.'

My eyes kept hazing open and shut without seeing anything; things were in them but didn't have the power to stay or be remembered. The world was a kind of colored no-dream with objects in it. Then, one of the times that my eyelids lifted without any command, I stared straight out with my brain asleep but my eyes wide. We were going out the far edge of a little town, swinging to the right through the twiggy grayish stuff that is always growing near southern highways. Up ahead, the road ran between two hills. Lined up dead center between them was a mountain, high, broad and blue, the color of concentrated woodsmoke. There were others farther back from it, falling back, receding left and right.

'Funny thing,' Lewis said.

I leaned around, hearing him. 'What?'

'Funny thing about up yonder,' he said. 'The whole thing's different. I mean the whole way of taking life and the terms you take it on.'

'What should I know about that?' I said.

'The trouble is,' he said, 'that you not only don't know anything about it, you don't *want* to know anything about it.'

'Why should I?'

'Because, for the Lord's sake, there may be something important in the hills. Do you know what?'

'No; I don't know anything. I don't mind going down a few rapids with you, and drinking a little whiskey by a campfire. But I don't give a fiddler's fuck about those hills.'

'But do you know,' he said, and his quietness made me listen, although with the reservation that it had better be good if he put that much emphasis on it, 'there are songs in those hills that collectors have never put on tape. And I've seen one family with a dulcimer.'

'So, what does that prove?'

'Maybe nothing, maybe a lot.'

'I'll leave that to Drew,' I said. 'But do *you* know something, Lewis? If those people in the hills, the ones with the folk songs and dulcimers, came out of the hills and led us all toward a new heaven and a new earth, it would not make a particle of difference to me. I am a get-through-the-day man. I don't think I was ever anything else. I am not a great art director. I am not a great archer. I am mainly interested in sliding. Do you know what sliding is?'

'No. You want me to guess?'

'I'll tell you. Sliding is living antifriction. Or, no, sliding is living *by* antifriction. It is finding a modest thing you can do, and then greasing that thing. On both sides. It is grooving with comfort.'

'You don't believe in madness, eh?'

'I don't, at all. I know better than to fool with it.'

'So what you do . . .'

'So what you do is go on by it. What you do is get done what you ought to be doing. And what you do rarely – and I *mean* rarely – is to flirt with it.'

'We'll see,' Lewis said, glancing at me as though he had me. 'We'll see. You've had all that office furniture in front of you, desks and bookcases and filing cabinets and the rest. You've been sitting in a chair that won't move. You've been steady. But when that river is under you, all that is going to change. There's nothing you do as vice-president of Emerson-Gentry that's going to make any difference at all, when the water starts to foam up. Then, it's not going to be what your title says you do, but what you end up doing. You know: *doing*.'

Then he waited, and I woke up fully, where I had not been before.

'I know,' he said. 'You think I'm some kind of narcissistic fanatic. But I'm not.'

'I wouldn't put it that way, exactly,' I said.

'I just believe,' he said, 'that the whole thing is going to be reduced to the human body, once and for all. I want to be ready.'

'*What* whole thing?'

'The human race thing. I think the machines are going to fail, the political systems are going to fail, and a few men are going to take to the hills and start over.'

I looked at him. He lived in the suburbs, like the rest of us. He had money, a good-looking wife and three children. I could not really believe that he came in from placating his tenants every evening and gave himself solemnly to the business of survival, insofar as it involved his body. What kind of fantasy led to this? I asked myself. Did he have long dreams of atomic holocaust in which he had to raise himself and his family out of the debris of less strong folk and head toward the same blue hills we were approaching?

'I had an air-raid shelter built,' he said. 'I'll take you down there sometime. We've got double doors and stocks of bouillon and bully beef for a couple of years at least. We've got games for the kids, and a record player and a whole set of records on how to play the recorder and get up a family recorder group. But I went down there one day and sat for a while. I decided that survival was not in the rivets and the metal, and not in the double-sealed doors and not in the marbles of Chinese checkers. It was in me. It came down to the man, and what he could do. The body is the one thing you can't fake; it's just got to be there.'

'Suppose there was a lot of fallout, and there was no way to breathe? Suppose the radiation didn't have any respect for your physique?'

'In that case, buddy,' he said, 'I'd be prepared to throw in the jock. But if it comes to a situation where I can operate, I don't want to crap out. You know me pretty well, Ed. You know I'd go up in those hills, and I believe I'd make out where many another wouldn't.'

'You're ready, are you?'

'I think I am,' he said. 'I sure am, psychologically. At times I get the feeling that I can't wait. Life is so fucked-up now, and so complicated, that I wouldn't mind if it came down, right quick, to the bare survival of who was ready to survive. You might say I've got the survival craze, the real bug. And to tell the truth I don't think most other people have. They might cry and tear their hair and be ready for some short hysterical violence or other, but I think most of them wouldn't be too unhappy to give down and get it over with.'

'Is this just something you think about on your own? Does your wife know all this?'

'Sure. She was very interested in the shelter. Now she's learning open-air cooking. She's doing damned good, too. She even talks about taking her paints along, and making a new kind of art, where things are reduced to essentials – like in cave painting – and there's none of this frou-frou in art anymore.'

I had the clear sense that he'd both talked this up too much with his wife and maybe a few other people, and had never really talked about it at all.

'Where would you go?' he asked. 'Where would you go when the radios died? When there was nobody to tell you where to go?'

'Well,' I said, 'I'd probably head south, where the climate

would be better. I'd try to beat my way down to the Florida coast, where there'd be some fish around, even if there wasn't anything else to eat.'

He pointed ahead, where the hills were moving from one side of the road to the other, and growing solid. 'That's where I'd go,' he said. 'Right where we're going. You could make something up there. You could make something, and not have to build it on sand.'

'What could you make?'

'If everything wasn't dead, you could make a kind of life that wasn't out of touch with everything, with the other forms of life. Where the seasons would mean something, would mean everything. Where you could hunt as you needed to, and maybe do a little light farming, and get along. You'd die early, and you'd suffer, and your children would suffer, but you'd be in touch.'

'Oh, I don't know,' I said. 'If you wanted to, you could go up in the hills and live right now. You could have all those same conditions. You could hunt, you could farm. You could suffer just as much now as if they dropped the H-bomb. You could even start a colony. How do you think Carolyn would like that life?'

'It's not the same,' Lewis said. 'Don't you see? It would just be eccentric. Survival depends – well, it depends on *having* to survive. The kind of life I'm talking about depends on its being the last chance. The very last of all.'

'I hope you don't get it,' I said. 'It's too big a price to pay.'

'No price is too big,' Lewis said, and I knew that part of the conversation was over.

'What's the life like up there, now?' I asked. 'I mean, before you take to the mountains and set up the Kingdom of Sensibility?'

'Probably not too much different from what it's liable to

be then,' he said. 'Some hunting and a lot of screwing and a little farming. Some whiskey-making. There's lots of music, it's practically coming out of the trees. Everybody plays something: the guitar, the banjo, the autoharp, the spoons, the dulcimer – or the dulcimore, as they call it. I'll be disappointed if Drew doesn't get to hear some of that stuff while we're up here. These are good people, Ed. But they're awfully clannish, they're set in their ways. They'll do what they want to do, no matter what. Every family I've ever met up here has at least one relative in the penitentiary. Some of them are in for making liquor or running it, but most of them are in for murder. They don't think a whole lot about killing people up here. They really don't. But they'll generally leave you alone if you do the same thing, and if one of them likes you he'll do anything in the world for you. So will his family. Let me tell you about something that happened two years ago.'

'All right.'

'Shad Mackey and I were running Blackwell Creek. The creek was low and things got sort of dull. We were doing nothing but paddling and it was hot as hell. Shad said he'd rather take his bow and hunt rabbits down-stream. He got out, and we said we'd meet where the creek comes into the Cahula River, way down below where we're going to be. He took off into the woods on the east side, and I went on down the creek. Saw a wildcat drinking that day, I remember.

'Anyway, I got on down to the river and pulled the canoe up on the bank and stretched out on a rock to wait for him. Nothing happened. I kept listening, but outside the regular woods noises, I couldn't hear a thing. It started to get dark, and I was beginning to get worried. I didn't want him out there by himself in the dark, and I didn't want to be out there either. I wasn't ready for it. You know, I wasn't *ready*. I didn't have anything to eat. I didn't have

39

a bow with me, like a damned fool. I had a pocketknife and a ball of string, and that's all.'

'You should have looked on that as a challenge, Lewis,' I said, not able to resist.

He was not touchy about these things at all; he knew he couldn't be swayed. 'It wasn't the right kind,' he said.

'Anyway,' he went on, 'I was lying on a big rock, and the cold was coming up into me, bone by bone. I happened to look around, and there was a fellow standing there looking at me. "What you want, boy, down around here?" he said. He was skinny, and had on overall pants and a white shirt with the sleeves rolled up. I told him I was going down the river with another guy, and that I was waiting for Shad to show up. It wasn't easy for him to believe that, but gradually we got to talking. Sure enough, he had a still near there. He and his boy were working it. He took me back about a quarter of a mile from the river. His boy was building a fire. We sat down and talked. "You say you got a man back up there hunting with a bow and arrow. Does he know what's up there?" he asked me. "No," I said. "It's rougher than a night in jail in south Georgia," he said, "and I know what I'm talking about. You have any idea whereabouts he is?" I said no, "Just up that way someplace, the last time I saw him." '

I felt like laughing. For all his fanaticism about pre-paredness, Lewis was forever getting himself and other people into situations like this. And I was damned well hoping that this wouldn't be another one. 'What happened then?' I asked.

'The fire was blazing up. The shadows were jumping. The fellow stood up and went over to his boy, who was about fifteen. He talked to him for a while, and then came about halfway back to me before he turned around and said, "Son, go find that man." The hackles on my neck stood up. The boy didn't say a thing. He went and got a flashlight and an old single-shot twenty-two. He picked up a handful of bullets from a box and put them in his pocket. He called his dog, and then he just faded away.'

'He did? Just went off?'

'He went off where I pointed. That's all he had. That and his father. That's the something I'm talking about. I don't care how much you argue with me. I *know* it. Dependability. The kind of life that *guarantees* it. That fellow wasn't commanding his son against his will. The boy just knew what to do. He walked out into the dark.'

'So?'

'So we're lesser men, Ed. I'm sorry, but we are. Do you think Dean would do something like that when he's fifteen? First of all, he won't have to. But if he did, he couldn't do it, couldn't be that boy walking off into the dark with his dog.'

'He could have been killed. And maybe the father was an asshole, anyway,' I said.

'Maybe he was, but the boy didn't think so,' Lewis said. 'This kind of thing is just as hard on the parents as on the children. If both of them recognize it, it works. You know?'

I didn't quite, though I didn't say so. 'Does the story have any end?'

'It does,' Lewis said. 'About two o'clock in the morning, when the fire was about burned out and I was leaned up against a tree asleep, the boy came back with Shad. Shad'd broken his leg and was in the bushes in the dark, trying to do something for himself, when the boy found him. God knows how he did it.'

'What if he hadn't done it?'

'It wouldn't make any difference,' Lewis said. 'He went, and he tried. He didn't have to. Or rather he did have to. But anyway, he went, and Shad would have been in a bad way if he hadn't.'

'I saw Shad at a better business meeting last month,' I said.

'He may be a friend of yours, but I can't see that anything so much was saved, up there in the woods.'

'That's pretty callous, Ed.'

'Sure it is,' I said. 'So what?'

'As it happens, I agree with you,' he said after a moment. 'Not a good man. Drinks too much in an uncreative way. Talks too much. Doesn't deliver enough, either on the river or in business or, I'm fairly sure, in bed with his wife or anybody else, either. But that's not the point. His own life and his own values are up to him to make. The boy went and hauled him out of the woods because of *his* values. And his old man and his old man's way of life, both of them ignorant and full of superstition and bloodshed and murder and liquor and hook-worm and ghosts and early deaths, were the cause of it. I admire it, and I admire the men that it makes, and that make it, and if you don't, why, fuck you.'

'OK,' I said, 'fuck me. I'll still stay with the city.'

'I reckon you will,' Lewis said. 'But you'll have doubts.'

'I may, but they won't bother me.'

'That's the trouble. The city's got you where you live.'

'Sure it does. But it's also got you, Lewis. I hate to say this, but you put in your time playing games. I may play games, like being an art director. But I put my life and the lives of my family on the line. I have to do it, and I do it. I don't have any dreams of a new society. I'll take what I've got. I don't read books and I don't have theories. What'd be the use? What you've got is a fantasy life.'

'That's all anybody has got. It depends on how strong your fantasy is, and whether you really – *really* – in your own mind, fit into your own fantasy, whether you measure up to what you've fantasized. I don't know what yours is, but I'll bet you don't come up to it.'

'Mine is simple,' I said. I didn't say, though, what forms it had taken recently, nor anything about the moon-slice of somebody else's gold eye in the middle of my wife's back as she labored for us.

'So is mine, and I work for it. A gut-survival situation may never happen. Probably it won't. But you know something? I sleep at night. I have no worries. I am becoming myself, as inconsequential as that may be. I am not something somebody shoved off on me. I am what I choose to be, and I am *it*.'

'There're a lot of other kinds of people to be, than what you are,' I said.

'Sure there are. But this is my kind. It feels right, like when you turn loose the arrow, and you know when you let go that you've done everything right. You know where the arrow is going. There's not any other place that it can go.'

'Lord,' I said. 'Lewis, you're out of sight.'

'Who knows,' he said. 'But I believe in survival. All kinds. Every time I come up here, I believe in it more. You know, with all the so-called modern conveniences, a man can still fall down. His leg will break, like Shad Mackey's. He can lie there in the woods with night coming on, knowing he's got two cars in the garage, one of them an XKE, a wife and three children watching "Star Trek" as he lies trying to get his breath under a bush. The old human body is the same as it always was. It still feels that old fear, and that old pain. The last time I was near here . . .'

'You know that old broken-leg thing, don't you, buddy?'

'I know it,' he said. 'I broke it like a goddamned fool, up here by myself. There was a trout stream I wanted to fish, and it was hard to get to. I took thirty feet of rope and let myself down to the creek and fished . . . well, I *fished*. It was one of the best afternoons I ever had with man or woman or beast.

I was climbing back up when the rope worked into my right hand and began to hurt like hell, and I slacked up on that hand and tried to wrap the rope around it a different way, and the next thing I knew, the damned rope slicked through the other hand and I was going down. In fact, I was already down. I hit on one leg, and I could hear something go in that right ankle. I had a hard time getting up from the bottom of the creek, with those waders on, and when I tried to stand up, I knew I had it to do.'

'How'd you get out?'

'I went up the rope. I just armed it out, hand over hand, and then started hobbling and hopping and crawling. And you damned well better hope you never have to one-leg it through any woods. I was holding on to every tree like it was my brother.'

'Maybe it was.'

'No,' Lewis said. 'But I got out, finally. You know the rest.'

'Yeah. And now you're going back.'

'You better believe it. But you know something, Ed? That intensity; well, that's something special. That was a great trip, broken ankle and all. I heard old Tom McCaskill, the night before. That was worth it.'

'Who is that?'

'Well, let me tell you. You come up here camping in the woods, on the river in some places, or back off in the bush, hunting or whatever you're doing, and in the middle of the night you're liable to hear the most God-awful scream that ever got loose from a human mouth. There's no explanation for it. You just hear it, and that's all. Sometimes you just hear it once, and sometimes it keeps on for a while.'

'What is it, for the Lord's sake?'

'There's this old guy up here who just gets himself – or makes himself – a jug every couple of weeks, and goes off in the woods at night. From what I hear, he doesn't have any idea where he's going. He just goes off the road and keeps going till he's ready to stop. Then he builds himself a fire and sits down with the jug. When he gets drunk enough he starts out to hollering. That's the way he gets his kicks. As they say, don't knock it if you ain't tried it. You tried it?'

'No, but maybe on this trip. I doubt if I'll ever get another chance. Maybe we don't even have to go down the river. Maybe we should just go off and drink and holler. And Drew could play the guitar. I'll bet he'd just as soon. I'll bet he'd rather.'

'Well, I wouldn't. Would you?'

'Don't knock it if you ain't tried it,' I said. 'But no, I wouldn't. In fact, I'm looking forward to getting on the river. I'm so tanked up with your river-mystique that I'm sure I'll go through some fantastic change as soon as I dig the paddle in the first time.'

'Just wait, buddy,' he said. 'You'll want to come back. It's real.'

I looked off at the blue forms of the mountains, growing less transparent and cloudlike, shifting their positions, rolling from side to side off the road, coming back and centering in our path, and then sliding off the road again, but strengthening all the time. We went through some brush and then out across a huge flat field that ran before us for miles, going straight at the bulging range of hills, which was now turning mile by mile from blue to a light green-gold, the color of billions of hardwood leaves.

Around noon we started up among them, still on the highway. At an intersection we turned off onto a black-top state road, and from that onto a badly cracked and weedy concrete highway of the old days – the thirties as nearly as I could tell – with the old splattered tar centerline wavering onward. From that we turned onto another concrete road that sagged and slewed and holed-out and bumped ahead, not worth maintaining at all.

It was still about forty miles to Oree. We had to get there, hire two men to drive the cars back down to Aintry and then go downriver and find a campsite and set up camp. If possible, we also wanted to buy some more supplies. We had time, but we didn't have any to waste. Lewis speeded up; a bad road always challenged him. The canoe bumped and grated overhead.

We were among trees now, lots of them. I could have told you with my eyes closed; I could hear them whish, then open to space and then close with another whish. I was surprised at how much color there was in them. I had thought that the pine tree was about the only tree in the state, but that wasn't the case, as I saw. I had no notion what the trees were, but they were beautiful, flaming and turning color almost as I looked at them. They were just beginning to turn, and the flame was not hot yet. But it was there, beginning to come on.

'You look at these trees,' Lew said. 'I've been up here in April when you could see the most amazing thing about them.'

'They look pretty amazing now,' I said. 'What do you mean?'

'Have you ever heard of the larva of the linden moth?'

'Sure,' I said. 'All the time. Tell you the truth, no.'

'Every year when the larvae are ambitious – larvas is *larvae* – you can look at the trees and you see something happening.'

'What?'

'You can see a mass hanging. A self-hanging of millions of 'em.'

'Is this another put-on?'

'No, buddy. They let themselves down on threads. You can look anywhere you like and see 'em wringing and twisting on the ends of the threads like men that can't die. Some of them are black and some are brown. And everything is quiet. It's so quiet. And they're there, twisting. But they're bad news. They eat the hardwood leaves. The government's trying to figure some way to get rid of 'em.'

It was a warm day. Everything was green, and through the green there was that subtle gold-coming color that makes the green hurt to look at. We passed through Whitepath and Pelham, towns smaller than the others, and Pelham smaller than Whitepath, and then began to wind and climb. The woods were heavy between the towns, and closed in around them.

'Look for deer,' Lewis said. 'When there's not much mast, they come down to the cornfields and along the roads.'

I looked but didn't see any, though at one curve in the road I thought I saw something dart back into the woods to the right. But the leaves where I thought it had gone in were not moving, so probably it was my imagination.

Finally we came to Oree. It was evidently the county seat, for it had a little whitewashed building it called the town hall; the jail was part of it, and an old-fashioned fire engine was parked at one side. We went to a Texaco station and asked if there was anybody there who'd like to make some money. When Lewis killed the engine, the air came alive and shook with insects, even in the center of town, an in-and-out responding silence of noise. An old man with a straw hat and work shirt appeared at Lewis' window, talking in. He looked like a hillbilly in some badly cast movie, a character actor too much in character to be believed. I wondered where the excitement was that intrigued Lewis so much; everything in Oree was sleepy and hookwormy and ugly, and most of all, inconsequential. Nobody worth a damn could ever come from such a place. It was nothing, like most places and people are nothing. Lewis asked the fellow if he and somebody else would drive our cars down to Aintry for twenty dollars.

'Take two of you to drive this thing?' the man asked.

'If that was the case we'd need four,' Lewis said, and didn't explain. He just sat there and waited. I glanced up at the prow of the canoe, the hook coming at us from above.

After a long minute Drew and Bobby drove up beside us.

'See what I mean?' Lewis said.

The other two got out and came over. The old man turned as though he were being surrounded. His movements were very slow, like those of someone whose energies have been taken by some other thing than old age. It was humiliating to be around him, especially with Lewis' huge pumped-up bicep shoving out its veins in the sun, where it lay casually on the window of the car. Out of the side of my eye I saw the old man's spotted hands trembling like he was deliberately making them do it. There is always something wrong with people in the country, I thought. In the comparatively few times I had ever been in the rural South I had been struck by the number of missing fingers. Offhand, I had counted around twenty, at least. There had also been several people with some form of crippling or twisting illness, and some blind or one-eyed. No adequate medical treatment, maybe. But there was something else. You'd think that farming was a healthy life, with fresh air and fresh food and plenty of exercise, but I never saw a farmer who didn't have something wrong with him, and most of the time obviously wrong; I never saw one who was physically powerful, either. Certainly there were none like Lewis. The work with the hands must be fantastically dangerous, in all that fresh air and sunshine, I thought: the catching of an arm in a tractor part somewhere off in the middle of a field where nothing happened but that the sun blazed back more fiercely down the open mouth of one's screams. And so many snakebites deep in the woods as one stepped over a rotten log, so many domestic animals suddenly turning and crushing one against the splintering side of a barn stall. I wanted none of it, and I didn't want to be around where it happened either. But I

48

was there, and there was no way for me to escape, except by water, from the country of nine-fingered people.

I looked off into the woods, then, and shot an eye corner back at my bow. This trip would sure be the farthest off in the woods I had ever been; there would be more animals than I had ever been close to, and they would be wilder. Lewis said he believed there were even a few bears and wild hogs in the mountains, though he said that the hogs were more likely to be domestic pigs that had run off. But they revert fast, he said; they grow that ruff up the back of the neck and the snout stretches out and the tushes get long, and in six or seven years you can't tell them from the ones in Russia, except maybe by a notch in the ear or a ring in the nose. I knew there was not much chance of our running into a bear or a hog; that was romance. But then, the idea of hunting, for me, was also a kind of romance. The death of a real deer at my hands was just a vaporous, remote presence that hovered over the figure of the paper deer forty-five yards away at target six of our archery range, as I tried to hit the heart-lung section marked out in heavy black.

'Man, I like the way you wear that hat,' Bobby said to the old man.

The man took off the hat and looked at it carefully; there was nothing remarkable about it, but when it was on his head it had the curious awkward-arrogant tilt that you find only in the country South. He put the hat back on the other side of his head with the same tilt.

'You don't know nothin',' he said to Bobby.

Drew said, 'Can you tell us something about the land around here? I mean, suppose we wanted to get down the river to Aintry. Could we do it?'

The man turned away from Bobby, and the finality with which he did it made me glance at Bobby to see if he had disappeared

49

as a result. Bobby was smiling the kind of smile that might or might not come before a mean remark.

'Well,' the man said, 'it's right rocky, on down a piece. If there's been a rain it raises way up, but it don't come over the banks, leastways in most places. There ain't no danger of the valley floodin'; ain't nothin' in it anyway. Furthest down I been is Walker's Point, about fifteen miles, where the land starts gettin' high. In a dry spell the river drops on down out of sight; you got to lean way out over the rocks to see it. And they say there's another big gorge on down south, but I ain't never been there.'

'Do you think we can get down the river?' Drew asked.

'In whut?'

'In these two canoes.'

'I wouldn't want to try it,' he said, and straightened up. 'If it rains, you're liable to be in bad trouble. The water climbs them rock walls like a monkey.'

'What the hell,' Lewis said. 'It's not going to rain. Look up yonder.'

I looked up yonder. It was clear, hazy-hot blue with no clouds. It seemed all right, if it stayed that way.

'If it rains, we'll just find us a place and hole up,' Lewis said. 'I've done it before.'

'You'll have a time holing up if you get down in that gorge.'

'We'll make out.'

'All right,' the old man said. 'You asked me. I told you.'

Drew and Bobby turned to go back to the Olds, and the Texaco man walked back alongside of Drew. I heard him ask, 'Whose guitar is that-there yonder?' Then he was jumping like a dog on its hind legs back into the filling station. 'Lonnie,' he hollered, 'come on out chere.'

He came back and behind him was an albino boy with pink

50

eyes like a white rabbit's; one of them stared off at a furious and complicated angle. That was the eye he looked at us with, with his face set in another direction. The sane, rational eye was fixed on something that wasn't there, somewhere in the dust of the road.

'Git yer banjo,' the old man said, and then to Drew, 'Come on, play us a little something.'

Drew grinned, rolled down the back window of the wagon, got out the big cracked Martin and put on his finger picks. He came back to the front of the Olds and hiked himself onto the hood with one leg up to hold the guitar. He tuned for a minute, and Lonnie came back holding up a five-string banjo with a capo made out of rags and rubber bands.

'Lonnie don't know nothin' but banjo-pickin',' the old man said. 'He ain't never been to school; when he was little he used to sit out in the yard and beat on a lard can with a stick.'

'What're we going to play, Lonnie?' Drew asked, his glasses opaque with pleasure.

Lonnie stood holding the banjo, looking off from us now with both eyes, the eyes splitting apart and all of us in the blind spot.

'Anything,' the old man said. 'Play anything.'

Drew started in on 'Wildwood Flower,' picking it out at medium tempo and not putting in many runs. Lonnie dragged on the rubber bands and slipped the capo up. Drew started to come on with the volume; the Martin boomed out and over the dusty filling station. I had never heard him play so well, and I really began to listen deeply, moved as an unmusical person is moved when he sees that the music is meant. After a little while it sounded as though Drew were adding another kind of sound to every note he played, a higher, tinny echo of the melody, and then it broke in on me that this was the banjo, played so softly and rightly that it sounded like Drew's own fingering. I could not see Drew's face, but the back of his neck was sheer joy. He eased out of the melody and played rhythm, and Lonnie took it. He emphasized nothing, but through everything he played there was a lovely unimpeded flowing that seemed endless. His hands, full of long scratches, took time; the fingers moved only slightly, about like those of a good typist; the music was just there. Drew came back in the new key and they finished, riding together. For the last couple of minutes of the song, Drew slid down and went over and stood beside Lonnie. They put the instruments together and leaned close to each other in the pose you see vocal groups and phony folk singers take on TV programs, and something rare and unrepeatable took hold of the way I saw them, the demented country kid and the big-faced decent city man, the minor civic leader and hedge clipper. I was glad for Drew's sake we had come. Just this incident would be plenty to satisfy him.

'God*damn*,' he said as they finished.

'Come on, Drew,' Lewis said. 'Put that thing away. We got to get water under us.'

'I could play with this guy all day,' Drew said. 'Can you wait just a minute? I'd like to get his name and address.'

He turned to Lonnie, then quickly to the old man; he was, I guess, afraid that Lonnie didn't know his name and address. They walked together a few steps, almost out of the area of the filling station, and stood talking. Then Drew passed the Martin to the old man and took a pencil and his wallet out of his pocket and wrote carefully what the old man told him. Once the man touched Drew's shoulder. Drew came back, and the old man and Lonnie went inside.

'You know,' Drew said to all of us, 'I'd like to come back up here, just to hear some more music. I thought all the real country pickers had long since gone to Nashville.'

'How about the river?' Lewis asked.

'He tells me you can't get down to the river anywhere in town here. It's too steep. But eight or ten miles north of here the land's flat. We might be able to find us a road through the woods. There was a logging operation up there a few years back, and he thinks there are still some roads that go down to the river, or somewhere around it.'

'How about drivers?'

'He doesn't have anybody here, but there are a couple of brothers who run a garage out the way we're going to have to go, and they might be able to do it.'

We drove out of town. We were higher up than I thought. We went over a bridge, and through the whirling girders of the supports the river was flickering. It was green, peaceful, slow, and I thought, very narrow. It didn't look deep or dangerous, just picturesque. It was hard to imagine that it flowed through woods anywhere, or that animals drank from it, or that it was going to be dammed up and become a lake.

North of town about half a mile we stopped. Lewis thought it would be a good idea for Drew and Bobby to buy supplies while Lewis and I made the deal about the cars. We could see the Griner Brothers' Garage from where we were, and Lewis told Drew to meet us there in half an hour. We drove up to the garage and parked.

There was a frame house connected to the garage, and we went to it and knocked on the door. No one answered. A doghead came around a jamb inside. We could hear hammering from the galvanized tin garage, but when we went over there we saw that the front of it was locked with a big chain and padlock. We walked around to the back. Half of the double door was sagging open. We went in, Lewis first.

It was dark and iron-smelling, hot with the closed-in heat that brings the sweat out as though it had been waiting all over your body for the right signal. Anvils stood around or lay on their sides, and chains hung down, covered with coarse, deep grease. The air was full of hooks; there were sharp points everywhere – tools and nails and ripped-open rusty tin cans. Batteries stood on benches and on the floor, luminous and green, and through everything, out of the high roof, mostly, came this clanging hammering, meant to deafen and even blind. It was odd to be there, not yet seen, paining with the metal harshness in the half-dark.

We went toward the hammering, which seemed to be done also on the outside of the shed, on the roof and tin sides and us at the same time, who got it all. We were close enough to the source of the sound to flinch each time it came, when it stopped. The air around our heads closed in. By this time we could see a few more things, though it was actually darker there than where the batteries and anvils were. The hub of what looked like a truck wheel was on a table, and a big figure was bending over it. We were still invisible. I was about to say something when the figure straightened and turned.

Not saying anything and holding one hand in the other, the man stepped forward between us and went toward the slant light that stood for the door. I instinctively let him go by, though for a second I thought I saw Lewis move toward his path, and my heart-blood jumped in place, not able to understand what was happening or about to happen. Lewis' move toward blocking the man, if it was a move, appeared as instinctive on his part as my own move away, but I can't to this day remember if it really happened; it might have been just a trick of perspective or darkness. We followed the man out.

When we broke into the sun in the half-grass and gray dirt of the yard, he was standing spread-legged looking at his hand, which was cut in the thin webbing between the left thumb and

54

forefinger. He was a huge creature, twenty pounds heavier than Lewis, dressed in overall pants and an old-fashioned sleeveless undershirt, with a train engineer's cap on and cut-down army boots. He held his hand low in the sun, right at his waist, turning it one way and then another. He held it like he was having to keep it down by all the strength in his other hand and the rest of his body.

There is no very good way to start a conversation under conditions like that; all I wanted to do was disappear, so as not to have to explain what I was doing there, but Lewis walked up to the man and asked, very civilly for him, if he could help.

'No,' the big man said, looking squarely at me instead of Lewis.

'It ain't as bad as I thought.'

He pulled a gray handkerchief out of his pocket and wrapped it around his hand, jerking the knot tight with his teeth.

Lewis waited until the second half of the knot was tied and said, 'I was wondering if you and somebody else, maybe your brother, would drive two cars down to Aintry for us for twenty dollars. Or if you wanted to get a third fellow to drive another car so you'd have a way to get back to Oree, we'd give all three of you ten dollars apiece.'

'Drive them down there for *what?*'

'We want to take a canoe trip down the Cahulawassee, and we'd like for our cars to be in Aintry when we get there day after tomorrow.'

'A *canoe* trip?' he said, looking back and forth between us.

'That's right,' Lewis said, narrowing his eyes a little. 'A canoe trip.'

'You ever been down in there?'

'No,' Lewis said. 'Have you?'

Griner set his heavy-hanging face on Lewis; they battled in

midair; the sound of crickets in the grass around the garage clashed like shields and armor plate. I could see the man was insulted; Lewis himself had told me that the worst thing you can do is to throw something back at these mountain people.

'No,' Griner answered slowly. 'I ain't never been down in there much. There ain't nothing to go down there for. Fishing's no good.'

'How about hunting?'

'Never been. But I don't believe I'd go there if I was you. What's the use of it?'

'Because it's there,' Lewis said, for my benefit.

'It's there, all right,' Griner said. 'If you git in there and can't get out, you're goin' to wish it wudn't.'

My chest felt hollow, and my heart was ringing like iron. I wanted to back out; just go back to town and forget it. I hated what we were doing.

'Listen, Lewis,' I said, 'to hell with it. Let's go back and play golf.'

He didn't pay any attention. 'Well, can you do it?' he asked Griner.

'How much did you say?'

'Twenty dollars for two men, thirty for three.'

'Fifty,' Griner said.

'Fifty, my ass,' Lewis said.

Good God, I thought, why is he like this? I was scared to death, and I resented insanely Lewis' getting me into such a situation. Well, you didn't have to come, I told myself. But never again. Never.

'How about forty?' Griner said.

Lewis kicked the ground and turned to me. 'Are you good for ten?'

I took out the money and gave it to him.

'Twenty now,' Lewis said to Griner. 'We'll send the rest to you. If we're good for this, we're good for the rest. Take it or leave it.'

'Good enough,' Griner said, but it was hard not to believe he was saying something mean. He took the bills and looked at them and put them in his pocket. He went across the yard toward the house, and we went around front, back to the car.

'What do you think?' I asked Lew. 'You reckon we'll ever see these cars? This is a rough son of a bitch. Why wouldn't he and his brother just go off and sell them?'

'Because we know who he is,' Lewis said matter-of-factly. 'And he doesn't come by twenty dollars so easy as all that. Sure, the cars'll be right there when we get there. Don't worry about it.'

After a few minutes Griner came out of the house with his even bigger brother alongside. They were like two pro football linemen in their first season after retirement when they are beginning to soften up, working as night watchmen. We didn't try to introduce ourselves; the thought of asking them to shake hands with us never occurred to me until years later. I still wonder what would have happened if we had tried.

Drew's car came into sight from behind us. We told them what the arrangements were. The brothers and another man – who just simply materialized – got into an old Ford pickup with the paint seared off in patches clear down to the naked metal, and followed us. It seemed to me that we should have been following them, but from the filling station Lewis had the information he wanted; it was not much, but it was enough for him. He knew where the river was, approximately, he knew that the land flattened to the north and that there had been logging in the woods near the river. That all this might possibly be misinformation did not make the slightest difference to him. He was going there.

After a while he turned off on a dirt road. We ran along on this for a time, covering the truck behind us with ocher dust swirling up in a thick cloud from Lewis' too-fast driving. We ran past some farms and out over the crest of an open field on a section of road as straight as a plow furrow through two stands of rotten corn on either side, and then into some hot pinewoods that dropped off and kept dropping off. The road got worse. It began to curve back in the general direction of the highway, and Lewis craned his head out the window, trying to make the road bend back toward where he believed the river was. When he turned I was not expecting it, and thought we had hit something. We swayed off the road and down, everything going with us rattling. Lewis rose a little higher in the seat. Bushes whacked up under the car. I turned to look back. The other cars weren't behind us, as far as I could tell. I thought perhaps Lew's speed had lost them at the turn-off, but if they'd turned off with us they'd surely be in sight by now, and they weren't.

The road slung in a tight half-circle and gave out. In front of us were a few blackened boards on the ground and a rock chimney sinking into the weeds. A lizard ran over the biggest stone, and stopped with his head up. A dead sawhorse stood, off by itself in what looked like a sandpit.

'Well,' Lewis said, 'we screwed up.'

'Maybe we'd better let them show us where the river is.'

'We'll see.'

He backed into the weeds and manhandled the car around until we could get back on the track we had come down. When we reached the other road, the truck was waiting for us, with Drew's car behind it. I had wondered why Drew hadn't followed us, but it was like him to drop behind the truck; he didn't know anything about where he was going, and he was willing to listen to somebody who did.

The first Griner leaned out of the cab. 'Where you goin', city boy?'

Lewis flushed. 'Get on with it,' he said.

'Naw, naw,' Griner said. 'Go on ahead. You'll find it. Ain't nothin' but the biggest river in the state.'

Lewis gunned ahead again. We swung with the road to the right, then back to the left and down. Suddenly it hit me that there were some stumps among the trees going by.

'Maybe this is where they were logging,' I said.

Lewis nodded. 'This land has been sawmilled, all right,' he said. 'I figure we're getting there.'

The road kept dropping and failing. Finally it was only the ghost of a road; it was hard to believe that there had ever been any vehicles on it; it was almost like the rest of the woods. We eased on down. Once we had to crawl over a washout with the wheels barely balanced on each side. It would have been tough going in a jeep, even.

All at once the road fell away and slid down a kind of bank. I didn't see how it would be possible to get back up.

'Hold on,' Lewis said, and tipped the car over forward. Rhododendron and laurel bushes closed in on us with a soft limber rush. A branch of something jumped in the window and stayed, lying across my chest.

We had stopped, and I sat with the pressure of the woods against me; when I looked down I saw that one leaf was shaking with my heart.

Lewis held up a finger next to his ear. 'Listen,' he said.

I listened, not pushing away the limb. At first I didn't hear anything. Yet the silence sounded like something was coming up under it, something steady and even and unendable. Lewis started the engine, and I helped the branch off me and out the window as we crawled down, rustling with many leaves. A high bank rose up, and the road went straight to it and quit. There was a gully in front of the bank. I got out, looking at the ground for snakes. Why on God's earth am I here? I thought. But when I turned back to the car to see what Lewis was doing, I caught a glimpse of myself in the rear window. I was light green, a tall forest man, an explorer, guerrilla, hunter. I liked the idea and the image, I must say. Even if this was just a game, a charade, I had let myself in for it, and I was here in the woods, where such people as I had got myself up as were supposed to be. Something or other was being made good. I touched the knife hilt at my side, and remembered that all men were once boys, and that boys are always looking for ways to become men. Some of the ways are easy, too; all you have to do is be satisfied that it has happened.

Lewis went forward from me and jumped the gully. He climbed the bank and then stood for a moment the tallest man in the woods, his hands on his hips, looking down on the other side. I started up, too; I wanted to see what he was seeing. He went down the other side as I came up, feeling dirt on my hands for the first time in years. At the top there was nothing to see but more woods, and Lewis in his camouflage and Australian hat going through them. I went down in two or three soft, collapsing jumps that filled my tennis shoes with leaf mold. There was water at the bottom. Trees with thin leaves, like willows – maybe willows – were growing thickly there; I couldn't see beyond the puddle at the bottom, but it was stirring faintly, not stagnant. And then I realized that there was plenty of sound going on; we had come into it almost imperceptibly, and now it seemed all around us.

Lewis crow-hopped over the water and I followed, holding on to saplings when I could. He stopped and I came up beside him. He pulled an armload of arrowy leaves out of the way. I edged up more, looking out – or in – through the ragged, ashen window he made.

The river opened and was there. It was gray-green, very clear and yet with a certain milkiness, too; it looked as though it would turn white and foam at rocks more easily than other water. It was about forty yards wide, and shallow, about two and a half or three feet deep. The bed was full of clean brown pebbles. We couldn't see very far upstream or down because of our position and because of the willows, but just watched the part in front of us going by and by carrying nothing, not even a twig, as it lay in the branches and leaves in Lewis' arms. He let the limbs fall; they swept in gracefully and closed the river off again.

'There she is,' Lewis said, still looking straight ahead.

'Pretty,' I said. 'Pretty indeed.'

It took us a good long time to get the canoes off the cars and over the gully and the bank. Lew and Bobby pulled the canoes up the bank by the nose, hauling on the bow ropes, and Drew and I shoved from behind. Finally we slid them out through the willows. We put the wooden canoe in first. Lewis got down in the water, up to his knees in the bank mud, and supervised the loading. Both canoes had floorboards, though they were held in only by gravity and by the seats. We put in the perishables first and then the waterproof tents over everything, lashing them to the floorboard slats. Drew slid down into the water, and finally so did I. Then Lewis left.

'How about your guitar?' Bobby hollered from the top of the bank.

'Bring it,' Drew said, and then to me, 'I don't mind losing that old Martin in the river, but I'll be goddamned if I want those characters to run off with it.'

'I hope we don't ruin it, by spilling our foolish asses in this river,' I said.

'I don't know about you,' Drew said, as mock-country as he could talk, 'but I ain't planning to spill in this-here river. I'm a-goin' with you, and not Mr. Lewis Medlock. I done seen how he drove these roads he don't know nothin' about.'

'OK,' I said. 'Fine. But you probably ought to know that he can handle a canoe pretty well, and I can't. He's strong as the devil, too, and he's in shape. I'm not.'

'I'll take my chances,' he said. 'So will Miss Martin.'

Lewis and Bobby kept coming through the willows, carrying stuff, and Drew and I kept cramming it under the lashed-down tents, any way we could. Lewis should have stayed down here in the water with us, I thought. He could surely have done a better job of loading than we were doing. We floundered around in the slime, our feet deep in the mud.

Finally Bobby came through the leaves for the last time. 'We're ready,' he said.

'Everything all set about the cars?'

'Far as I can tell,' he said. 'Lewis is dealing with those guys now. I'm sure glad we're getting rid of them.'

Far off we heard a car start. It occurred to me that I had no idea at all of who the third driver in the truck was; I had not seen his face, or not noticed it.

'Personally,' Bobby said, 'I damn well doubt whether they can get the cars back up the road we came down.'

'That's a nice thought,' Drew said. 'What if they can't?'

'We'll be gone,' I said. 'Then it's their problem.'

'Damned if it's *their* problem,' Bobby said. 'What're we going to do if we come off this river, and there're no cars, down at what's-its-name?'

Lewis spoke through the branches. 'They'll be there,' he said. 'Don't worry about a thing.'

We now had our life jackets on and I held the wooden canoe

steady for Bobby to get in. He swayed out over the river and got into the bow seat. Lewis followed. The weight sank the canoe far enough into the water to make it as stable as it ever could be.

'OK,' Lew said. 'Turn loose.'

I did; they floated free. I stood watching over my shoulder. My feet were pointed toward the bank; I was mired down so far that I began to wonder how I was going to get out. I stayed rooted, holding on to the aluminum canoe while Drew got into the front and picked up the paddle.

'This how you hold this thing?' he asked me.

'I reckon,' I said. 'You hold it . . . like you hold it.'

I got one foot out of the mud by driving the other one about twice as far down, and then grabbed a long branch and pulled myself up as best I could with the river holding on to me hard by the left leg.

'It's got me,' I said.

'What's got you?'

'It.'

I scrambled and pulled on the branch until I was out. I kicked a foothold into the bank and stepped wide from it into the stern of Lewis' canoe and was in, everything rocking and wallowing. We pushed out with the paddles from the bank.

A slow force took hold of us; the bank began to go backward. I felt the complicated urgency of the current, like a thing made of many threads being pulled, and with this came the feeling I always had at the moment of losing consciousness at night, going toward something thing unknown that I could not avoid, but form which I would return. I dipped the paddle in.

Movies and pictures of Indians on calendars gave me a general idea of what to do, and I waved the paddle slowly through the water, down and along the left side of the canoe. The nose with Drew in it – I saw now that moving *him* to one side or the other, to turn the canoe, was going to be a big part of the problem – swung heavily out toward midstream, where the current began to pick us up and move us a little faster. The sensation of pure *riding* could not have been greater though we were doing not much more than drifting, bogged with the weight of gear, and with uncertainty. Downstream, Lewis and Bobby were hardly any better off, their strokes uncoordinated and helpless, though Lewis was trying. I supposed that he was letting Bobby get the feel of the water, and find which side he would rather paddle on. I told Drew to keep his paddle on the right, and we tried a few sweeps together, running over a very shallow place where the water quickened and broke and foamed over gray-brown gravel. We rocked and scraped on the stones.

'Go ahead and try a little stronger pull,' I said. 'We've got to find a way to make this thing move like we want it to.'

He dug in, and I swept with him. We settled into a good motion that moved us toward a curve. Once or twice my paddle hit the bottom-rocks; this put an odd, dissonant, intimate feeling into my hands. We started into the curve just as the other canoe disappeared around it. I plowed a little harder to turn us exactly with the current. Drew glanced back, his glasses flashing, the life preserver not turning. His face-side had a big grin. 'Hey, hey,' he said. 'How about this?'

'How about it, is right.'

As we straightened out of the curve I had a quick sensation of something wrong. Either the river was wrong or the green canoe was. Lewis and Bobby were traveling broadside to the gentle water, and Lewis was doing his best to bring the bow around. Bobby was totally confused, as nearly as I could tell, though he was trying to help. But they were going down the river backward. Drew put his hand over his face. I thought of hollering something to Lewis, but I couldn't bring myself to do it. Sometimes I could laugh at him, but I felt that it wouldn't be right to do it now. Drew and I rested, the paddles pulled up, keeping our mouths shut. The stream was with us, and we could watch. Bobby quit trying to paddle, and Lewis, by the sheer desire to do it, managed to swing the canoe broadside again, but just as he lifted it side-on to the current a paired set of rocks stopped it. Lewis banged and shoved at the rocks with his paddle and with his hands, and then tried to hunch the canoe free with his weight. Finally, though, he stepped off into the river and took hold of the canoe. Drew and I came alongside and I backwatered. On impulse I got out to help. Lew and I hauled and shoved, with Bobby sitting in the bow with his face absolutely perfect as an expression of dead weight.

Loading the canoe, I had not really been aware of the water, but now I was. It felt profound, its motion built into it by the composition of the earth for hundreds of miles upstream and down, and by thousands of years. The standing there was so good, so fresh and various and continuous, so vital and uncaring around my genitals, that I hated to leave it.

'Let's have a beer,' I said.

Lewis wiped off the sweat and rummaged around under the tents and the tarps. He came up with four twelve-ounce cans of beer from a polyethylene sack of melting ice, and we hung our forefingers in the rings and dragged them open. We were all thirsty from the work and anxiety of the loading, and my thirst and Lewis' went all the way back to the Griner Brothers' Garage, where I had shed more liquid than I thought I had in my system. I drank the whole can in one long, unhurried epical swallow.

I looked around. We were in the middle of a farm that backed steeply up on the river on two sides, one more than the other, and seemed to be battling the woods for existence. In a gully to my right as I faced downstream a cow was drinking; on top of a little grassy bluff others were lying down. Cow dung shone in the late heat, and there was a small misty, insane glimmering of insects wherever it had fallen.

I held the wavering color of the can under water until it filled enough to sink, and let it go, down and on past my ballooning nylon legs.

Lew and I started the canoe off the rocks with one three-armed shove, and I climbed back in with Drew. We entered a long straight stretch, moving with the fresh sweat that had sprung up from the beer as much as with the current.

The land on both sides climbed, and the river pulled us steadily toward a silver highway bridge. We went under, and the bridge clattered its boards as a pickup truck went over.

We were civilized again. On the right bank some tin sheds backed down to the water; the mud was covered with rusted pieces of metal, engine parts and the blue and green blinks of broken bottles. But there was something worse than any of this; some of the color was not only color; it was bright, unchangeable. Drew had been hit the same way, for another reason. 'Plastic,' he said. 'Doesn't decompose.'

'Does that mean you can't get rid of it,' I said, 'at *all?*'

'Doesn't go back to its elements,' he said, as though that were all right.

In the dark light the broken plastic pitchers shot out their rays like batteries. One was orange, one was yellow, and a water container was blue; what Martha, referring to clothes, would have called electric blue. The plastic throwaways were invulnerable in their colors, amongst the split, splintering boards and the brown-gold tin cans in the mud flats under the town, their lids pried-up and cruel, but going back to the earth.

The sky was beginning to smoke up with night, with complete, unlighted night. For a little while I thought that was the reason the water didn't have the clean sparkle, the deep-milk-but-clear that it had had when we got on it. The current lacked the arrowy drive, the sense of purpose that had been part of it in the willow woods. There was something in the texture of it.

I pulled my paddle out of the water; a white feather was stuck to the end of it. I shook it off and peered into the river. Off to the right and getting ready to go by under water was a vague choked whiteness. It was a log completely covered with chicken feathers, with all the feather-hairs weaving and wavering in a perfect physical representation of nausea. When you are sick enough, I said truly to myself, *that* is the thing you feel.

'There must be a poultry processing plant in this town,' Drew half turned and said.

'Sure.'

The river was feathering itself night and day. The rocks were full of feathers, drift on drift; even the down-river sides were streaming and bannered with them. Every shape under the river was a sick off-white; the water around us was full of little prim, dry feathers curled up like things set sail by children, all going at about the same speed we were. And out among them to the right, convoyed by six or eight feathers, was a chicken head with its glazed eye half-open, looking right at me and through me. If there had been more heads it would not have been so remarkable, but I saw only the one, going with us, turning its other eye as though the result of a movement of its gone body, drinking the sad water with a half-opened bill, pinwheeling and floating upside down, then turning over downstream again. I half hit at it with the paddle flat, but it only moved off a foot or so and settled back into the current beside us.

On a patchy flow of feathers we went down, over the unplucked rocks and logs in the deep, slow water, and I was resigned to going along that way for a while until I noticed, for no particular reason, that the depth of my ears was increasing in some way. I concentrated, and the sound of water both deepened and went up a tone. There was another bend ahead, and the river seemed to strain to get there, and we with it.

Around the turn it came into view, and broadened in white. Everywhere we were going was filled with spring-bubblings, with lively rufflings, not dangerous-looking but sprightly and vivid. There was not the sensation of the water's raging, but rather that of its alertness and resourcefulness as it split apart at rocks, frothed lightly, corkscrewed, fluted, fell, recovered, jostled into helmet-shapes over smoothed stones, and then ran out of sight down long garden-staircase steps around another turn.

I looked for a way through. Drew pointed straight ahead, and it was better done that way than saying it. I sank the paddle into the river. The main current V'd ahead of us, and looked to be straight, as far as I could tell, though the V that indicated the fastest water disappeared about halfway along down the rapids.

'Call the rocks,' I hollered. 'We want to go straight down the middle.'

'Ay, ay,' Drew said. 'Let's go there.'

We headed into the waist of the V. The canoe shifted gears underneath, and the water began to throw us. We rode into the funnel-neck and were sucked into the main rapids so suddenly that it felt as though the ordinary river had been snatched from under us like a rug, and we were tossing and bucking and banging on stones, trying to hold the head of the canoe downriver any way we could. Drew bobbed in front of me, leaping toward a place that could be reached in no other way. He was incompetent but cool; no panic came back from him. Every time he changed sides with his paddle, I changed to the opposite side. Once we began to go cater-cornered; the water began to swing us broadside like mania, and I felt control sliding away, off somewhere in the bank-bushes looking at us, but Drew made half the right move and I made the other half, and we righted. The hull scraped and banged over the rocks, but we hung straight in the current, trembling with force and luck, past the deadly, vibrant rocks we overflowed.

I yelled to Drew to keep his paddle on one side or the other. He chose the right – the biggest rocks seemed to be there; they kept looming up, through the water and just under it – while I alternated between sweeping us forward, adding to our speed wherever I could, and pulling backward on the river whenever we got too close to the rocks on the right. Already it was beginning to be like work I knew, and I felt safer because of that.

Now I could look on past Drew and see the white water lapse and riffle out into green and dark. There was a short flourish of nervous rippling that took us between two black boulders, and we were through.

Drew hiked up his hand on the gunwale of the canoe and looked back, with a surprised pleasure.

'Old Lewis,' he said. 'He knows something.'

I looked for the other canoe, which was not far ahead of us. Bobby and Lewis were plowing away at water that looked curiously dead, after the rapids.

But it was evening water. There was no sun on it, and the light that made the reflections was going fast. Far off ahead was the pouring of another set of rapids or falls with – I was already ready to bet – a curve in it.

I was awfully tired, though not sore. As the sun lost energy, so did I, and the edge of night-cold clinched it. I wanted to let go of the river.

69

We drifted slowly. The current entered my muscles and body as though I were carrying it; it came up through the paddle. I fished up a couple of beers from our pack and opened them and passed one to Drew. He twisted back and took it, one lens of his glasses dark with the sunset.

'It's a hard life with us pioneers,' he said, and whistled a line from 'In My Birch-Bark Canoe.'

I lifted my beer and drank, keeping the beer coming in as fast as I could get it down. The nylon of my legs was drying out and clinging to my calves and shins. I pulled the cloth legs loose from me and took up the paddle again. I felt marvelous.

We were about even with the other canoe. Like that we went down more drifting than paddling, into the dark coming upriver to meet us. There were no rapids – though we kept hearing them – and we were riding through rocky banks and tall mournful long-leaf pines. Once a little road, overgrown with weeds and bushes, ran along the left bank for a few hundred yards and then gave out at a fallen tree. A hawk circled in the dying blue, the trailing edge of his wings standing out sharply in the deep intensification of the evening sky.

It was beginning to be very wild and quiet. I remembered to be frightened and right away I was. It was the beautiful impersonality of the place that struck me the hardest; I would not have believed that it could hit me all at once like this, or with such force. The silence and the silence-sound of the river had nothing to do with any of us. It had nothing to do with the town we had just left, with its few streetlights in the mountain darkness, its cafes and the faces of farmers in the tired glow of rigged wires in the town square, and the one theater showing a film that was appearing on late television in the city. I dozed, much as I had done with Lewis in the car in the morning, and I saw again our approach to the blue hills, the changing shapes and colors and positions as we came toward them, except that in some way or another my mind got turned around and I was going backwards, away from the hills and through the Clabber Girl signs and away from the country Jesuses and back to the buildup of roadhouses and motels and shopping centers around the city. Martha was there, and Dean, and it was a shock for me to realize, all of a sudden, that I was not with them; that I was looking onward into curves of water. Martha was worrying now, watching TV with Dean. She was not used to being without me at night, and I could see her sitting with her hands folded, in the position of a woman bravely suffering. Not suffering badly, but suffering just the same, her feet in hot mules.

I backwatered a little, and drove us with a long stroke up alongside the green canoe. An insect hit my lips like a bullet.

'Don't you think we ought to make camp pretty soon?' I said to Lewis.

'Yeah, I do. I'm afraid if we go any farther the banks might begin to get too high for us to get out on. You-all look for a place on the left, and we'll look over here.'

We ran some small rapids, phosphorescent in the twilight, feeling hardly more than a slight alteration of the stream under us, but it was enough to remind us of the trouble that would result if we were to dump the equipment in the water in the dark. The trees and bushes where I was looking were connecting, becoming one solid thing; it was very hard to make out what the details were like. But there did seem to be a kind of shelf about four feet up from the water. I pointed this out to Lewis, and he nodded. I swung the canoe toward the place, working cater-cornered against the bias of the stream. We hit the bank with a soft yielding bump. I got squeamishly out into the water and held the canoe, the sliding cold around me full of the presence of night-creatures. Drew scrambled out and tied us to a sapling. I pulled myself up and out as Bobby and Lewis maneuvered alongside; the hair on my shoulders crawled with discomfort.

We unlashed the stuff and began to make camp. Lewis had brought some long flashlights, and he set these up on stumps and in the forks of bushes to form an area of concentrated light. In and out of this we moved, working at strange duties. Lewis seemed to know where everything was, and went around placing articles on the ground in the positions from which he expected them to rise and create a camp: the two tents, the grill, the air mattresses, the sleeping bags. They tried to be useful, but Drew and Bobby did not seem to be getting much done, and I saw the folly of just standing around and letting Lewis do everything, though it would have been all right with him if I had. I was sleepy, and I went to the equipment that had to do with that. I blew up the air mattresses with a hand pump, all four of them; it took a good half an hour, and I was pumping steadily all the time, while the river lightened in front of me and the woods at my back got thicker and thicker with blackness.

Lewis pitched the tents and Bobby and Drew made a show of looking around for firewood. When we had the tents up and the air sacks and sleeping bags inside them, with a flashlight in each tent and the snake guards up, I felt a good deal better; we had colonized the place. I went out with a flashlight to pick up some wood. Whenever I met one of the others I would shine the light into his chest or to one side of him so as not to shine it in his eyes, but I didn't like that. The upcast light gave Bobby's face a greased, Mongoloid cast; Drew's looked sand-blasted, with pins of deep shadow stuck all through it in the places where he'd had acne. Lewis' face didn't change much, and somehow this did not surprise me at all. The long shadow of his nose crawled upward between his eyes, his brow-ridges hung forward more, but his low voice seemed to come from the right place in the light, or from the right place just beside it.

He and I stood shining our beams out onto the river, the light curling and foaming like white water at the surface of the calm current. It was a lovely, melancholy camp. I liked standing there with the light going out of my hand for no reason and sliding up and down along the current, but I thought I probably ought to be doing something more useful, so I got my unstrung bow and hung it on a branch to make the spot look like a real hunting camp, first greasing the broadheads against the dew. Lewis came over and ran his palm over the handle section.

'The old catapult, eh?'

'Sure enough,' I said.

'You like these Howard Hill broadheads?'

'Yeah, I think they're fine. The last archery magazine I read said a two-bladed head has better penetration. That's good enough for me. Those guys know.'

'These don't windplane?'

'I've only shot 'em at stumps and earthwork targets, but they go straight, nearly as I can tell. They do out of this bow, anyway.'

Bobby poured everybody a stiff drink of bourbon, and we drank while Lewis made a fire against a bank of stones he had pulled up out of the ground or gathered from around the tents. He had brought steaks. He built up a big blaze, let it die down some and then put the meat on in a buttered pan.

The smell of the meat-smoke was wonderful. We all had another drink and sat on the bank, watching the firelight uncertain and persistent on the water. Fear and excitement and the prospect of eating all became forms of each other in my mind. There was a kind of comfort in knowing that we were where no one – no matter what issues were involved in other places – could find us, that night was around us and there was nothing we could do about it.

The pale fire on the water was not subject to the current, and this seemed wonderful to me. It played and danced where it was, an invulnerable spirit that would die. We all sat without saying anything, and I was proud of us for that, and especially proud of Lewis, who I was afraid was going to expound. I stretched out on my back, paralleling the river.

There was a darkness on my inland side when I opened my eyes; I thought I had been lying there a long time. But then something filled the space again. It was Drew with his guitar. I sat up, and the water, though it still swarmed weightlessly with the cave-images of fire, now seemed on the point of swirling them down.

Drew tuned softly, then raked out a soft chord that flowed and floated away.

'I've always wanted to do this,' he said. 'Only I didn't know it.'

He moved up the neck, drawing out chord after chord. These built and shimmered on each other in the darkness, in lonely harmony. Then he began to pick individual notes, and put the bass under them.

'It's woods music,' he said. 'Don't you think so?'

'Sure do.'

I loved the powerful nasal country clang, the steely humming and the strings hit like hammers on rails. Drew played deep and clean, and neither of us could have been happier. He played 'Expert Town' and 'Lord Bateman'; he played 'He Was a Friend of Mine' and 'Shaggy Dad' and Leadbelly's 'Easy, Mr. Tom.'

'I really ought to have a twelve-string for this one,' he explained, but it sounded good anyway.

Lewis brought over the cooked steaks while Drew played, and

then we ate, two little steaks apiece and big wedges of cake that Lewis' wife had made. We all had another drink. The fire was leaving us; in the river it had already died.

'You know,' Lewis said, 'we don't have too many more years for this kind of thing.'

'I guess not,' I said. 'But I can tell you, I'm glad we came. I'm glad to be here. I wouldn't be anywhere else, the way I feel.'

'It's true, Lewis,' Bobby said. 'It's all true, what you said. It's great. And I think we did real good on the river. I mean, for amateurs.'

'Yeah, good enough, I reckon,' Lewis said. 'But I'm sure glad you and I didn't get that damned sluggish wood canoe turned around backward just before we hit some white water. That might have been bad.'

'We didn't though,' Bobby said. 'And I don't think it'll happen again, do you?'

'I hope not,' Lewis said.

'Well, to the sleeping bags, men,' I said, stretching.

'Had my first wet dream in a sleeping bag,' Lewis said. 'I surely did.'

'How was it?' Bobby asked.

'Great. There's no repeating it.'

I stood up, finally, and creaked and stooped into the tent. I was massively tired, and hated the laces of my tennis shoes which had hardened in the water until I couldn't untie them. I pulled the shoes off by main-strength, shucked off everything else as well and got into the bag and zipped it up. Drew was still playing, out on the bank; I could hear him trying out some high minor, far away. I lay back in the soft down, crinkling into the elastic resistance of the air mattress. I snapped out the flashlight and closed my eyes.

I was out and in. I was stone dead and also, for a while, lying there listening, not knowing what I was listening for. It might have been a human voice with fire in it, an unearthly drunken man-howl; it might have been old Tom McCaskill screaming into the night from his fire.

Then there was nothing. I turned and saw Drew now beside me with his hand down along the seam of the bag.

I could hear the river running at my feet, and behind my head the woods were unimaginably dense and dark; there was nothing in them that knew me. There were creatures with one forepaw lifted, not wanting yet to put the other down on a dry leaf, for fear of the sound. There were the eyes made for seeing in this blackness; I opened my eyes and saw the dark in all its original color. In it I saw Martha's back heaving and working and dissolving into the studio, where we had finally decided that the photographs we had taken were no good and had asked the model back. We had also gone ahead with the Kitts' sales manager's idea to make the ad like the Coppertone scene of the little girl and the dog. There was Wilma holding the cat and forcing its claws out of its pads and fastening them into the back of the girl's panties. There was Thad; there was I. The panties stretched, the cat pulled, trying to get its claws out of the artificial silk, and then all at once leapt and clawed the girl's buttocks. She screamed, the room erupted with panic, she slung the cat round and round, a little orange concretion of pure horror, still hanging by one paw from the girl's panties, pulling them down, clawing and spitting in the middle of the air, raking the girl's buttocks and her legbacks. I was paralyzed. Nobody moved to do anything. The girl screamed and cavorted, reaching behind her.

Something hit the top of the tent. I thought it was part of what I had been thinking, for the studio was no dream. I put out a hand. The material was humming like a sail. Something seemed to have hold of the top of the tent; the cloth was trembling in a huge grasp. The sickening memory of where I was took hold of me from the inside of the heart. I groped down for the cold shank of the flashlight between the air sacks and snapped it on, running the weak glow up from the door of the tent. I kept seeing nothing but gray-green stitches until I got right above my head. The canvas was punctured there, and through it came one knuckle of a deformed fist, a long curving of claws that turned on themselves. Those are called talons, I said out loud.

I lay with the sweat ready to break, looking up through almost-closed lids, full now of a dread that was at least partly humorous. There was nothing, after all, so dangerous about an owl. Its other foot punctured the tent slowly and deliberately, and it shifted its weight until I could feel it come even. The claws did not relax, but the tent quivered less. Still, it shuddered lightly, as though we were about to be carried away in it. I dozed for a minute and tried to see what the tent must look like from the outside, with the big night bird – surely it was very big, from the size of the nails and feet – sitting in its own silence and equilibrium, holding us fast inside what it took to be our sleep.

The nails tightened a very little, the canvas tore slightly and then beat in a huge tent-beat; it seemed strange that we were still on the ground. I fell back, realizing that I had heard the first downstroke of the owl's wings, urgent and practically soundless; the stroke that hung it in the air as it set out.

Sometime later, from some deep place, I heard the woods beating. In the middle of this sound the tent shook; the owl had hold of it in the same place. I knew this before I cut the light on – it was still in my hand, exactly as warm as I was – and saw the feet, with the heel talons now also coming in. I pulled one hand out of the sleeping bag and saw it wander fraily up through the thin light until a finger touched the cold reptilian nail of one talon below the leg-scales. I had no idea of whether the owl felt me; I thought perhaps it would fly, but it didn't. Instead, it shifted its weight again, and the claws on the foot I was touching loosened for a second. I slipped my forefinger between the claw and the tent, and half around the stony toe. The claw tightened; the strength had something nervous and tentative about it. It tightened more, very strongly but not painfully. I pulled back until the hand came away, and this time the owl took off.

All night the owl kept coming back to hunt from the top of the tent. I not only saw his feet when he came to us; I imagined what he was doing while he was gone, floating through the trees, seeing everything. I hunted with him as well as I could, there in my weightlessness. The woods burned in my head. Toward morning I could reach up and touch the claw without turning on the light.

September 15th

I KEPT waking, and waking again, but when I was alive for good, the screen wire of the tent-front was gray and steady. Drew was deep in his sack, his head away from me. I lay with the flashlight still in one hand, and tried to shape the day. The river ran through it, but before we got back into the current other things were possible. What I thought about mainly was that I was in a place where none – or almost none – of my daily ways of living my life would work; there was no habit I could call on. Is this freedom? I wondered.

I zipped the sleeping bag down and rolled out, holding my breath, my own heat rising from me and fading away as I crawled free, with one quick look upward through the owl-hole. I pulled on my tennis shoes and bent toward the river sound, then stood up.

It was oddly warm and still and close, and the river was running with a heavy smoke of fog that moved just a little slower than the current must have been doing, rolling down the water in huge bodiless billows from upstream. It hovered at the bank while I watched, and overflowed, and in its silence I realized that I had been waiting for it to make a sound when it did this. I looked at my legs and they were gone, and my hands at my sides also; I stood with the fog eating me alive.

An idea came to me. I went back to my duffel bag, got out a two-piece suit of long underwear and put it on; it was almost exactly the color of the fog. My bow was backed and faced with white fiber glass, usually a disadvantage in green or brown woods but a very good thing now. I strung the bow, leaning on the live weight and resistance, took an arrow out of the bow quiver and went around behind the tents. The fog was seeping up over the canvas, swirling a little with the motion of deep water around Lewis and the others. It went back into the woods up what looked to be a long thin draw or little ravine, and I followed it, giving up my idea of waking Lewis and concentrating on being quiet. I couldn't see far ahead, but I knew that if I stayed in the draw, all I would have to do to get back down to camp, even if the fog got worse, would be to turn around and come back down until I practically – or actually – stumbled over the tents. I concentrated on getting into some kind of relation to the woods under these conditions; I was as invisible as a tree.

At first I didn't have any idea of really hunting. I had no firm notion of what I was doing, except walking forward carefully, away from the river and into more and more silence and blindness – for the fog was now coming up past me and thickening straight back into my face – and carrying a bow and a nocked arrow and three other arrows in one hand and fingering the bowstring with the other. It tingled like a wire in my right-hand fingers, giving off an electric current that came from the woods and the fog and the fact that hunting and pretending to hunt had come together and I could not now tell them apart. Behind the tents, before I had got into the woods, I had figured that since I had the equipment to hunt and knew to some extent how to use it, I might as well make some show of doing what I said I had come for. All I had really wanted was to stay away a reasonable length of time, long enough for the others to wake and find me gone – I thought of just sitting down on the bank of the ravine and waiting for half an hour by my watch – and then walk back into camp with my bow strung and say I'd been out taking a look around. That would satisfy honor.

But now not; not quite. I was really looking and really listening, and a good many things came together in my legs and arms and fingers. I was a good shot, at least up to thirty-five yards, and the visibility I had was not going to be anything like that in the next half hour. I could do it, if I came on a deer; I felt certain I could, and would.

The fog was still heavy, but the draw-bottom began to climb, and as I went upward there was more light, first light through the fog and then things through the fog – leaves and twigs. The walls of the ditch – which I now saw was what I was in – were not as high now, barely to my shoulders, and I could see levelly along the ground into the woods a little way on both sides. Nothing moved, and there was also the quiet of nothing being there, though I did my best not to make a sound in case there was. The wet ground helped me; as far as I could tell I caused very little sound to come into the place, and thought perhaps that technically I didn't make such a bad hunter after all, at least for a little while.

Now I was walking up what was hardly more than a sunken track, caved in on both sides, with the last rags of mist around me. I knew I had better not go much farther or I might lose the ditch. I stopped to turn around. There was nothing in any direction I hadn't already seen.

I started back, still looking as far off as I could into the woods rising slowly up to eye level right and left. The mist began to roll into my face in thin puffs. I was beginning to worry about walking right off past the tents into the river when to the left I saw something move. I stopped, and the fog rose exactly to my teeth. About fifteen yards from me, right at the limit of my vision, was a small deer, a spike buck as nearly as I could tell from the shape of his head. He was browsing, the ghost of a deer but a deer just the same. He lifted his head and looked directly at my face, which from his angle must have seemed like a curious stone on the ground, if he saw it. I stood there, buried to the neck in the ditch, in the floor of the forest.

He was broadside to me; I had shot a thousand targets one-quarter his size at the same distance, and when I recalled this – when my eyes and hands got together on it – I knew I could kill him just as easily as I could hit his outline on cardboard. I raised the bow.

He brought his head a little higher and lowered it again. I pulled the string back to the right side of my face and began to steady down. For a moment I braced there at the fullest tension of the bow, which brought out of me and into the bow about three fourths of my own strength, with the arrow pointing directly into his heart. It was a slight upshot, and I allowed for this, though at the range it wouldn't matter much.

I let go, but as I released I knew it was a wrong shot, not very wrong but wrong enough. I had done the same thing on key shots in archery tournaments: lifted my bow hand just as the shot went. At the sound of the bowstring the deer jumped and wheeled at about the time the arrow should have gone through him. I thought I might have hit him high, but actually I had seen the orange feathers flick and disappear over his shoulder. I may even have touched him, but I was fairly sure I had not drawn blood. He ran a few steps and turned, looking back around his side at me. I jerked loose another arrow and strung it, but my heart was gone. I was shaking, and I had trouble getting the arrow nocked. I had it only about halfway back when he took off for good. I turned loose anyway and saw the arrow whip badly and disappear somewhere above where he had been.

I was heaving and sweating as I drew in the fog and let it

back out, a sick, steaming gas. Like that, I went downhill, part of the time with my hand at arm's length in front of my face. I saw the tents – one of them, then another thing like it – as low dark patches with something structured about them, clearly out of place here.

Lewis was up, trying to make a fire with wet twigs and branches. As I unstrung the bow, the others came out too.

'What about it, buddy?' Lewis said, looking at the two empty slots in the quiver.

'I got a shot.'

'You did?' Lewis said, straightening.

'I did. A spectacular miss at fifteen yards.'

'What happened? We could'a had meat.'

'I boosted my bow hand, I think. I psyched out. I'll be damned if I know how. I had him. He was getting bigger all the time. It was like shooting at the wall of a room. But I missed, all right. It was just that little second, right when I turned loose. Something said raise your hand, and before I could do anything about it, I did it.'

'Damn,' Bobby said. 'Psychology. The delicate art of the forest.'

'You'll get another chance,' Drew said. 'We got a long ways to go yet.'

'What the hell,' I said. 'If I'd hit him I'd be back in the woods now, tracking. He'd be hard to find in this fog. So would I.'

'You could've marked the place you shot from and come back and got us,' Lewis said. 'We could've found him.'

'You'd have a time finding him now,' I said. 'He's probably in the next county.'

'I guess so,' Lewis said. 'But it's a shame. Where's my old steady buddy?'

'Your old steady buddy exploded,' I said. 'High and wide.'
Lewis looked at me.

'I know you wouldn't have, Lewis,' I said. 'You don't need to tell me. We'd have meat. We'd all live forever. And you know something? I wish you'd been up there and I'd been with you. I would'a just unstrung my bow and watched you put it right into the heart-lung area. Right into the boiler room. The pinwheel, at fifteen yards. What I was really thinking about up there was you.'

'Well, next time don't think about me. Think about the deer.'

I let that ride and went to drag the stuff out of the tents. Lewis finally got a kind of fire started. When the sun began to take on height and force, the mist burned off in a few minutes. Through it the river, which we could hardly make out at first, showed itself more and more until we could see not only the flat of it and the stitches of the current but down through it into the pebbles of the stream-bed near the bank.

We had pancakes with butter and sorghum. After we finished, Lewis went over to the stream to wash out the cooking stuff. I pulled all the air mattresses out on the ground, unscrewed their caps and lay on each in turn until the ground came up to me through it and I was lying on the last sigh of air I had pumped into it the night before. We rolled the tents, wet and covered with leaves and pieces of bark, and lashed them into the canoes. I asked the others if they thought we might team up differently this time, for I was afraid that Lewis in his impatience might say something unpleasant to Bobby, and, since Bobby suddenly seemed to me on the edge of exasperation with himself for coming, I thought it would probably be best if I took him on. Drew would not have laughed, or laughed in the right way, at the cracks that were Bobby's only means of salvaging his civility, and I figured I would.

'How about it, tiger?' I said to Bobby.

'OK,' he said. 'How far can we get today, do you reckon?'

'Beats me,' I said. 'We'll get as far as we can. Depends on the water, and how many places we have to walk through. Everybody including the map says there's a gorge down below here, and that sort of bothers me. But there's nothing we can do about it now.'

Bobby and I got in and shoved off, and right away I could tell I was in for a hard time. I was not in awfully good shape myself, but Bobby was wheezing and panting after the first hundred yards. He had no coordination at all, and changed the canoe from what it had been with Drew's steady, serious weight in front to a nervous, unstable craft that seemed bound and determined to do everything wrong, to get rid of us. I was sure that Lewis was disgusted with Bobby, and just as sure that I would be, also, before much longer.

'Easy,' I said. 'Easy. You're trying too hard. All we want to do is hold this thing straight. We don't need to be pulling our guts out to get there. Just let the river do it. Let George do it.'

'George ain't doing it fast enough. I want to get the hell and gone out of this goddamned place.'

'Ah, now. It's not all that bad.'

'It's *not?* Mosquitoes ate me up last night. My bites have got bites. I'm catching a fucking cold from sleeping on the fucking ground. I'm hungry as hell for something that tastes good. And I don't mean sorghum.'

'Just steady down a little, and we'll get there . . . when we get there. It's not going to do your cold any good to dump in this river, you can bloody well bet.'

'Fuck it,' he said. 'Let's get on with it. I'm tired of this woods scene; I'm tired of shitting in a hole in the ground. This is for the Indians.'

After a while he settled down a little, and the back of his neck lightened its red. We dug a couple of strokes for every twenty-five yards, and the river moved us along. But I thought that the chances were pretty good, with my high center of gravity and his nerves, that we would spill before the day was out, especially if there were any fast stretches with lots of rocks. With the equipment and with Bobby and me, who were at least fifty pounds heavier than the other two, we were riding far too low in the water. We had too much stuff with us for the way we were teamed, and I signaled back to Lewis to pull over to the bank. He did, and we wallowed alongside the other canoe and tied up.

'Getting hot,' Lewis said.

'Hot as the hinges,' I said.

'Did you see that big snake back yonder?'

'No. Where?'

'He was lying up in the limbs of that old oak tree you went under about a mile and a half back. I didn't see him till you were right under him, and he lifted his head. I didn't want to make any fuss; thought it might make him nervous. I'm pretty sure it was a moccasin. I've heard of them dropping in boats.'

'Shit fire,' Bobby said. 'That's all we need.'

'Yeah,' said Lewis. 'I can imagine.'

'Can you take on some of the stuff in our canoe, Lewis?' I asked. 'We're awful low and logy.'

'Sure. Go get the cooking equipment and the bedrolls. That ought to equalize us, just about. You can also let us have about half the beer that's left.'

'Happy to. Everybody's going to need something to cool off with, today.'

'Why do it just with beer?' Lewis said, unbuttoning his shirt. 'It's shallow and slow here. I'm going to get wet.'

I transferred the bedrolls and beer and the primus and other cooking equipment to the other canoe. Lewis was already in the water naked, booming overhand down the current with a lot of back showing, like Johnny Weismuller in the old Tarzan movies. He swam as well as he did everything else, and outran the current easily. Then he came back, his eyes glaring with effort at water level. I shucked off my coveralls and dived in, and so did Drew.

The river was very cold; it felt as though it had snow and ice in it, and had only just turned then to water. But it was marvelously clear and alive, and broke like glass around you and came together unhurt. I swam a little way into the current, and would gladly have given up all human effort – I was tired of human efforts of all kinds, especially my own – and gone on downstream either dead or alive, to wherever it would take me. But I swam back, a hard forty yards against the subtle tearing and downstream insistence, and stood up next to Lewis, who was waist deep with water crumpling and flopping at his belly. I looked at him, for I have never seen him with his clothes off.

Everything he had done for himself for years paid off as he stood there in his tracks, in the water. I could tell by the way he glanced at me; the payoff was in my eyes. I had never seen such a male body in my life, even in the pictures in the weight-lifting magazines, for most of those fellows are short, and Lewis was about an even six feet. I'd say he weighed about 190. The muscles were bound up in him smoothly, and when he moved, the veins in the moving part would surface. If you looked at him that way, he seemed made out of well-matched redbrown chunks wrapped in blue wire. You could even see the veins in his gut, and I knew I could not even begin to conceive how many sit-ups and leg-raises – and how much dieting – had gone into bringing them into view.

He dropped a hand on my shoulder and stirred the fur around. 'What do you think, Bolgani the Gorilla?'

'I think Tarzan speak with forked tongue,' I said. 'I think Lord of Jungle speak with tongue of Histah the Snake. I think we never get out of woods. He bring us here to stay and found kingdom.'

'Yeah,' said Bobby from the bank. 'Kingdom of Snakes is right.'

Drew came out of the river near us. 'Gosh that feels good,' he said. 'It really does. I never felt anything more wonderful in my life. Refreshing. You know, that's just what it is. I feel like I can go all day, now. You better come on in for a minute, Bobby.'

'No thanks. Whenever you're ready, me and the other Fatso will just Fatso on down, the washed and the unwashed.'

He sat with his knees drawn up, self-protective in the sun against the water-chill he could see on us. Our nipples were blue and drawn up, and my stomach muscles were beginning to heave against the moving underwater freeze. I climbed out and pulled on my sweaty coveralls. My head was fresh and cool while my body heated up, and I wanted to get back on the river before I began to melt again.

Bobby and I went over to our canoe and tried to figure out what else we might be able to transfer to the other one. We finally ended up taking only one tent, my bow, a six-pack of beer and Drew's guitar, for the wooden canoe was leaking a little and ours was more or less dry. We wrapped the guitar in the tent, got in and pushed off.

We rode a lot better now, and Bobby's paddling improved a good deal because of this, and maybe because he had convinced himself that the less trouble he was the quicker we'd get off the river.

The water was calm for a long time. We made turn after turn, sometime near one bank, and sometime near the other. I tried not to go under any more limbs, and this was easy enough to do. The river spread and slowed and quieted, and we had to paddle more than we had been doing. We could hardly feel any current at all; it was very faint, and when we rested it was as though we were drawn forward by something invisible underneath us, while the water around us stood still. We could hear sound far off in front, but it kept retreating down-stream. Each turn opened out only on another stretch of river, gradually unfolding its woods along both banks. A heron of some kind flushed on the right. He swept downstream in front of us, going left, then right, then left-right, dipping quickly and indecisively. He would disappear around the next turn, then, as we came around it, would spring up again from leaves where we had not seen him and muscle himself into the air on long blue wings, giving a hoarse agonized inhuman cry and making a magnificent half-turn over the river ahead of us, then start downstream again with long wingbeats, the tips of his wings all but touching the water, so that wherever he was his shadow started up under him at each downstroke, vague and misshapen with the river. This continued through four or five turns, until we came around another one like the others and did not see him. He may have veered into the woods, but I thought that most probably he had learned to sit still, maybe nearing hysterical flight once again as we approached and went past, but managing to keep that long-necked, desperate cry in his throat until we had gone.

In the new silence the river seemed to go deeper and deeper under us; the colors changed toward denser greens as the sun got higher. The pace of the water began to pick up; we slid farther and farther with each stroke. I thought to myself that anyone fighting the brush along the bank could not keep up with us.

Every now and then I glanced down at the bow at my feet, big-handled and tense-looking, and at its two arrows slathered with house paint. The big orange feathers spiraled out of them, and the emery-wheeled edges of the broadheads shone in the sun like radium. Though I would have had to do a good deal of curious balancing to string the bow, I keep looking on both sides of the river for deer, hoping that we might float in on a big buck drinking. It was something to do.

We went through some deep, quickened water and floated out into a calm broad stretch of a long turn that slid us into a dim underpass of enormous trees, conifers of some kind, spruce or fir. It was dark and heavy in there; the packed greenness seemed to suck the breath out of your lungs. Bobby and I lifted our paddles clear of the river as by a signal, and we eased through the place the way the river wanted to go. Intense needles of light shook on the ripples, gold, hot enough to burn and almost solid enough to pick up from the surface like nails.

We came out among some fields grown up six or seven feet high in grass. A mottled part of the bank slipped into the water, and it took me a minute to realize it was a snake. He went across about twenty feet in front of us, swimming as if crawling, his head high, and came out on the opposite bank without changing his motion at all, a thing with a single spell, a single movement, and no barriers.

We went on, taking Jong slow swings at the water. I had fitted my stroke to Bobby's the best I could; I moved when he moved, and had got to the point where I could put my paddle in the water and lift it out at the same time he did. I thought he must surely be taking some satisfaction in the improvement, but I didn't say anything for fear of upsetting the rhythm.

After two hours from the time the heron left us we had drunk all the beer we had. The sun was eating my bald spot, and my nylon outfit was soaking with me. My tongue began to balloon in my mouth, and my backbone was splintering through the skin; I kept touching it between strokes to see if anything had given way. The edge of the seat was digging into my right thigh, for that was the only position in which I could get a good grip on the river. All the pains began to try to link up with each other and there was nothing I could do about it.

I looked back. The other canoe was just coming around. Lewis had lagged behind us because, I suppose, he wanted us in sight in case we got into trouble. Anyway, they were about half a mile back and disappeared as we rounded another curve, and I pointed with my paddle to the left bank. I didn't know whether they saw me or not, but I figured to flag them in when they came by. I wanted to lie up in the shade and rest for a while. I was hungry, and I sure would've liked to have had another beer. We dug in and swung over.

As we closed in on the left bank, a pouring sound came from under the trees; the leaves at a certain place moved as if in a little wind. The fresh green-white of a creek was frothing into the river. We sailed past it half-broadside and came to the bank about seventy-five yards downstream. I put the nose against it and paddled hard to hold it there while Bobby got out and moored us.

'This is too much like work,' Bobby said, as he gave me a hand up.

'Lord, Lord,' I said. 'I'm getting too old for this kind of business. I suppose you could call it learning the hard way.'

Bobby sat down on the ground and untied a handkerchief

from around his neck. He leaned down to the river and sopped it, then swabbed his face and neck down, rubbing a long time in the nose area. I bent over and touched my toes a couple of times to get rid of the position that had been maiming my back, and then looked upstream. I still couldn't see the other canoe. I turned to say something to Bobby.

Two men stepped out of the woods, one of them trailing a shotgun by the barrel.

Bobby had no notion they were there until he looked at me. Then he turned his head until he could see over his shoulder and got up, brushing at himself.

'How goes it?' he said.

One of them, the taller one, narrowed in the eyes and face. They came forward, moving in a kind of half circle as though they were stepping around something. The shorter one was older, with big white eyes and a half-white stubble that grew in whorls on his cheeks. His face seemed to spin in many directions. He had on overalls, and his stomach looked like it was falling through them. The other was lean and tall, and peered as though out of a cave or some dim simple place far back in his yellow-tinged eyeballs. When he moved his jaws the lower bone came up too far for him to have teeth. 'Escaped convicts' flashed up in my mind on one side, 'Bootleggers' on the other. But they still could have been hunting.

They came on, and were ridiculously close for some reason. I tried not to give ground; some principle may have been involved.

The older one, looming and spinning his sick-looking face in front of me, said, 'What the *hail* you think you're doin'?'

'Going downriver. Been going since yesterday.'

I hoped that the fact that we were at least talking to each other would do some good of some kind.

He looked at the tall man; either something or nothing was passing between them. I could not feel Bobby anywhere near, and the other canoe was not in sight. I shrank to my own true size, a physical movement known only to me, and with the strain my solar plexus failed. I said, 'We started from Oree yesterday afternoon, and we hope we can get to Aintry sometime late today or early tomorrow.'

'*Aintry?*'

Bobby said, and I could have killed him, 'Sure. This river just runs one way, cap'n. Haven't you heard?'

'You ain't never going to get down to Aintry,' he said, without any emphasis on any word.

'Why not?' I asked, scared but also curious; in a strange way it was interesting to cause him to explain.

'Because this river don't go to Aintry,' he said. 'You done taken a wrong turn somewhere. This-here river don't go nowhere near Aintry.'

'Where does it go?'

'It goes . . . it goes . . .'

'It goes to Circle Gap,' the other man said, missing his teeth and not caring. ''Bout fifty miles.'

'Boy,' said the whorl-faced man, 'you don't know *where* you are.'

'Well,' I said, 'we're going where the river's going. We'll come out somewhere, I reckon.'

The other man moved closer to Bobby.

'Hell,' I said, 'we don't have anything to do with you. We sure don't want any trouble. If you've got a still near here, that's fine with us. We could never tell anybody where it is, because you know something? You're right. We don't know where we are.'

'A *stee*-ul?' the tall man said, and seemed honestly surprised.

'Sure,' I said. 'If you're making whiskey, we'll buy some from you. We could sure use it.'

The drop-gutted man faced me squarely. 'Do you know what the *hail* you're talkin' about?'

'I don't know what you're talking about,' I said.

'You done said something about makin' whiskey. You think we're makin' whiskey. Now come on. Ain't that right?'

'Shit,' I said. 'I don't know whether you're making whiskey or hunting or rambling around in the woods for your whole fucking life. I don't know and I don't care what you're doing. It's not any of my business.'

I looked at the river, but we were a little back from the bank, and I couldn't see the other canoe. I didn't think it could have gone past, but I was not really sure that it hadn't. I shook my head in a complete void, at the thought that it might have; we had got too far ahead, maybe.

With the greatest effort in the world, I came back into the man's face and tried to cope with it. He had noticed something about the way I had looked at the river.

'Anybody else with you?' he asked me.

I swallowed and thought, with possibilities shooting through each other. If I said yes, and they meant trouble, we would bring Lewis and Drew into it with no defenses. Or it might mean that we would be left alone, four being too many to handle. On the other hand, if I said no, then Lewis and Drew – especially Lewis – might be able to . . . well, to do something. Lewis' pectorals loomed up in my mind, and his leg, with the veins bulging out of the divided muscles of his thigh, his leg under water wavering small-ankled and massive as a centaur's. I would go with that.

'No,' I said, and took a couple of steps inland to draw them away from the river.

The lean man reached over and touched Bobby's arm, feeling

94

it with strange delicacy. Bobby jerked back, and when he did the gun barrel came up, almost casually but decisively.

'We'd better get on with it,' I said. 'We got a long ways to go.' I took part of a step toward the canoe.

'You ain't goin' nowhere,' the man in front of me said, and leveled the shotgun straight into my chest. My heart quailed away from the blast tamped into both barrels, and I wondered what the barrel openings would look like at the exact instant they went off: if fire would come out of them, or if they would just be a gray blur or if they would change at all between the time you lived and died, blown in half. He took a turn around his hand with the string he used for a trigger.

'You come on back in here 'less you want your guts all over this-here woods.'

I half-raised my hands like a character in a movie. Bobby looked at me, but I was helpless, my bladder quavering. I stepped forward into the woods through some big bushes that I saw but didn't feel. They were all behind me.

The voice of one of them said, 'Back up to that saplin'.'

I picked out a tree. 'This one?' I said.

There was no answer. I backed up to the tree I had selected. The lean man came up to me and took off my web belt with the knife and rope on it. Moving his hands very quickly, he unfastened the rope, let the belt out and put it around me and the tree so tight I could hardly breathe, with the buckle on the other side of the tree. He came back holding the knife. It occurred to me that they must have done this before; it was not a technique they would just have thought of for the occasion.

The lean man held up the knife, and I looked for the sun to strike it, but there was no sun where we were. Even so, in the intense shadow, I could see the edge I had put on it with a suburban grindstone: the minute crosshatching of high-speed abrasions, the wearing-away of metal into a murderous edge.

'Look at that,' the tall man said to the other. 'I bet that'll shave h'ar.'

'Why'ont you try it? Looks like that'n's got plenty of it. 'Cept on his head.'

The tall man took hold of the zipper of my coveralls, breathing lightly, and zipped it down to the belt as though tearing me open.

'Good God Amighty,' said the older one. 'He's like a god-damned monkey. You ever see anything like that?'

The lean man put the point of the knife under my chin and lifted it. 'You ever had your balls cut off, you fuckin' ape?'

'Not lately,' I said, clinging to the city. 'What good would they do you?'

He put the flat of the knife against my chest and scraped it across. He held it up, covered with black hair and a little blood. 'It's sharp,' he said. 'Could be sharper, but it's sharp.'

The blood was running down from under my jaw where the point had been. I had never felt such brutality and carelessness of touch, or such disregard for another person's body. It was not the steel or the edge of the steel that was frightening; the man's fingernail, used in any gesture of his, would have been just as brutal; the knife only magnified his unconcern. I shook my head again, trying to get my breath in a gray void full of leaves. I looked straight up into the branches of the sapling I was tied to, and then down into the clearing at Bobby.

He was watching me with his mouth open as I gasped for enough breath to live on from second to second. There was nothing he could do, but as he looked at the blood on my chest and under my throat, I could see that his position terrified him more than mine did; the fact that he was not tied mattered in some way.

They both went toward Bobby, the lean man with the gun this time. The white-bearded one took him by the shoulders and turned him around toward downstream.

'Now let's you just drop them pants,' he said.

Bobby lowered his hands hesitantly. 'Drop . . . ?' he began.

My rectum and intestines contracted. Lord God.

The toothless man put the barrels of the shotgun under Bobby's right ear and shoved a little. 'Just take 'em right on off,' he said.

'I mean, what's this all . . .' Bobby started again weakly.

'Don't say nothin',' the older man said. 'Just do it.'

The man with the gun gave Bobby's head a vicious shove, so quick that I thought the gun had gone off. Bobby unbuckled his belt and unbuttoned his pants. He took them off, looking around ridiculously for a place to put them.

'Them panties too,' the man with the belly said.

Bobby took off his shorts like a boy undressing for the first time in a gym, and stood there plump and pink, his hairless thighs shaking, his legs close together.

'See that log? Walk over yonder.'

Wincing from the feet, Bobby went slowly over to a big fallen tree and stood near it with his head bowed.

'Now git on down crost it.'

The tall man followed Bobby's head down with the gun as Bobby knelt over the log.

'Pull your shirt-tail up, fat-ass.'

Bobby reached back with one hand and pulled his shirt up to his lower back. I could not imagine what he was thinking.

'I said *up*,' the tall man said. He took the shotgun and shoved the back of the shirt up to Bobby's neck, scraping a long red mark along his spine.

The white-bearded man was suddenly also naked up to the waist. There was no need to justify or rationalize anything; they were going to do what they wanted to. I struggled for life in the air, and Bobby's body was still and pink in an obscene posture that no one could help. The tall man restored the gun to Bobby's head, and the other one knelt behind him.

A scream hit me, and I would have thought it was mine except for the lack of breath. It was a sound of pain and outrage, and was followed by one of simple and wordless pain. Again it came out of him, higher and more carrying. I let all the breath out of myself and brought my head down to look at the river. Where are they, every vein stood out to ask, and as I looked the bushes broke a little in a place I would not have thought of and made a kind of complicated alleyway out onto the stream – I was not sure for a moment whether it was water or leaves – and Lewis' canoe was in it. He and Drew both had their paddles out of water, and then they turned and disappeared.

The white-haired man worked steadily on Bobby, every now and then getting a better grip on the ground with his knees. At last he raised his face as though to howl with all his strength into the leaves and the sky, and quivered silently while the man with the gun looked on with an odd mixture of approval and sympathy. The whorl-faced man drew back, drew out.

The standing man backed up a step and took the gun from behind Bobby's ear. Bobby let go of the log and fell to his side, both arms over his face.

We all sighed. I could get better breath, but only a little.

The two of them turned to me. I drew up as straight as I could and waited with the tree. It was up to them. I could sense my knife sticking in the bark next to my head and I could see the blood vessels in the eyes of the tall man. That was all; I was blank.

The bearded man came to me and disappeared around me. The tree jerked and air came into my lungs in great gratitude. I fell forward and caught up short, for the tall man had put the gun up under my nose; it was a very odd sensation, funnier than it might have been when I thought of my brain as thinking of Dean and Martha at that instant and also of its being scattered, material of some sort, over the bush-leaves and twigs in the next second.

'You're kind of ball-headed and fat, ain't you?' the tall man said.

'What do you want me to say?' I said. 'Yeah. I'm bald-headed and fat. That OK?'

'You're hairy as a goddamned dog, ain't you?'

'Some dogs, I suppose.'

'What the *hail* . . .' he said, half turning to the other man.

'Ain't no hair in his mouth,' the other one said.

'That's the truth,' the tall one said. 'Hold this on him.'

Then he turned to me, handing the gun off without looking. It stood in the middle of the air at the end of his extended arm. He said to me, 'Fall down on your knees and pray, boy. And you better pray good.'

I knelt down. As my knees hit, I heard a sound, a snap-slap off in the woods, a sound like a rubber band popping or a sickle-blade cutting quick. The older man was standing with the gun barrel in his hand and no change in the stupid, advantage-taking expression of his face, and a foot and a half of bright red arrow was shoved forward from the middle of his chest. It was there so suddenly it seemed to have come from within him.

None of us understood; we just hung where we were, the tall man in front of me unbuttoning his pants, me on my knees with my eyelids clouding the forest, and Bobby rolling back and forth, off in the leaves in the corner of my eye. The gun fell, and I made a slowmotion grab for it as the tall man sprang like an animal in the same direction. I had it by the stock with both hands, and if I could pull it in to me I would have blown him in half in the next second. But he only gripped the barrel lightly and must have felt that I had it better, and felt also what every part of me was concentrated on doing; he jumped aside and was gone into the woods opposite where the arrow must have come from.

I got up with the gun and the power, wrapping the string around my right hand. I swung the barrel back and forth to cover everything, the woods and the world. There was nothing in the clearing but Bobby and the shot man and me. Bobby was still on the ground, though now he was lifting his head. I could understand that much, but something kept blurring the clear idea of Bobby and myself and the leaves and the river. The shot man was still standing. He wouldn't concentrate in my vision; I couldn't believe him. He was like a film over the scene, gray and vague, with the force gone out of him; I was amazed at how he did everything. He touched the arrow experimentally, and I could tell that it was set in him as solidly as his breastbone. It was in him tight and unwobbling, coming out front and back. He took hold of it with both hands, but compared to the arrow's strength his hands were weak; they weakened more as I looked, and began to melt. He was on his knees, and then fell to his side, pulling his legs up. He rolled back and forth like a man with the wind knocked out of him, all the time making a bubbling, gritting sound. His lips turned red, but from his convulsions – in which there was something comical and unspeakable – he seemed to gain strength. He got up on one knee and then to his feet again while I stood with the shotgun at port arms. He took a couple of strides toward the woods and then seemed to change his mind and danced back to me, lurching and clog-stepping in a secret circle. He held out a hand to me, like a prophet, and I pointed the shotgun straight at the head of the arrow, ice coming into my teeth. I was ready to put it all behind me with one act, with one pull of a string.

But there was no need. He crouched and fell forward with his face on my white tennis shoe tops, trembled away into his legs and shook down to stillness. He opened his mouth and it was full of blood like an apple. A clear bubble formed on his lips and stayed there.

I stepped back and looked at the whole scene again, trying to place things. Bobby was propped up on one elbow, with his eyes as red as the bubble in the dead man's mouth. He got up, looking at me. I realized that I was swinging the gun toward him; that I pointed wherever I looked: I lowered the barrel. What to say?

'Well.'

'Lord God,' Bobby said. 'Lord God.'

'You all right?' I asked, since I needed to know even though I cringed with the directness.

Bobby's face expanded its crimson, and he shook his head. 'I don't know,' he said. 'I don't know.'

I stood and he lay with his head on his palm, both of us looking straight ahead. Everything was quiet. The man with the aluminum shaft in him lay with his head on one shoulder and his right hand relaxedly holding the barb of the arrow. Behind him the blue and silver of Lewis' fancy arrow crest shone, unnatural in the woods.

Nothing happened for ten minutes. I wondered if maybe the other man wouldn't come back before Lewis showed himself, and I began to compose a scene in which Lewis would step out of the woods on one side of the clearing with his bow and the tall man would show on the other, and they would have it out in some way that it was hard to imagine. I was working on the details when I heard something move. Part of the bark of a big water oak moved at leg level, and Lewis moved with it out into the open, stepping sideways into the clearing with another bright-crested arrow on the string of his bow. Drew followed him, holding a canoe paddle like a baseball bat.

Lewis walked out between me and Bobby, over the man on the ground, and put his bow tip on a leaf. Drew moved to Bobby. I had been holding the gun ready for so long that it felt strange to lower the barrels so that they were pointing down and could kill nothing but the ground. I did, though, and Lewis and I faced each other across the dead man. His eyes were vivid and alive; he was smiling easily and with great friendliness.

'Well now, how about this? Just . . . how *about* this?'

I went over to Bobby and Drew, though I had no notion of what to do when I got there. I had watched everything that had happened to Bobby, had heard him scream and squall, and wanted to reassure him that we could set all that aside; that it would be forgotten as soon as we left the woods, or as soon as we got back in the canoes. But there was no way to say this, or to ask him how his lower intestine felt or whether he thought he was bleeding internally. Any examination of him would be unthinkably ridiculous and humiliating.

There was no question of that, though; he was furiously closed off from all of us. He stood up and backed away, still naked from the middle down, his sexual organs wasted with pain. I picked up his pants and shorts and handed them to him, and he reached for them in wonderment. He took out a handkerchief and went behind some bushes.

Still holding the gun at trail, as the tall man had been doing when I first saw him step out of the woods, I went back to Lewis, who was leaning on his bow and gazing out over the river.

Without looking at me, he said, 'I figured it was the only thing to do.'

'It was,' I agreed, though I wasn't all that sure. 'I thought we'd had it.'

Lewis glanced in the direction Bobby had taken and I realized I could have put it better.

'I thought sure they'd kill us.'

'Probably they would have. The penalty for sodomy in this state is death, anyway. And at the point of a gun . . . No, they wouldn't have let you go. Why should they?'

'How did you figure it?'

'We heard Bobby, and the only thing we could think of was that one of you had been bit by a snake. We started to come right in, but all at once it hit me that if it was something like snakebite, the other one of you could take care of the one that was bit just as well as three of us could, at least for a little while. And if there were other people involved, I told Drew I had just as soon come in on them without them knowing it.'

'What did you do?'

'We turned in that little creek and went up it about fifty yards. Then we shoved the canoe in some bushes and got out; I strung up and nocked an arrow, and we came on up to about thirty yards from where you were. As soon as I saw four people there, I began to shift around to find a place I could shoot through the leaves. I couldn't tell what was going on at first, though I thought it was probably what it was. I'm sorry I couldn't do anything for Bobby, but at least I didn't make a mismove and get his head blown off. When the guy started getting back up on his feet, I drew down on him, and waited.'

'How did you know when to shoot?'

'Any time that the gun wasn't pointed at you and Bobby would have been all right. I just had to wait till that time came. The other guy hadn't had any action yet, and I was pretty sure they'd swap the gun. The only thing I was worried about was that you might get in between me and him. But I was on him all the time, looking right down the arrow. I must have been at full draw for at least a minute. It would've been a much easier shot if I hadn't had to hold so long. But it was fairly easy anyway. I knew I was right on him; I tried to hit him halfway up the back and a little to the left. He moved, or that's just where it would have caught him. I knew I had him when I let go.'

'You had him,' I said. 'And now what're we going to do with him?'

Drew moved up to us, washing his hands with dirt and beating them against the sides of his legs.

'There's not but one thing *to* do,' he said. 'Put the body in one of the canoes and take it on down to Aintry and turn it over to the highway patrol. Tell them the whole story.'

'Tell them what, exactly?' Lewis asked.

'Just what happened,' Drew said, his voice rising a tone. 'This is justifiable homicide if anything is. They were sexually assaulting two members of our party at gunpoint. Like you said, there was nothing else we could do.'

'Nothing else but shoot him in the back with an arrow?' Lewis asked pleasantly.

'It was your doing, Lewis,' Drew said.

'What would you have done?'

'It doesn't make any difference what I would have done,' Drew said stoutly. 'But I can tell you, I don't believe . . .'

'Don't believe what?'

'Wait a minute,' I broke in. 'What we should or shouldn't have done is beside the point. He's there, and we're here. We didn't start any of this. We didn't ask for it. But what happens now?'

Something close to my feet moved. I looked down, and the

man shook his head as though at something past belief, gave a long sigh and slumped again. Drew and Lewis bent down on him.

'Is he dead?' I asked. I had already fixed him as dead in my mind, and couldn't imagine how he could have moved and sighed.

'He is now,' Lewis said, without looking up. 'He's mighty dead. We couldn't have saved him, though. He's center-shot.'

Lewis and Drew got up, and we tried to think our way back into the conversation.

'Let's just figure for a minute,' Lewis said. 'Let's just calm down and think about it. Does anybody know anything about the law?'

'I've been on jury duty exactly once,' Drew said.

'That's once more than I have,' I said. 'And about all the different degrees of murder and homicide and manslaughter I don't know anything at all.'

We all turned to Bobby, who had rejoined us. He shook his fiery face.

'You don't have to know much law to know that if we take this guy down out of these mountains and turn him over to the sheriff, there's going to be an investigation, and I would bet we'd go on trial,' Lewis said. 'I don't know what the charge would be, technically, but we'd be up against a jury, sure as hell.'

'Well, so what?' Drew said.

'All right, now,' said Lewis, shifting to the other leg. 'We've killed a man. Shot him in the back. And we not only killed a man, we killed a cracker, a mountain man. Let's consider what might happen.'

'All right,' Drew said. 'Consider it. We're listening.'

Lewis sighed and scratched his head. 'We just ought to wait

a minute before we decide to be so all-fired boy scoutish and do the right thing. There's not any right thing.'

'You bet there is,' Drew said. 'There's only *one* thing.'

I tried to think ahead, and I couldn't see anything but desperate trouble, and for the rest of my life. I have always been scared to death of anything to do with the police; the sight of a police uniform turns my saliva cold. I could feel myself beginning to breathe fast in the stillness, and I noticed the sound of the river for a moment, like something heard through a door.

'We ought to do some hard decision-making before we let ourselves in for standing trial up in these hills. We don't know who this man is, but we know that he lived up here. He may be an escaped convict, or he may have a still, or he may be everybody in the county's father, or brother or cousin. I can almost guarantee you that he's got relatives all over the place. Everybody up here is kin to everybody else, in one way or another. And consider this, too: there's a lot of resentment in these hill counties about the dam. There are going to have to be some cemeteries moved, like in the old TVA days. Things like that. These people don't want any "furriners" around. And I'm goddamned if I want to come back up here for shooting this guy in the back, with a jury made up of his cousins and brothers, maybe his mother and father too, for all I know.'

He had a point. I listened to the woods and the river to see if I could get an answer. I saw myself and the others rotting for weeks in some county jail with country drunks, feeding on sorghum, salt pork and sowbelly, trying to pass the time without dying of worry, negotiating with lawyers, paying their fees month after month, or maybe posting bond – I had no idea whether that was allowable in a case like this, or not – and drawing my family into the whole sickening, unresolvable mess, getting them all more and more deeply entangled in the life, death and identity of the repulsive, useless man at my feet, who was holding the head of the arrow thoughtfully, the red bubble at his lips collapsed into a small weak stream of blood that gathered slowly under his ear into a drop. Granted, Lewis was in more trouble than the rest of us were, but we all had a lot to lose. Just the publicity of being connected with a killing would be long-lasting trouble. I didn't want it, if there was any way out.

'What do you think, Bobby?' Lewis asked, and there was a tone in his voice which suggested that Bobby's decision would be final. Bobby was sitting on the same log he had been forced to lean over, one hand propping up his chin and the other over his eyes. He got up, twenty years older, and walked over to the dead man. Then, in an explosion so sudden that it was like something bursting through from another world, he kicked the body in the face, and again.

Lewis pulled him back, his hands on Bobby's shoulders. Then he let him go, and Bobby turned his back and walked away.

'How about you, Ed?' Lewis asked me.

'God, I don't know. I really don't.'

Drew moved over to the other side of the dead man and pointed down at him very deliberately. 'I don't know what you have in mind, Lewis,' he said. 'But if you conceal this body you're setting yourself up for a murder charge. That much law I *do* know. And a murder charge is going to be a little bit more than you're going to want to deal with, particularly with conditions like they are; I mean, like you've just been describing them. You better think about it, unless you want to start thinking about the electric chair.'

Lewis looked at him with an interested expression. 'Suppose there's no body?' he said. 'No body, no crime. Isn't that right?'

'I think so, but I'm not sure,' Drew said, peering closely at Lewis and then looking down at the man. 'What are you thinking about, Lewis?' he said. 'We've got a right to know. And we damned well better get to doing something right quick. We can't just stand around and wring our hands.'

'Nobody's wringing his hands,' Lewis said. 'I've just been thinking, while you've been giving out with what we might call the conventional point of view.'

'Thinking what?' I asked.

'Thinking of what we might do with the body.'

'You're a goddamned fool,' Drew said in a low voice. 'Doing *what* with the body? Throwing it in the river? That's the first place they'd look.'

'*Who'd* look?'

'Anybody who was looking for him. Family, friends, police. The fellow who was with him, maybe.'

'We don't have to put him in the river,' Lewis said.

'Lewis,' Drew said, 'I mean it. You level with us. This is not one of your fucking games. You killed somebody. There he is.'

'I did kill him,' Lewis said. 'But you're wrong when you say that there's nothing like a game connected with the position we're in now. It may be the most serious kind of game there is, but if you don't see it as a game, you're missing an important point.'

'Come on, Lewis,' I said. 'For once let's not carry on this way.'

Lewis turned to me. 'Ed, *you* listen, and listen good. We can get out of this, I think. Get out without any questions asked, and no troubles of any kind, if we just take hold in the next hour and do a couple of things right. If we think it through, and act it through and don't make any mistakes, we can get out without a thing ever being said about it. If we connect up with the law, we'll be connected to this man, this body, for the rest of our lives. We've got to get rid of him.'

'How?' I asked. 'Where?'

Lewis turned his head to the river, then half lifted his hand and moved it in a wide gesture inland, taking in the woods in a sweep obviously meant to include miles of them, hundreds of acres. Another expression – a new color – came into his eyes, a humorous conspiratorial craftiness, his look of calculated pleasure, his enthusiast's look. He dropped the hand and rested it easily on the bow, having given Drew and me the woods, the whole wilderness. 'Everywhere,' he said. 'Anywhere. Nowhere.'

'Yes,' Drew went on excitedly, 'we could do *something* with him. We could throw him in the river. We could bury him. We could even burn him up. But they'd find him, or find something, if they came looking. And how about the other one, the one who was with him? All he's got to do is to go and bring . . .'

'Bring who?' Lewis asked. 'I doubt if he'd want anybody, much less the sheriff or the state police, to know what he was doing when this character was shot. He may bring *somebody* back here, though I doubt it, but it won't be the law. And if he does come back, so what?'

Lewis touched the corpse with his bow tip and put his eyes squarely into Drew's. 'He won't be here.'

'Where'll he be?' Drew asked, his jaw setting blackly. 'And how do you know that other guy is not around here right now? It just might be that he's watching everything you do. We wouldn't be so hard to follow, dragging a corpse off somewhere and ditching it. He could bring them right back here. You look around, Lewis. He could be anywhere.'

Lewis didn't look around, but I did. The other side of the river was not dangerous, but the side where we were was becoming more and more terrifying to stand on. A powerful unseen presence seemed to flow and float in on us from three directions – upstream, downstream and inland. Drew was right, he could be anywhere. The trees and leaves were so thick that the eye gave up easily, lost in the useless tangle of plants living out their time in this choked darkness; among them the thin, stupid and crafty body of the other man could flow as naturally as a snake or fog, going where we went, watching what we did. What we had against him – I was shocked by the hope of it – was Lewis. The assurance with which he had killed a man was desperately frightening to me, but the same quality was also calming, and I moved, without being completely aware of movement, nearer to him. I would have liked nothing better than to touch that big relaxed forearm as he stood there, one hip raised until the leg made longer by the position bent gracefully at the knee. I would have followed him anywhere, and I realized that I was going to have to do just that.

Still looking off at the river, Lewis said, 'Let's figure.'

Bobby got off the log and stood with us, all facing Lewis over the corpse. I moved away from Bobby's red face. None of this was his fault, but he felt tainted to me. I remembered how he had looked over the log, how willing to let anything be done to him, and how high his voice was when he screamed.

Lewis crouched down over the dead man, a wisp of dry weed in his mouth. 'If we take him on the river in the canoe we'll be out in the open. If somebody was watching he could see where we dropped him in. Besides, like Drew says, the river's the first place anybody'd look. Where does that leave us?'

'Upstream or down,' I said.

'Or in,' Lewis said. 'Or maybe a combination.'

'*Which* combination?'

'I'd say a combination of in and up. Suppose we took him

downstream along the bank. We're heading down-river, and if we wanted to get rid of him as fast as possible, we'd bury him or leave him somewhere along the way.'

Again, his idea fitted. The woods upstream became more mysterious than those downstream; the future opened only on that side.

'So . . . we take him inland, and upstream. We carry him to that little creek and up it until we find a good place, and then we bury him and the gun. And I'd be willing to bet that nothing will ever come of it. These woods are full of more human bones than anybody'll ever know; people disappear up here all the time, and nobody ever hears about it. And in a month or six weeks the valley'll be flooded, and the whole area will be hundreds of feet under water. Do you think the state is going to hold up this project just to look for some hillbilly? Especially if they don't know where he is, or even if he's in the woods at all? It's not likely. And in six weeks . . . well, did you ever look out over a lake? There's plenty of water. Something buried under it – *under* it – is as buried as it can get.'

Drew shook his head. 'I'm telling you, I don't want any part of it.'

'What do you mean?' Lewis turned on him sharply and said, 'You *are* part of it. *You* want to be honest, *you* want to make a clean breast, *you* want to do the right thing. But you haven't got the guts to take a chance. Believe me, if we do this right we'll go home as clean as we came. That is, if somebody doesn't crap out.'

'You know better than that, Lewis,' Drew said, his glasses deepening with anger. 'But I can't go along with this. It's not a matter of guts; it's a matter of the law.'

'You see any law around here?' Lewis said. 'We're the law. What we decide is going to be the way things are. So let's vote on it. I'll go along with the vote. And so will you, Drew. You've got no choice.'

Lewis turned to Bobby again. 'How about it?'

'I say get rid of the son of a bitch,' Bobby said, his voice thick and strangled. 'Do you think I want this to get around?'

'Ed?'

Drew put the tense flat of his hand before my face and shook it. 'Think what you're doing, Ed, for God's sake,' he said. 'This self-hypnotized maniac is going to get us all in jail for life, if he doesn't get us killed. You're a reasonable man. You've got a family. You're not implicated in this unless you go along with what Lewis wants to do. Listen to reason, don't do this thing. Ed, *don't*. I'm *begging* you. Don't.'

But I was ready to gamble. After all, I hadn't done anything but stand tied to a tree, and nobody could prove anything else, no matter what it came to. I believed Lewis could get us out. If I went along with concealing the body and we got caught it could be made to seem a matter of necessity, of simply being outvoted.

'I'm with you,' I said, around Drew.

'All right then,' Lewis said, and reached for the dead man's shoulder. He rolled him over, took hold of the arrow shaft where it came out of the chest and began to pull. He added his other hand and jerked to get it started out and then hauled strongly with one hand again as the arrow slowly slithered from the body, painted a dark uneven red. Lewis stood up, went to the river and washed it, then came back. He clipped the shaft into his bow quiver.

I handed the shotgun to Bobby and went and got my belt and the knife and rope. Then Drew and I bent to the shoulders and lifted, and Bobby and Lewis took a foot apiece, with their free hands carrying the gun and the bow and an entrenching tool from the loaded canoe. The corpse sagged between us, extremely heavy, and the full meaning of the words *dead weight* dragged at me as I tried to straighten. We moved toward the place where Lewis had come from.

Before we had gone twenty yards Drew and I were staggering, our feet going any way they could through the dry grass. Once I heard a racheting I was sure was a rattlesnake, and looked right and left of the body sliding feet-first ahead of me into the woods. The man's head hung back and rolled between Drew and me, dragging at everything it could touch.

It was not believable. I had never done anything like it even in my mind. To say that it was like a game would not describe exactly how it felt. I knew it was not a game, and yet, whenever I could, I glanced at the corpse to see if it would come out of the phony trance it was in, and stand up and shake hands all around, someone new we'd met in the woods, who could give us some idea where we were. But the head kept dropping back, and we kept having to keep it up, clear of the weeds and briars, so that we could go wherever we were going with it.

We came out finally at the creek bank near Lewis' canoe. The water was pushing through the leaves, and the whole stream looked as though it was about half slow water and half bushes and branches. There was nothing in my life like it, but I was there. I helped Lewis and the others put the body into the canoe. The hull rode deep and low in the leafy water, and we began to push it up the creek, deeper into the woods. I could feel every pebble through the city rubber of my tennis shoes, and the creek flowed as untouchable as a shadow around my legs. There was nothing else to do except what we were doing.

Lewis led, drawing the canoe by the bow painter, plodding bent-over upstream with the veins popping, the rope over his shoulder like a bag of gold. The trees, mostly mountain laurel and rhododendron, made an arch over the creek, so that at times we had to get down on one knee or both knees and grope through leaves and branches, going right into the most direct push of water against our chests as it came through the foliage. At some places it was like a tunnel where nothing human had ever been expected to come, and at others it was like a long green hall where the water changed tones and temperatures and was much quieter than it would have been in the open.

In this endless water-floored cave of leaves we kept going for twenty minutes by my watch, until the only point at all was to keep going, to find the creek our feet were in when the leaves of the rhododendrons dropped in our faces and hid it. I wondered what on earth I would do if the others disappeared, the creek disappeared and left only me and the woods and the corpse. Which way would I go? Without the creek to go back down, could I find the river? Probably not, and I bound myself with my brain and heart to the others; with them was the only way I would ever get out.

Every now and then I looked into the canoe and saw the body riding there, slumped back with its hand over its face and its feet crossed, a caricature of the southern small-town bum too lazy to do anything but sleep.

Lewis held up his hand. We all straightened up around the canoe, holding it lightly head-on into the current. Lewis went up the far bank like a creature. Drew and Bobby and I stood with the canoe at our hips and the sleeping man rocking softly between. Around us the woods were so thick that there would have been trouble putting an arm into it in places. We could have been watched from anywhere, any angle, any tree or bush, but nothing happened. I could feel the others' hands on the canoe, keeping it steady.

In about ten minutes Lewis came back, lifting a limb out of the water and appearing. It was as though the tree raised its own limb out of the water like a man. I had the feeling that such things happened all the time to branches in woods that were deep enough. The leaves lifted carefully but decisively, and Lewis Medlock came through.

We tied the canoe to a bush and picked up the body, each of us having the same relationship to it as before. I don't believe I could have brought myself to take hold of it in any other way.

Lewis had not found a path, but he had come on an opening between trees that went back inland and, he said, upstream. That was good enough; it was as good as anything. We hauled and labored away from the creek between the big water oak trunks and the sweetgums standing there forever, falling down, lurching this way and the other with the corpse, thick and slick with sweat, trying to make good a senselessly complicated pattern of movement between the bushes and trees. After the first few turns I had no idea where we were, and in a curious way I enjoyed being *that* lost. If you were in something as deep as we were in, it was better to go all the way. When I quit hearing the creek I knew I was lost, wandering foolishly in the woods holding a corpse by the sleeve.

Lewis lifted his hand again, and we let the body down on the ground. We were by a sump of some kind, a blue-black seepage of rotten water that had either crawled in from some other place or came up from the ground where it was. The earth around it was soft and squelchy, and I kept backing off from it, even though I had been walking in the creek with the others.

Lewis motioned to me. I went up to him and he took the arrow he had killed the man with out of his quiver. I expected it to vibrate, but it didn't; it was like the others – civilized and expert. I tested it; it was straight. I handed it back, but for some reason didn't feel like turning loose of it. Lewis made an odd motion with his head, somewhere between disbelief and determination, and we stood holding the arrow. There was no blood on it, but the feathers were still wet from the river where he had washed it off. It looked just like any arrow that had been carried in the rain, or in heavy dew or fog. I let go.

Lewis put it on the string of his bow. He came back to full draw as I had seen him do hundreds of times, in his classic, knowledgeable form so much more functional and accurate than the form of an archer on an urn, and stood, concentrating. There was nothing there but the black water, but he was aiming at a definite part of it: a single drop, maybe, as it moved and would have to stop, sooner or later, for an instant.

It went. The arrow leapt with a breathtaking instant silver and disappeared at almost the same time, while Lewis held his follow-through, standing with the bow as though the arrow were still in it. There was no sense of the arrow's being stopped by anything under the water – log or rock. It was gone, and could have been traveling down through muck to the soft center of the earth.

We picked up the body and went on. In a while more we came out against the side of a bank that shelved up, covered with ferns and leaves that were mulchy like shit. Lewis turned to us and narrowed one eye. We put the body down. One of its arms was wrenched around backwards, and it seemed odd and more terrible than anything that had happened that such a position didn't hurt it.

Lewis fell. He started to dig with the collapsible GI shovel we had brought for digging latrines. The ground came up easily, or what was on the ground. There was no earth; it was all leaves and rotten stuff. It had the smell of generations of mold. They might as well let the water in on it, I thought; this stuff is no good to anybody.

Drew and I got down and helped with our hands. Bobby

stood looking off into the trees. Drew dug in, losing himself in a practical job, figuring the best way to do it. The sweat stood in the holes of his blocky, pitted face, and his black hair, solid with thickness and hair lotion, shone sideways, hanging over one ear.

It was a dark place, quiet and almost airless. When we were finished with the hole there was not a dry spot anywhere on my nylon. We had hollowed out a narrow trench about two feet deep.

We hauled the body over and rolled it in on its side, unbelievably far from us. Lewis reached his hand and Bobby handed him the shotgun. Lewis put the gun in and pulled back his hands to his knees, looking. Then his right hand went back into the grave, and he gave the gun a turn, arranging it in some kind of way.

'OK,' he said.

We shoveled and scrambled the dirt back in, working wildly. I kept throwing the stuff in his face, to get it covered up quick. But it was easy, in double handfuls. He disappeared slowly, into the general sloppiness and uselessness of the woods. When he was gone, Lewis smoothed out the leaf mold over him.

We stood on our knees. We leaned forward, panting, our hands on the fronts of our thighs or on the ground. I had a tremendous driving moment of wanting to dig him up again, of siding with Drew. Now, if not later, we knew where he was. But there was already too much to explain: the dirt, the delay, and the rest of it. Or should we take him and wash him in the river? The thought of doing that convinced me; it was impossible, and I stood up with the others.

'Ferns'll be growing here in a few days,' Lewis said. It was good to hear a voice, especially his. 'Nobody'd ever come on him in a million years. I doubt if we could even find this place again.'

'There's still time, Lewis,' Drew said. 'You better be sure you know what you're doing.'

'I'm sure,' Lewis said. 'The first rain will kill every sign we made. There's not a dog can follow us here. When we get off this river, we'll be all right. Believe me.'

We started back. I couldn't tell anything about our back trail, but Lewis kept stopping and looking at a wrist compass, and it seemed to me that we were going more or less in the right direction; it was the direction I would have followed if I had been by myself.

We came out upstream of where the canoe was. The water was running toward the river, and we went with it, down the secret pebbles of the creek-bed, stooping under the leaves of low branches, mumbling to ourselves. I felt separated from the others, and especially from Lewis. There was no feeling any longer of helping each other; I believed that if I had stepped into a hole and disappeared the others would not have noticed, but would have gone on faster and faster. Each of us wanted to get out of the woods in the quickest way he could. I know I did, and it would have taken a great physical effort for me to turn back and take one step upstream, no matter what trouble one of the others was in.

When we got to the canoe we all got in. Drew and Lewis paddled, and I felt the long surges of Lewis' strokes move us as I wanted us to move. Drew fended off the low branches, and we went back to the river faster than I thought possible.

The other canoe was where we had left it, softly shaking against the bank.

'Let's get the hell out of here,' Bobby said.

'Let me figure a minute,' Lewis said. 'This is no time for vanity or hurt feelings. How much work can you do, Bobby?'

'I don't know, Lewis,' Bobby said. 'I'll try.'

'It's not your fault,' Lewis said. 'But trying is not going to be enough. We've got to get the best combinations we can get. I expected I'd better take Bobby with me. Ed, how much have you got left?'

'I don't know. Some.'

'All right. You and Drew take my boat. Bobby and I will take everything we can in the other one. We'll try to keep up with you, but it'll be better if you lead off, so that we can see you if you get into trouble. I hate to tell you, but from what little I know, we haven't hit the rough part of this river yet.'

'The part that was going to be fun,' Bobby said.

'The part that's going to knock your stupid brains out if you don't do exactly what I tell you to do,' Lewis said, without raising his voice. 'Come on; let's get whatever else we can carry out of my canoe. You want out of this, don't you?'

We took about ten minutes shifting equipment around.

'Take everything, if you can take it, Lewis,' I said. 'If Drew and I have to go through these damned rapids first, I want a boat I can at least halfway handle. And I don't want things wrapping around me in the water.'

'I don't blame you,' Lew said. 'We'll take all we can.'

'All I want is a weapon,' I said. 'I'll take my bow.'

'I'd think twice about that,' Lewis said. 'If you think tents can be bad, you wait'll those bare broadheads gore you a few times when you're in the water with them.'

'I'll take it anyway,' I said. 'And I sure wish we still had that guy's gun. Why the hell did we leave it with *him*?'

'The gun is better right where it is,' Lewis said.

'We could have got rid of it later.'

'No, too risky. Every mile we carried that shotgun with us would increase the danger of our being caught with it. That could be the thing, buddy. That could be the thing.'

We were ready. Drew crawled into the front of the aluminum canoe. I was glad he was there; I could work with him. He sat with the paddle just out of the river, shaking his head. Neither of us said anything until I told him to push off.

It was about four o'clock, and the thought of spending another night in the woods paralyzed me. The problems and the physical work of the burial had taken my mind off our situation, but now the thought of it and of what might happen to us surrounded me; I felt driven into it by a hammer. But something came to an edge in me, also. The leaves glittered, all mysterious points, and the river and the light on it were nothing but pure energy. I had never lived sheerly on nerves before, and a gigantic steadiness took me over, a constant trembling or awareness in a hundred places that added up to a kind of equilibrium, that made my arms move in long steady motions and showed me where the rocks were by the differences in the swirling of the water.

We moved well for the better part of an hour. Lewis was keeping up, too, driving the almost-buried canoe forward with an effort I could not even guess at. He liked to take things on himself and, because he could, do more than anyone else. And I was glad to see that in an emergency his self-system didn't fold up on him, but carried on the same, or even stronger.

But I was also very glad that Drew and I were light and maneuverable. There were no rapids, but the river seemed to be moving faster. There was an odd but definite sensation of going downhill in a long curving slant like a ramp. I noticed this more and more, and finally it occurred to me that the feeling was caused by what the land on both sides was doing. At first it had lifted into higher banks, the left higher than the right, and now it was going up raggedly and steadily, higher and higher, changing the sound of the river to include a kind of deep beating noise, the tone coming out more and more as the walls climbed, shedding their trees and all but a few bushes and turning to stone. Most of the time the sides were not vertical, but were very steep, and I knew we would be in real trouble if we spilled. I prayed that there would be no rapids while we were in the gorge, or that they would be easy ones.

We pulled and pulled at the river. Drew was hunched forward in a studious position like a man at a desk, and at every stroke the old GI shirt he wore took a new hold across his shoulders, one which was the old hold as well.

I looked back. We had opened up a little distance on the other canoe; it was about thirty yards behind us. I thought I heard Lewis holler to us, probably to slow down, but the voice, thinly floating through the boom of wall-sound, had no authority and very little being at all.

The walls were at least 150 feet high on both sides of us now. The cross-reverberation seemed to hold us on course as much as the current did; it was part of the same thing – the way we had to move to get through the gorge.

I looked around again, and Lewis and Bobby had gained a little. They were too close to us for running rapids, but there was nothing I could do about it; as far as I was concerned they were going to have to take their chances.

As we cleared each turn, before Drew swung across in front of me I kept looking for white water, and when I'd checked for that I looked along both banks as far downriver as I could see, to try to tell if either of them was lowering. There was no white water, and the walls stayed like they were, gray and scrubby, limestonish, pitted and scabby.

But the sound was changing, getting deeper and more massively frantic and authoritative. It was the old sound, but it was also new, it was a fuller one even than the reverberations off the walls, with their overtones and undertones; it was like a ground-bass that was made of all the sounds of the river we'd heard since we'd been on it. God, God, I thought, I know what it is. If it's a falls we're gone.

The sun fell behind the right side of the gorge, and the shadow of the bank crossed the water so fast that it was like a quick step from one side to the other. The beginning of darkness was thrown over us like a sheet, and in it the water ran even faster, frothing and near-foaming under the canoe. My teeth were chattering; I felt them shaking my skull, as though I had already been in the river and now had to suffer in the stone shade of the bank. We seemed to leap, and then leap from that leap to another down the immense ditch, like flying down an underground stream with the ceiling ripped off.

We couldn't make it to Aintry by dark; I knew that now. And we couldn't survive on the river, even as it was here, without being able to see. The last place I wanted to be was on the river in the gorge in the dark. It might be better to pull over while there was still light and find a flat rock or a sandbar to camp on, or get ready to sleep in the canoes.

We came around one more bend, and at the far end of it the river-bed began to step down. There was a succession of small, rough rapids; I couldn't tell how far they went on. About the only thing I had learned about canoeing was to head into the part of the rapids that seemed to be moving the fastest, where the most white water was. There was not much light left, and I had already made up my mind to get through this stretch of water and pull over to the bank, no matter what Lewis and Bobby decided to do.

The water was throwing us mercilessly. We came out in a short stretch between rapids, but we were going too fast to get out of the middle of the river before the next rocks. I didn't want to risk getting the canoe broadside to the river and then be sucked into the rocks. That would not only spill us, but would probably wedge the canoe on the rocks, and the force of water against it would keep it there. And we couldn't make it downriver with four of us in one canoe, as low in the water and hard to turn as it would be. I tried to hold Drew centered on the white water, to line him up and shoot him through the rocks; if I could get him through, I'd be with him.

'Give me some speed, baby,' I hollered.

Drew lifted his paddle and started to dig in long and hard.

Something happened to him. It looked at first – I can see it in my mind in three dimensions and slow motion and stop action – as if something, a puff of wind, but much more definite and concentrated, snatched at some of the hair at the back of his head. For a second I thought he had just shaken his head, or had been jarred by the canoe in some way I hadn't felt, but at the same instant I saw this happen I felt all control of the canoe go out of it. The river whirled the paddle from Drew's hand as though it had never been there. His right arm shot straight out, and he followed it, turning the whole canoe with him. There was nothing I could do; I rolled with the rest.

In a reflex, just before my head smashed face-first into the white water with the whole river turning around in midair and beginning to swing upside down, I let go the paddle and grabbed for the bow at my feet, for even in panic I knew I would rather have a weapon than the paddle, as dangerous as it would be to have the naked broadheads near me in such water.

The river took me in, and I had the bow. My life jacket brought me up, and Lewis' canoe was on top of me like a whale, rising up on the current. It hit me in the shoulder, driving me down where the rocks swirled like marbles, and something, probably a paddle, thrust into the side of my head as Lewis or Bobby

123

fended me off like a rock. I kicked at the rushing stones and rose up. Downstream, the green canoe drove over the broadside other one, reared nearly straight up, and Bobby and Lewis pitched out on opposite sides. A rock hit me and I felt some necessary thing – a muscle or bone – go in my leg. I kicked back with both feet and caught something solid. I must have been upside down, for there was no air. I opened my eyes but there was nothing to see. I threw my head, hoping I would be throwing it clear of the water, but it did not clear. I was not breathing and was being beaten from all sides, being hit and hit at and brushed by in the most unlikely and unexpected places in my body, rushing forward to be kicked and stomped by everything in the river.

I turned over and over. I rolled, I tried to crawl along the flying bottom. Nothing worked. I was dead. I felt myself fading out into the unbelievable violence and brutality of the river, joining it. This is not such a bad way to go, I thought; maybe I'm already there.

My head came out of the water, and I actually thought of putting it under again. But I got a glimpse of the two canoes, and that interested me enough to keep me alive. They were together, the green one buckled, rolling over and over each other like logs. Something was nailing one of my hands, the left one, to the water. The wooden canoe burst open on a rock and disappeared, and the aluminum one leapt free and went on.

Get your feet forward of you, boy, I said, with my mouth dragging through the current. Get on your back.

I tried, but every time I came up with my feet I hit a rock either with my shins or thighs. I went under again, and faintly I heard what must have been the aluminum canoe banging on the stones, a ringing, distant, beautiful sound.

I got on my back and poured with the river, sliding over the stones like a creature I had always contained but never released.

With my life preserver the upper part of my body drew almost no water. If I could get my feet – my heels – over the stones I slid over like a moccasin, feeling the moss flutter lightly against the back of my neck before I cascaded down into the next rapids.

Body-surfing and skidding along, I realized that we could never have got through this stretch in canoes. There were too many rocks, they were too haphazardly jumbled, and the water was too fast; faster and faster. We couldn't have portaged, either, because of the banks, and we couldn't have got out and walked the canoes through. We would have spilled one way or the other, and strangely I was just as glad. Everything told me that the way I was doing it was the only way, and I was doing it.

It was terrifyingly enjoyable, except that I hurt in so many places. The river would shoot me along; I'd see a big boulder looming up, raise my feet and slick over, crash down on my ass in a foaming pool, pick up speed and go on. I got banged on the back of the head a couple of times until I learned to bend forward as I was coming down off the rock, but after that nothing new hurt me.

I was already hurt, I knew. But I was not sure where. My left hand hurt pretty bad, and I was more worried about it than anywhere else, for I couldn't remember having hit it with anything. I held it up and saw that I had hold of the bow by the broadheads and was getting cut in the palm every time I flinched and grabbed. The bow was also clamped under my left arm, and now I took it out and swung the heads away from me, just before I went over another rock. As I slid down I saw calm water below, through another stretch of rapids: broad calm, then more white water farther down, far off into evening. I relaxed again, not even touching the stones of the passage this time, but riding easily along through the flurrying cold ripples into the calm water, cradling the bow.

I was floating, not flowing anymore. Turning idly in the immense dark bed, I looked up at the gorge side rising and rising. My legs were killing me, but I could kick them both, and as far as I could tell neither was broken. I lifted my hand from the water; it was nicked and chopped a little in places, but not as badly as it might have been; there was a diagonal cut across the palm, but not a deep one – a long slice.

I floated on, trying to recover enough to think what to do. Finally I started to struggle weakly around to look upstream for the others. My body was heavy and hard to move without the tremendous authority of the rapids to help it and tell it what to do.

Either upstream or down, there was nobody in the river but me. I kept watching the last of the falls, for I had an idea that I might have passed the others, somewhere along. There had probably been several places where the water split and came down through the rocks in different ways; all three of them might be back there somewhere, dead or alive.

As I thought that, Bobby tumbled out of the rapids, rolling over and over on the slick rocks, and then flopped belly-down into the calm. I pointed to the bank and he began feebly to work toward it. So did I.

'Where is Lewis?' I yelled.

He shook his head, and I stopped pulling on the water and turned to wait in midstream.

After a minute or two Lewis came, doubled-up and broken-looking, one hand still holding his paddle and the other on his face, clasping something intolerable. I breaststroked to him and lay beside him in the cold coiling water under the falls. He was writhing and twisting uselessly, caught by something that didn't have hold of me, something that seemed not present.

'Lewis,' I said.

'My leg's broke,' he gasped. 'It feels like it broke off.'

The water where we were did not change. 'Hold on to me,' I said.

He moved his free hand through the river and fixed the fingers into the collar of my slick nylon outfit, and I moved gradually crossways on the water toward the big boulders under the cliff. The dark came on us faster and faster as I hauled on the crossgrain of the current with Lewis' choking weight dragging at my throat.

From where we were the cliff looked something like a gigantic drive-in movie screen waiting for an epic film to begin. I listened for interim music, glancing now and again up the pale curved stone for Victor Mature's stupendous image, wondering where it would appear, or if the whole thing were not now already playing, and I hadn't yet managed to put it together.

As we neared the wall, I saw that there were a few random rocks and a tiny sand beach where we were going to come out; where Bobby was, another rock. I motioned to him, and he unfolded and came to the edge of the water, his hands embarrassing.

He gave me one of them, and I dragged us out. Lewis hopped up onto a huge placid stone, working hard, and then failed and crumpled again. The rock, still warm with the last of the sun that had crossed the river on its way down, held him easily, and I turned him on his back with his hand still over his face.

'Drew was shot,' Lewis said with no lips. 'I saw it. He's dead.'

'I'm not sure,' I said, but I was afraid that's what it was. 'Something happened to him. But I don't know. I don't know.'

'Let's take his pants down,' I said to Bobby.

He looked at me.

'God*damn* phraseology,' I said. 'We're in another bag, now, baby. Get his pants off him and see if you can tell how bad he's hurt. I've got to try to get that goddamned canoe, or we'll stay here.'

I turned back to the river. I waded in, feeling the possibility of a rifle shot die with the very last light, moving back into the current like an out-of-shape animal, taking on the familiar weight and lack-of-weight of water. Very clear-headed, I sank down.

The depth came to me, increasing – no one can tell me different – with the darkness. The aluminum canoe floated palely, bulging half out of the total dark, making slowly for the next rapids, but idly, and unnaturally slowed and stogged with calm water. Nearly there, I ran into a thing of wood that turned out to be a broken paddle. I took it on.

I swam slow-motion around the canoe, listening for the rifle shot I would never hear if it killed me; that I had not heard when it killed Drew, if it did. Nothing from that high up could see me, and I knew it, though it might see the canoe. Even that was doubtful, though, and the conviction enlarged on me that I could circle the canoe all night, if I chose, in the open.

The calm was deep; there was no place to stand to dump the water out. I hung to the upside-down gunwale, tipping it this way and that, trying to slip the river out of the factory metal. Finally it rolled luckily, and the stream that had been in it began to flow again; the hull lightened and climbed out of the water, and was mostly on top of it. I pushed on the sharp stern, keeping it going with excruciating frog legs. The current went around me, heading into the darkness downstream. I could see a little white foaming, but it was peacefully beyond, another problem for another time. I turned to the cliff and called softly out to Bobby, and he answered.

I looked up and could barely make out his face. The canoe went in to him, guided by the same kind of shove I gave Dean when he was first learning to walk. He waded and drew it up onto the sand by the bow rope, and we beached it under the overhang.

I moved onto land, not saying anything.

'For God's sake,' Bobby said, 'don't be so damned quiet. I'm flipping already.'

Though my mouth was open, I closed it against the blackness and moved to Lewis, who was now down off the rock and lying in the sand. His bare legs were luminous, and the right leg of his drawers was lifted up to the groin. I could tell by its outline that his thigh was broken; I reached down and felt of it very softly. Against the back of my hand his penis stirred with pain. His hair gritted in sand, turning from one side to the other.

It was not a compound fracture; I couldn't feel any of the bone splinters I had been taught to look for in innumerable compulsory first-aid courses, but there was a great profound human swelling under my hand. It felt like a thing that was trying to open, to split, to let something out.

'Hold on, Lew,' I said. 'We're all right now.'

It was all-dark. The river-sound enveloped us as it never could have in light. I sat down beside Lewis and motioned to Bobby. He crouched down as well.

'Where is Drew?' Bobby asked.

'Lewis says he's dead,' I said. 'Probably he is. He may have been shot. But I can't really say. I was looking right at him, but I can't say.'

Lewis' hand was pulling at me from underneath. I bent down near his face. He tried to say something, but couldn't. Then he said, 'It's you. It's got to be you.'

'Sure it's me,' I said. 'I'm right here. Nothing can touch us.'

'No. That's not . . .' The river had the rest of what he said, but Bobby picked it up.

'What are we going to do?' he made the dark say; night had taken his red face.

'I think,' I said, 'that we'll never get out of this gorge alive.'

Did I say that? I thought. Yes, a dream-man said, you did. You did say it, and you believe it.

'I think he means to pick the rest of us off tomorrow,' I said out loud, still stranger than anything I had ever imagined. When do the movies start, Lord?

'What . . . ?'

'That's what I'd do. Wouldn't you?'

'I don't . . .'

'If Lewis is right, and I think he is, that toothless bastard drew down on us while we were lining up to go through the rapids, and before we were going too fast. He killed the first man in the first boat. Next would have been me. Then you.'

'In other words, it's lucky we spilled.'

'Right. Lucky. Very lucky.'

It was an odd word to use, where we were. It was a good thing that we couldn't see faces. Mine felt calm and narrow-eyed, but it might not have been. There was something to act out.

'What are we going to do?' Bobby said again.

'The question is, what is *he* going to do?'

Nothing came back. I went on.

'What can he lose now? He's got exactly the same thing going for him that we had going for us when we buried his buddy back in the woods. There won't be any witnesses. There's no motive to trace him by. As far as anybody else knows, he's never seen us and we've never seen him. If all four of us wind up in the river, that'll just even things out. Who in the hell cares? What kind of search party could get up into these rapids? A helicopter's not going to do any good, even if you could see into the river from one, which you can't. You think anybody's going to fly a helicopter down into this gorge, just on the chance that he *might* see something? Not a chance in the world. There might be an investigation, but you can bet nothing will come of it. This is a wild goddamned river, as you might know. What is going to happen to us, if he kills us, is that we are going to become a legend. You bet, baby: one of those unsolved things.'

'You think he's up there? Do you really?'

'I'm thinking we better believe he's up there.'

'But then what?'

'We're caught in this gorge. He can't come down here, but the only way out of this place for us is down the river. We can't run out of here at night, and when we move in the morning he'll be up there somewhere.'

'Jesus Christ Almighty.'

'Yes,' I said. 'You might say that. As Lewis might say, "Come on, Jesus boy, walk on down to us over that white water. But if you don't, we've got to do whatever there is to do." '

'But listen, Ed,' he said, and the pathetic human tone against the river-sound made me cringe, 'you got to be sure.'

'Sure of what?'

'Sure you're right. What if you're wrong? I mean, we may not really be in any danger, at all, from anybody up . . . up there.' He gestured, but it was lost.

'You want to take a chance?'

'Well, no. Not if I don't have to. But what . . . ?'

'*What* what?'

'What can we do?'

'We can do three things,' I said, and some other person began to tell me what they were. 'We can just sit here and sweat and call for our mamas. We can appeal to the elements. Maybe we can put Lewis back up on the rock and do a rain dance around him, to cut down the visibility. But if we got rain, we couldn't get out through it, and Lewis would probably die of exposure. Look up yonder.'

I liked hearing the sound of my voice in the mountain speech, especially in the dark; it sounded like somebody who knew where he was and knew what he was doing. I thought of Drew and the albino boy picking and singing in the filling station.

There was a pause while we looked up between the wings of cliff and saw that the stars were beginning there, and no clouds at all.

'And then what?' Bobby said.

'Or somebody can try to go up there and wait for him on top.'

'What you mean is . . .'

'What I mean is like they say in the movies, especially on Saturday afternoon. It's either him or us. We've killed a man. So has he. Whoever gets out depends on who kills who. It's just that simple.'

'Well,' he said, 'all right. I don't want to die.'

'If you don't, help me figure. We've got to figure like he's figuring, up there. Everything depends on that.'

'I don't have any idea what he's figuring.'

'We can start out with the assumption that he's going to kill us.'

'I got that far.'

'The next thing is when. He can't do anything until it gets light. So that means we've got till morning to do whatever we're going to do.'

'I still don't know what that is.'

'Just let me go on a minute. My feeling is this. You can't hear a gunshot that far off, with all this goddamned noise down here. After he shot Drew, he might have shot at us some more, and we'd never have known it unless another one of us was hit. I don't have any idea how well he can see from where he is. But I think it's reasonable to suppose that he saw well enough to know that he hit Drew, and that the canoes turned over. He might believe that the rest of us drowned, but I don't believe he'd want to take a chance that we did. That's awful rough water, but the fact that you and Lewis and I got out of it proves that it can be done, and I'm thinking he probably knows it. Again, maybe the reason he didn't nail the rest of us was that by the time we got down here where we are now, we'd been carried a good ways past him, and also it was too dark. That's our good luck; it means we've got at least a couple of advantages, if we can figure how to work them.'

'*Advantages*? Some advantages. We've got a hurt man. We've got a waterlogged canoe with the bottom stove in. We've got two guys who don't know the first thing about the woods, who don't even know where in the hell they are. He's got a rifle, and he's up above us. He knows where we are and can't help being, and we don't have the slightest notion of where he is, or even who he is. We haven't got a goddamned chance, if you and Lewis are right. If he's up there and wants to kill us, he can kill us.'

'Well now, it hasn't happened yet. And we've got one big card.'

'What?'

'He thinks we can't get at him. And if we can, we can kill him.'

'How?'

'With either a knife or a bow. Or with bare hands, if we have to.'

'We?'

'No. One of us.'

'I can't even shoot a bow,' he said. He was saved for a little while.

133

'That narrows it down, sure enough,' I said. 'You see what I mean about solving our problems? If you just do a little figuring.'

It was a decision, and I could feel it set us apart. Even in the dark the separation was obvious.

'Ed, level with me. Do you really think you can get up there in the dark?'

'To tell the truth, I don't. But we haven't got any other choice.'

'I still think that maybe he's just gone away. Suppose he has?'

'Suppose he hasn't?' I said. 'Do you want to take the chance? Look, if I fall off this fucking cliff, it's not going to hurt you any. If I get shot, it's not going to be you getting shot. You've got two chances to live. If he's gone away, or if for some reason or other he doesn't shoot, or if he misses enough times for the canoe to get away downriver, you'll live. Or if I get up there and kill him, you'll live. So don't worry about it. Let me worry.'

'Ed . . .'

'Shut up and let me think some more.'

I looked up at the gorge side but I couldn't tell much about it, except that it was awfully high. But the lower part of it, at least, wasn't quite as steep as I had thought at first. Rather than being absolutely vertical, it was more of a very steep slant, and I believed I could get up it at least part of the way, when the moon came up enough for me to see a little better.

'Come here, Bobby. And listen to everything I tell you. I'm going to make you go back over it before I leave, because the whole thing has got to be done right, and done right the first time. Here's what I want you to do.'

'All right. I'm listening.'

'Keep Lewis as warm and comfortable as you can. When it

gets first light – and I mean just *barely* light: light enough for you to see where you're going – get Lewis into the canoe and move out. The whole business is going to have to be decided right there.'

I was the one. I walked up and down a little on the sandbar, for that should have been my privilege. Then for some reason I stepped into the edge of the river. In a way, I guess, I wanted to get a renewed feel of all the elements present, and also to look as far up the cliff as I could. I stood with the cold water flowing around my calves and my head back, watching the cliff slant up into the darkness. More stars had come out around the top of the gorge, a kind of river of them. I strung the bow.

I ran my right hand over the limbs, feeling for broken pieces and splinters of fiber glass. Part of the upper limb seemed a little rougher than it should have, but it had been that way before. I took out the arrows I had left. I had started with four but had wasted two on the deer. One of the remaining ones was fairly straight; I spun it through my fingers as Lewis had taught me to do, feeling for the passing tick and jump a crooked aluminum arrow has when it spins. It may have been a little bent up in the crest, just under the feathers, but it was shootable, and at short range it ought to be accurate. The other arrow was badly bent, and I straightened it as well as I could with my hands, but there was not much I could do in the dark. Holding it at eye level and pointing it toward the best of the light places in the sky, I could not see even well enough to tell exactly where and how badly it was bent. But the broadhead was all right.

I walked back to Bobby and leant the bow against the spur of stone that overhung the canoe. Bobby stepped over to me as I paid out and recoiled the thin rope that had been at my waist the whole time. I had made a lucky buy – considering that a cliff I had not counted on being involved *was* involved, and a rope was a good thing to have in such a situation – and I had a brief moment of believing that the luck would run through the other things that were coming. I ran the rope over and over my left thumb and elbow until I had a tight ring. I tied the ends and passed the belt that held the big knife through the coil.

'Don't go to sleep,' I said to Bobby.

'Not likely,' he said. 'O God.'

'Now listen. If you go at first light, you'll make a damned hard target from the top of the gorge. You should be safe as long as you're running these little rapids along here. If I'm going to get on top of the cliff, I'll be there by then, and the odds will be evened out a little, if our man the Human Fly really does find a way to climb up there. I'll do everything I can to see that he doesn't crack down on you. From the little I was able to tell about the cliff before it got dark, it's rough as hell up there, and if he misses you at one place – or if you can slip by him without his seeing you – he won't be able to keep up with you; all you have to do is get by him and get around one turn and you're home free.'

'Ed, will you tell me one thing? Have you ever thought there might be more than one?'

'Yes, I've thought of it. I must say I have.'

'What if there is?'

'Then we're likely to die, early tomorrow morning.'

'I believe you.'

'I don't believe, though, that there's more than one man. I'll tell you why. It's not a good idea to involve somebody else in a murder if you don't have to. That's one thing. The other is that I don't think there's been time for him to go and get anybody else. He's got all the advantages; he doesn't need anybody to help him.'

'I sure hope you're right.'

'We'll have to figure I am. Anything else?'

'Yes, I've got to say it. I don't think we're going about this the right way. We may have the whole thing wrong.'

'I'm staking my life on being right. Lewis would do it. Now I'm going to have to. Let me get going.'

'Listen,' Bobby said, grabbing at me weakly, 'I can't do it. I won't make a sitting duck out of myself so you can go off in the woods and leave us to be shot down. I can't. I just can't.'

'Listen, you son of a bitch. If you want to go up that cliff, you go right ahead. There it is; it's not going away. But if I go up it we're going to play this my way. And I swear to God that if you don't do exactly what I say I'll kill you myself. It's just that goddamned simple. And if you leave Lewis on this rock I'll do the same thing.'

'Ed, I'm not going to leave him. You know I wouldn't do that. It's just that I don't want to go out there in plain sight of some murderous hillbilly and set myself up to be killed like Drew.'

'If everything works right – and if you do what I tell you to do – you won't get killed. Just *listen* to me. I'm going through this one more time, and it's got to stick. I'm going to tell you what to do no matter what should happen.'

'All right,' he said at last.

'Number one, move out as soon as you can see the river well enough to get through the next set of rapids. It'll probably still be too dark to shoot from the top. Even if it isn't he doesn't stand much chance of hitting you when you're in the rapids. Whenever you're in calm water, pull like hell for a while, then slack off; don't hit a constant speed. If he does shoot at you, try your goddamndest to get to the next set of rapids, or around the next turn. If you see you can't possibly get away – that is, if you see he's got you bracketed, and the shots are coming closer and closer – dump the canoe and let it go. Try to get Lewis out, then stay with him and wait for a day, and I'll try to bring back help. If nothing happens by that time, you'll know I didn't make it. Then leave Lewis and try to get downriver the best way you can, even if you have to swim part of the way. Take all three life jackets and float yourself down. We can't be more than fifteen miles from a highway bridge. If you have to do that, though, for God's sake remember where you left Lewis. If you don't remember, he's going to die. And that's for sure.'

He looked at me, and for the first time since the sun had gone down I could see his eyes; they had some points of light in them.

'That's about it, then,' I said. I picked up the bow and went over to the canoe near where Lewis was lying, tirelessly grinding the back of his head into the sand. I crouched down beside him; he was shaking in a certain matter-of-fact way, with the false cold of pain, and some of it came into me as he reached up and touched me on the front of the shoulder.

'Do you know what the fuck you're doing?'

'No, creature,' I said. 'I'm going to try to make it up as I go along.'

'Don't let him see you,' he said. 'And don't have any mercy. Not any.'

'I won't if I can help it.'

'Help it.'

I held my breath.

'Kill him,' Lewis said with the river.

'I'll kill him if I can find him,' I said.

'Well,' he said, lying back, 'here we are, at the heart of the Lewis Medlock country.'

'Pure survival,' I said.

'This is what it comes to,' he said. 'I told you.'

'Yes. You told me.'

Everything around me changed. I put my left arm between the bowstring and the bow and slid the bow back over my shoulder with the broadheads turned down. Then I walked to the gorge side and put a hand on it, the same hand that had been cut by the arrow in the river, as though I might be able to feel what the whole cliff was like, the whole problem, and hold it in my palm. The rock was rough, and a part of it fell away under my hand. The river sound loudened as though the rocks in the channel had shifted their positions. Then it relaxed and the extra sound died or went away again into the middle distance, the middle of the stream.

I knew that was the sign, and I backed off and ran with a hard scramble at the bank, and stretched up far enough to get an elbow over the top side of the first low overhang. Scraping my sides and legs, I got up on it and stood up. Bobby and Lewis were directly beneath me, under a roof of stone, and might as well not have been there. I was standing in the most entire aloneness that I had ever been given.

My heart expanded with joy at the thought of where I was and what I was doing. There was a new light on the water; the moon was going up and up, and I stood watching the stream with my back to the rock for a few minutes, not thinking of anything, with a deep feeling of nakedness and helplessness and intimacy.

I turned around with many small foot movements and leaned close to the cliff, taking on its slant exactly. I put my cheek against it and raised both hands up into the darkness, letting the fingers crawl independently over the soft rock. It was this softness that bothered me more than anything else; I was afraid that anything I would stand on or hold to would give way. I got my right hand placed in what felt like a crack, and began to feel with my left toes for something, anything. There was an unevenness – a bulge – in the rock and I kicked at it and worried it to see how solid it was, then put my foot on it and pulled hard with my right arm.

I rose slowly off the top of the overhang, the bow dropping back further over my left shoulder – which made it necessary to depend more on my right arm than my left – got my right knee and then my foot into some kind of hole. I settled as well as I could into my new position and began to feel upward again. There was a bulge to the left, and I worked toward it, full of wonder at the whole situation.

The cliff was not as steep as I had thought, though from what I had been able to tell earlier, before we spilled, it would probably get steeper toward the top. If I had turned loose it would have been a slide rather than a fall back down to the river or the overhang, and this reassured me a little – though not much – as I watched it happen in my mind.

I got to the bulge and then went up over it and planted my left foot solidly on it and found a good hold on what felt like a root with my right hand. I looked down.

The top of the overhang was pale now, ten or twelve feet below. I turned and forgot about it, pulling upward, kneeing and toeing into the cliff, kicking steps into the shaly rock wherever I could, trying to position both hands and one foot before moving to a new position. Some of the time I could do this, and each time my confidence increased. Often I could only get one handhold and a foothold, or two handholds. Once I could only get one handhold, but it was a strong one, and I scrambled and shifted around it until I could get a toe into the rock and pull up.

The problem-interest of it absorbed me at first, but I began to notice that the solutions were getting harder and harder: the cliff was starting to shudder in my face and against my chest. I became aware of the sound of my breath, whistling and humming crazily into the stone: the cliff was steepening, and I was laboring backbreakingly for every inch. My arms were tiring and my calves were not so much trembling as jumping. I knew now that not looking down or back – the famous advice to people climbing things – was going to enter into it. Panic was getting near me. Not as near as it might have been, but near. I concentrated everything I had to become ultrasensitive to the cliff, feeling it more gently than before, though I was shaking badly. I kept inching up. With each shift to a newer and higher position I felt more and more tenderness toward the wall.

Despite everything, I looked down. The river had spread flat and filled with moonlight. It took up the whole of space under me, bearing in the center of itself a long coiling image of light, a chill, bending flame. I must have been seventy-five or a hundred feet above it, hanging poised over some kind of inescapable glory, a bright pit.

I turned back into the cliff and leaned my mouth against it, feeling all the way out through my nerves and muscles exactly how I had possession of the wall at four random points in a way that held the whole thing together.

It was about this time that I thought of going back down, working along the bank and looking for an easier way up, and I let one foot down behind me into the void. There was nothing. I stood with the foot groping for a hold in the air, then pulled it back to the place on the cliff where it had been. It burrowed in like an animal, and I started up again.

I caught something – part of the rock – with my left hand and started to pull. I could not rise. I let go with my right hand and grabbed the wrist of the left, my left-hand fingers shuddering and popping with weight. I got one toe into the cliff, but that was all I could do. I looked up and held on. The wall was giving me nothing. It no longer sent back any pressure against me. Something I had come to rely on had been taken away, and that was it. I was hanging, but just barely. I concentrated all my strength into the fingers of my left hand, but they were leaving me. I was on the perpendicular part of the cliff, and unless I could get over it soon I would just peel off the wall. I had what I thought of as a plan if this should happen; this was to kick out as strongly as I could from the cliff face and try to get clear of the overhang and out into the river, into the bright coiling of the pit. But even if I cleared the rocks, the river was probably shallow near the bank where I would land, and it would be about as bad as if I were to hit the rocks. And I would have to get rid of the bow.

I held on. By a lot of small tentative maneuvers I swapped hands in the crevice and touched upward with my left hand, weighted down by the bow hanging over my shoulder, along the wall, remembering scenes in movies where a close-up of a hand reaches desperately for something, through a prison grate for a key, or from quicksand toward someone or something on solid ground. There was nothing there. I swapped hands again and tried the wall to my right. There was nothing. I tried the loose foot, hoping that if I could get a good enough foothold, I could get up enough to explore a little more of the wall with my hands, but I couldn't find anything there either, though I searched as far as I could with the toe and the knee, up and down and back and forth. The back of my left leg was shaking badly. My mind began to speed up, in the useless energy of panic. The urine in my bladder turned solid and painful, and then ran with a delicious sexual voiding like a wet dream, something you can't help or be blamed for. There was nothing to do but fall. The last hope I had was that I might awaken.

I was going, but anger held me up a little longer. I would have done something desperate if I had had a little more mobility, but I

142

was practically nailed in one position; there was nothing desperate I could do. Yet I knew that if I were going to try something, I had better do it now.

I hunched down into what little power was left in my left leg muscles and drove as hard as it was possible for me to do; harder than it was possible. With no holds on the cliff, I fought with the wall for anything I could make it give me. For a second I tore at it with both hands. In a flash inside a flash I told myself not to double up my fists but to keep my hands open. I was up against a surface as smooth as monument stone, and I still believe that for a space of time I was held in the air by pure will, fighting an immense rock.

Then it seemed to spring a crack under one finger of my right hand; I thought surely I had split the stone myself. I thrust in other fingers and hung and, as I did, I got the other hand over, feeling for a continuation of the crack; it was there. I had both hands in the cliff to the palms, and strength from the stone flowed into me. I pulled up as though chinning on a sill and swung a leg in. I got the middle section of my body into the crevice as well, which was the hardest part to provide for, as it had been everywhere else. I wedged into the crack like a lizard, not able to get far enough in. As I flattened out on the floor of the crevice, with all my laborious verticality gone, the bow slid down my arm and I hooked upward just in time to stop it with my wrist. I pulled it into the cliff with me, the broadheads at my throat.

September 16th

W ITH MY cheek on one shoulder, I lay there on my side in the crevice, facing out, not thinking about anything, solid on one side with stone and open to the darkness on the other, as though I were in a sideways grave. The glass of the bow was cold in my hands, cold and familiar. The curves were beautiful to the touch, a smooth chill flowing, and beside the curves the arrow lay – or stood – rigidly, the feathers bristling when I moved a little, and the points pricking at me. But it was good pain; it was reality, and deep in the situation. I simply lay in nature, my pants' legs warm and sopping with my juices, not cold, not warm, but in a kind of hovering. Think, I said, think. But I could not. I won't think yet; I don't have to for a while. I closed my eyes and spoke some words, and they seemed to make sense, but were out of place. I believe I was saying something about some bank advertising Thad and I were not in agreement on, but it might not have been that at all; there is no way to tell.

The first words I really remember were said very clearly. What a view. *What* a view. But I had my eyes closed. The river was running in my mind, and I raised my lids and saw exactly what had been the image of my thought. For a second I did not know what I was seeing and what I was imagining; there was such an utter sameness that it didn't matter; both were the river. It spread there eternally, the moon so huge on it that it hurt the eyes, and the mind, too, flinched like an eye. What? I said.

Where? There was nowhere but here. Who, though? Unknown. Where can I start?

You can start with the bow, and work slowly into the situation, working back and working up. I held the bow as tightly as I could, coming by degrees into the realization that I was going to have to risk it again, before much longer. But not now. Let the river run.

And let the moonlight come down for a little while. I had the bow and I had one good arrow and another one I might risk on a short shot. The thought struck me with my full adrenaline supply, all hitting the veins at once. Angelic. Angelic. Is that what it means? It very likely does. And I have a lot of nylon rope, and a long knife that was held at my throat and stuck by a murderer in the tree beside my head. It is not in the tree now; it is at my side. It is not much duller for having been in the river, and if I wanted to shave hair with it, I could. Does it still hurt, where that woods rat, that unbelievable redneck shaved across me with it? I felt my chest, and it hurt. Good. Good. Am I ready? No. No. Not yet, Gentry. It doesn't have to be yet. But soon.

It was easy to say I don't understand, and I did say it. But that was not really relevant. It just came down to where I was, and what I was doing there. I was not much worried. I was about 150 feet over the river, as nearly as I could tell, and I believed that if I could get that far I could get the rest of the way, even though the cliff was steeper here than it was lower down. Let me look, now. That is all there is to do, right at this moment. That is all there is to do, and that is all that needs to be done.

What a view, I said again. The river was blank and mindless with beauty. It was the most glorious thing I have ever seen. But it was not seeing, really. For once it was not just seeing. It was beholding. I *beheld* the river in its icy pit of brightness, in its far-below sound and indifference, in its large coil and tiny points and flashes of the moon, in its long sinuous form, in its uncomprehending consequence. What was there?

Only that terrific brightness. Only a couple of rocks as big as islands, around one of which a thread of scarlet seemed to go, as though outlining a face, a kind of god, a layout for an ad, a sketch, an element of design. It was a thread like the color of sun-images underneath the eyelids. The rock quivered like a coal, because I wanted it to quiver, held in its pulsing border, and what it was pulsing with was me. It might have looked something like my face, in one of those photographs lit up from underneath. My face: why not? I can have it as I wish: a kind of three-quarter face view, set in the middle of the moon-pit, that might have looked a little posed or phony, but was yet different from what any mirror could show. I thought I saw the jaw set, breathing with the river and the stone, but it might also have been a smile of some kind. I closed my eyes and opened them again, and the thread around the rock was gone, but it had been there. I felt better; I felt wonderful, and fear was at the center of the feeling: fear and anticipation – there was no telling where it would end.

I turned back. I turned back to the wall and the cliff, and into my situation, trying to imagine how high the cliff had seemed to be the last time I had seen it by daylight, and trying to estimate where I was on it. I thought I surely must be three quarters of the way up. I believed I could stand upright in the crevice, and this would give me three or four more feet.

Why not? Was there a bulge above me? If I could get on top of that, who knows what might not be possible? I let my hand go up, and it felt the top of the crevice. What are you sending me? I said. It feels good. It feels like something I might be able to work up on top of, if I went to the left, and took one moment of pure death. There is going to be that moment, but that is not bad.

I have had so many in the past few hours: so many decisions, so many fingers groping over this insignificant, unwatched cliff, so many muscles straining against the stone.

Where was Drew? He used to say, in the only interesting idea I had ever heard him deal with, that the best guitar players were blind men: men like Reverend Gary Davis and Doc Watson and Brownie McGhee, who had developed the sense of touch beyond what a man with eyes could do. I have got something like that, I said. I have done what I have done, I have got up here mostly by the sense of touch, and in the dark.

Are they below? Is Lewis still twisting into the sand? Is Bobby sitting on the rock beside him trying to think what to do? Is his head in his hands? Or has his jaw set, believing that we can all get out, even now?

Who knows that? But we have laid a plan, and that is all we have been able to do. If that doesn't work, we will probably all be killed, or if I can get back down the cliff when nothing happens, we will all just go a few miles downriver in the canoe, take a few days in the city to recover, report Drew as drowned and get back into the long, declining routine of our lives. But we were cast in roles, and first we must do something about them.

I was a killer. There were deaths involved: one certain murder and probably another. I had the cold glass of the bow in my hand, and I was lying belly-up in a crevice in a cliff above a river, and it could be that everything was with me.

I could get there, in my mind. The whole thing focused, like an old movie that just barely held its own on the screen. The top of the gorge was wild and overgrown and lumpy, and I remembered it also thickly wooded. I wanted to give myself something definite to do when I got to the top, and lying there, I tried to fix on what would be the best thing and the first thing to do when I got there.

I had to admit it: I thought that there was really no danger involved, at least from anything human. I didn't actually believe that the man who had shot Drew would stay around all night for another shot at us, or that he would come back in the early light, either. But then I remembered what I had told Bobby, and I was troubled again. *If it were me* was the main thing I thought. I went over everything in my mind, and as far as I could tell, I was right. There was a lot more reason for him to kill the rest of us than there was for him to let us go. We were all acting it out.

I turned. Well, I said to the black stone at my face, when I get to the top the first thing I'll do will be not to think of Martha and Dean again, until I see them. And then I'll go down to the first stretch of calm water and take a look around before it gets light. When I finish that, I'll make a circle inland, very quiet, and look for him like I'm some kind of an animal. What kind? It doesn't matter, as long as I'm quiet and deadly. I could be a snake. Maybe I can kill him in his sleep. That would be the easiest thing to do, but could I do it? How? With the bow? Or would I put the hardware store knife through him? Could I do it? Or would I like to do it? I asked this.

But the circling – what about that? If I got too far from the river, and the sound of the river, I would almost surely lose myself. And then what? A circle? *What* circle? What principle guides you, when you try to make a circle – a *circle* – in the woods? I didn't have it. Suppose I got inland from the river far enough to lose track of myself? Had I shot the whole thing, right there?

But I could see myself killing, because I had no real notion I would have to. If he was close to the cliff edge, as he would at some place and time have to be, the high-rising sound of water would help me get close enough to him for a killing shot. I wanted to kill him exactly as Lewis had killed the other man:

I wanted him to suspect nothing at all until the sudden terrible pain in his chest that showed an arrow through him from behind, come from anywhere.

Oh what a circle, I thought. All in the woods, with the leaves waiting, the wind waiting, for me to draw it. That is leaving too much to chance. It won't work, I knew as I considered it. It will never work.

What then, art director? Graphics consultant? What is the layout? It is this: to shoot him from behind, somewhere on the top of the gorge. He almost certainly would get himself into the prone position in order to shoot down onto the river. There are these various kinds of concentration. While he was deep in his kind, I would try to get within twenty or thirty feet of him and put my one good arrow through his lower rib cage – for what would save the shot would be exactness – and then fall back and run for it into the woods, and sit down and wait until he had time enough to die.

That was as far ahead as I could think. In a way, it seemed already settled. It was settled as things in day-dreams always are, but it could be settled only because the reality was remote. It was the same state of mind I had had when I had hunted the deer in the fog. These were worthy motions I was going through, but only motions, and it was shocking to remind myself that if I came on him with the rifle I would have to carry them through or he would kill me.

I slid farther into the crack to draw from the stone a last encouragement, but I was already tired of being there. It would be best to stand up and get on with it.

I got on one knee and went cautiously outward, rising slowly with both hands palm-up on the underside of the fissure top. I was up, slanting backward, and I felt along and around the bulge over my head. To the right there was nothing I could do, but I was glad to be back. To the left the crevice went on beyond where I could reach, and the only thing to do was to edge along it, sidestepping inch by inch until only my toes, very tired again, were in the crack. But I was able to straighten from my back-leaning position to an upright one – really upright – and then to lean surprisingly forward at the waist, as I edged to the left. This was unexpected and exhilarating. The stone came back at me strong. I got on the rock with my knees instead of my toes and fingertips, and had a new body position. With it, I wormed. I went to the left and then to the right, and the river-pit blazed. It was slow going, for the handholds were not good, and the broadheads gored me under the arms a good deal, but there was a trembling and near-perfect balance between gravity – or my version of it – and the slant of the stone: I was at the place where staying on the wall and falling canceled each other out in my body, yet were slightly in favor of my staying where I was, and edging up. Time after time I lay there sweating, having no handhold or foothold, the rubber of my toes bending back against the soft rock, my hands open. Then I would begin to try to inch upward again, moving with the most intimate motions of my body, motions I had never dared use with Martha, or with any other human woman. Fear and a kind of enormous moon-blazing sexuality lifted me, millimeter by millimeter. And yet I held madly to the human. I looked for a slice of gold like the model's in the river: some kind of freckle, something lovable, in the huge serpent-shape of light.

Above me the darks changed, and in one of them was a star. On both sides of that small light the rocks went on up, black and solid as ever, but their power was broken. The high, deadly part of the cliff I was on bent and rocked steadily over toward life, and toward the hole with the star in it, where, as I went, more stars were added until a constellation like a crown began to form. I was now able to travel on knees – my knees after all – the bow scraping the ground beside me.

I was crying. What reason? There was not any, for I was really not ashamed or terrified; I was just there. But I lay down against the cliff to get my eyesight cleared. I turned and propped on my elbow like a tourist, and looked at it again. Lord, Lord. The river hazed and danced into the sparkle of my eyelashes, the more wonderful for being unbearable. This was something; it was something.

But eventually you have to turn back to your knees, and on cliffs they carry you better than any other part of the body, on cliffs of a certain slant; I got on my knees.

It was painful, but I was going. I was crawling, but it was no longer necessary to make love to the cliff, to fuck it for an extra inch or two in the moonlight, for I had some space between me and it. If I was discreet, I could offer it a kick or two, even, and get away with it.

My feet slanted painfully in one direction or another. Guided by what kind of guesswork I could not say, I kept scrambling and stumbling upward like a creature born on the cliff and coming home. Often a hand or foot would slide and then catch on something I knew, without knowing, would be there, and I would go on up. There was nothing it could do against me, in the end; there was nothing it could do that I could not match, and, in the twinkling of some kind of eye-beat, I was going.

By some such way as this, I got into a little canyon. Yes, and I stood up. I could not see much, but it *felt* like the little draw where I had hunted the deer in the fog. The bottom underfoot – under *foot* – was full of loose rocks and boulders, but I was walking it. At each shoulder, the walls were wanting to come down, but they did not. Instead, they started to fill with bushes and small, ghostly, dense trees. These were solid, and I came up to them, little by little. Then their limbs were above me. I was out.

I picked up the bow, out of the crook of my arm. Everything was with me; the knife at my side said what it was. And there was rope, for nothing, or for something. And I looked out, on the mindlessness and the beauty.

Upriver, I could see only the ragged, blinding V of the rapids that had thrown us, and there was nothing to look at there, except only the continual, almost-silent pouring of the water, through and through. I faced around and for what I judged an equal amount of time looked into the woods. I went back into the pines growing on solid ground, leaned my forehead on a tree and then put my forearm between the tree and it.

Where? I went back to look down on the river. Trees, fewer and fewer, were growing to the edge of the cliff. The moon shone down through their needles on the Cahulawassee. I thought for the first time seriously of the coming destruction on the river, of the water rising to the place I was standing now, lifting out of its natural bed up over the stones that had given us such a hard time in the white water, and slowly also up the cliff, the water patiently and inevitably searching out every handhold I had had, then coming to rest where I was standing in the moonlight. I sat on a cold rock at the edge, looking down. I believed, in the great light, that if I fell I could instinctively reach to the cliff and catch on to something that would hold: that, among all the places in the world that could kill me, there was one that could not.

I came back by degrees to the purpose.

First, I assumed that the man who had shot Drew knew that he had shot him. That was a beginning. I also assumed that he knew we hadn't all been killed in the rapids. What then? He might be waiting above the calm where Bobby and Lewis were – where I was, more or less – planning to draw down on them when they started out. If that were the case he would kill them both, though if Bobby gauged the change in the light well enough and set out when there was enough visibility to use the canoe but not enough to shoot by, they might have a chance to get past him, through the next stretch of rapids – the ones now a little downstream from me – and on down. Our whole hope rested on our being able to second-guess the man, and, now that I was on top of the gorge, it seemed to me that we had guessed right, or as right as it was possible for us to do. If Bobby moved out in the very early half-light, the chances of making a good shot down onto the water would be greatly reduced, and big gaps in the upper part of the wall, small deep ravines such as the one I had come up, would keep him from getting downstream at anything like the speed the canoe could make. I counted on his knowing this, and on the idea that he would try to solve the problem by setting up his shots downstream at calm water, where the target would be moving at a more constant speed and not leaping and bobbing. Below me, except for one rush of whiteness cramped between two big hedges of stone, the rapids seemed comparatively gentle, in places – so far as I could tell – scarcely more than a heavy-twilled rippling. But even this would be disconcerting for a marksman because of the bobbing it would cause. If I were going to kill somebody from this distance and this angle I would want to draw a long bead. Under those conditions, and if he was a good shot, there was no reason he couldn't get Bobby and Lewis both, and within a few seconds of each other, if he took his time and dropped the first one cleanly. That would take calm water, as slow as possible, and it would have to be down-stream, out of sight around the next turn.

That's it then, I thought. I had to ambush him in some way, if possible from behind, and this depended on my being able to locate the place he would pick to shoot from, and on luck. And I would have to get him as he was steadying down to fire, which cut the margin of safety for Bobby and Lewis very thin.

I had thought so long and hard about him that to this day I still believe I felt, in the moonlight, our minds fuse. It was not that I felt myself turning evil, but that an enormous physical indifference, as vast as the whole abyss of light at my feet, came to me: an indifference not only to the other man's body scrambling and kicking on the ground with an arrow through it, but also to mine. If Lewis had not shot his companion, he and I would have made a kind of love, painful and terrifying to me, in some dreadful way pleasurable to him, but we would have been together in the flesh, there on the floor of the woods, and it was strange to think of it. Who was he? An escaped convict? Just a dirt farmer out hunting? A bootlegger?

Since I needed to be in a place where I could see the river, and as much of it as possible, in order to know whether or not the canoe was in sight of the man, I wanted to get as high as possible, and out of sight, and that meant a rock with an overlook, or a tree. I remembered that when the bow-hunting of deer from tree stands first hit our state, a lot of hunters who had never been near an animal in the woods bagged deer the first time they tried it. Deer are supposed to have no natural enemies in trees, and so seldom look up. This was not much to go on, but there were plenty of trees growing near the edge of the cliff. First, though, I would have to get down the river and find the right spot.

I began to make my way over the boulders at the edge, paralleling the rapids, which went on and on as far as I could see. Most of the time it was not as hard going as I would have thought. The rocks were very big ones, and I stepped and jumped from one dark mass to another with a sureness of foot that astonished me, for there seemed nothing at all to be afraid of. The only thing that bothered me now and then was the harshness of my breath, in which there was still the sound of panic, and this appeared to have nothing to do with the actions of my body. It took me a good while – at least an hour, maybe two – to get down past the rapids. When the moon smoothed out below me, and the rising sound fell back, I had the river where I wanted it. What now?

The top was mostly boulders, and there were a lot of them I could have hidden behind, but I would have had almost no visibility. I decided to go downstream a little farther just to get a look at what was there, and then to come back to about where I was now standing.

This time the traveling was much rougher; there were some very bad places: big hacked-feeling boulders with fallen trees wedged between them, and at one spot there was a kind of natural wall, high like a stone barricade, that I didn't think I'd be able to get over. Both going downriver and coming back I had to feel my way inland twenty or thirty yards to find a way to get over it. There were saplings growing near it on both sides, though, and with the help of these – which gave me something to hold on to as my feet were climbing the rock – I got on top of it and slid down the other side. All the time I was traveling I was looking at the river, and unless the man lay on top of the stone wall – where visibility was not good, the river showing only as a faint movement like the leaves of a tree seen through another tree – he would have to get somewhere on the edge itself to have a wide enough view of the stream to sight and lead accurately. Of the part of the calm water I had been back and forth over, there was only one place that looked right for this. It was surrounded on the upstream side by jumbled rocks, but was easier to get to from inland, as far as I could tell. There was a pale sandy platform at the very edge that looked down on the river through a thicket of grass about a yard high. As far as I was concerned, this was it. We were still far enough from houses and highways not to be heard, but I was fairly sure that we were not awfully far, even so, and the closer we were the less likely he would be to take a chance. If he doesn't come here, I thought, but picks another calm place down-stream, Bobby and Lewis have had it.

Yes, I thought with a cowardly but good feeling, *they've* had it. After all, I would have done all I could, and as a last resort could work my way out of the woods, following the river down to the first highway bridge. I was not particularly afraid of the man's hunting me down after killing the others – though I was afraid to some extent, imagining suddenly his moving along my uncertain tracks in the windless underbrush and dark foliage – for he wouldn't know where I was. Though he most likely recalled that there'd been four people in the canoes, one of us could easily have been drowned in the rapids; after all, the three of us nearly *had* drowned there. My life was safer than anyone's unless the toothless man and I came on each other by chance.

Or unless I took a shot at him and missed. That chilled me; I felt my tongue thicken at the possibility. I thought about starting the trek out of the woods now, but the back of my mind told me that I had not gone through enough of the right motions yet; if Bobby and Lewis died, I wanted to be able to say to myself that I had done more than just climb up a gorge side and leave them helpless. But if the man I was looking for didn't come where I expected him to after I had done my best to find him and kill him, that was not my fault. And there was not much chance that I had really guessed right. It was just the best that I could do.

There was still no light in the sky but moonlight. I turned away from the river where the land shelved back to some boulders

157

and low trees, and felt around. Among the trees, which held the light from me, I could tell nothing except by touch. I put out a foot because I could reach farther that way. Something solid was there. I took a step toward it and was enveloped at once in branches and the stiff pine-hairs. I set the bow down and climbed into the lower limbs, which were very thick and close together, and went up until the tree swayed.

There was a little visibility through the needles, a little flickering light off the river, which the tree set twice as far off as it had been when I looked at it from the grasses at the edge of the cliff. I finally figured out that the part of the river I could see was where it came out of the turn from the last of the rapids below Lewis and Bobby, and calmed and smoothed out, losing its own thready silver for the broad-lying moonlight.

I went back down and got the bow and began to do what I could about setting up a blind in the tree. I had never shot anything – or at anything – from a tree before, not even a target, though I remembered someone's telling me to aim a little lower than seemed right. I thought about this while I worked.

Moving as though I was instructing myself – where does this hand go? Here? No, it would be better over here, or a little lower down – I cleared away the small-needled twigs between myself and the platform of sand. It was not hard to do; I just kept taking things away from between the river-light and my face until there were not any. When I was back against the bole of the tree, I was looking down a short, shaggy tunnel of needles; I would shoot right down that; it even seemed to help me aim. All the time I was clearing, I was aided by a totally different sense of touch than I had ever had, and it occurred to me that I must have developed it on the cliff. I seemed able to tell the exact shape and weight of anything at first touch, and had to put out no extra strength to break or strip off any part of the tree I wanted to. Being alive in the dark and doing what I was doing was like a powerful drunkenness, because I didn't believe it. There had never been anything in my life remotely like it. I felt the bark next to me with the most intimate part of my palm, then broke off a needle and put it in my mouth and bit down. It was the right taste.

I edged around the trunk one way and another to see if I could give myself any more advantages, or a slightly wider angle from which to shoot. I did not want to tear the tree up any more; it must look like a tree, with no danger in it; it must look like the others. I had my clear shot down onto the sand, down the dark tunnel, but I could not swing more than a foot or two either way. For me to kill him under these conditions, he would have to be thinking as I had thought for him, and not approximately but exactly. The minds would have to merge.

I took my good arrow off the bow quiver, nocked it by feel and drew it back, setting my feet firmly on two big branches and getting solid at full draw, leaning to the right a little from the trunk to clear my right elbow to go all the way back. I lined up the shot down onto the open place as accurately as I could, thought for a second about shooting the arrow down into the sand to make sure of my elevation, fought off the idea with a quick springing of sweat and relaxed the broadhead out from the bow, letting my breath come forward at the same time. It had been close; I had almost done it. Involuntary release would get me killed, and it was also likely to lose or damage the arrow so that I wouldn't have any chance at all, if the man came. If.

I got as comfortable as I could, and decided to stay in the tree until light. I began to practice stillness, for that was what I was up there for.

It was very quiet, almost out of hearing of the river; I heard the rapids upstream from me as no more than a persistent rustle,

159

mixing, I thought as I listened, with another sound that must certainly be coming from down-stream: more rapids, I would have bet, maybe even a falls. If that were true, it increased the chances of my being in the right place. Everything about it was logical, though through all the logic I still had no real belief that the man would come; it was far more likely that I had figured the whole thing wrong. I was just going through motions, even though they were the motions of life and death. I was awfully tired and not very excited, except when I thought that I might have guessed right, and I would have to get into the last motions of all and go through them: to turn that broadhead down the tunnel of pine needles on a human body and let it go, forever.

But mainly I was amazed at my situation. Just rather dumbly amazed. It was harder to imagine myself in a tree, like this, than it was to reach out and touch the bark or the needles and know that I actually was in one, in the middle of the night – or somewhere in the night – miles back in the woods, waiting to try to kill a man I had seen only once in my life. Nobody in the world knows where I am, I thought. I put tension on the bowstring, and the arrow came back a little. Who would believe it, I said, with no breath; who on earth?

It was slow waiting. I looked at my watch, but the river had killed it. My head bent forward, and seemed to want to keep on going down. I snapped awake two or three times, but slower each time, with less snap; once I leapt up out of the oldest dream of all – the oldest and most dreamlike – the one about starting to fall. For a second I had no idea what to do or to grab for, and simply put out a hand. I straightened again, wedged back, and tried to take stock once more. There was no arrow in the bow. My God, I thought, I've done it now. I don't think I can get this crooked one even clear of the tree. Without a weapon I knew I would huddle helplessly in the tree, praying he wouldn't notice me, and stay there while he killed Bobby and Lewis. I knew that I wouldn't take him on with just a knife, no matter what advantage of surprise I had.

It was as dark as it had been, even darker. I hung the bow on a limb and went down the trunk. The arrow should have been on the ground, probably sticking up, but it was not. I crawled around in the needles, sobbing with fear and frustration, feeling everything and everywhere I could with hands, arms, legs, body, everything I had, hoping the broadhead would cut me, anything, but just be there.

It wasn't, though, and I could now feel a little light. I would have to go back up the tree. Maybe, when I could see better, I could do some kind of job of straightening on the arrow I had left, but I also knew that the confidence I could hit what I was shooting at was going to be hurt; there is no skill or sport, not even surgery or golf, in which confidence is as important as it is in archery.

But I found the arrow I had dropped, stuck in a limb below where the bow hung, and the plan I had set up locked together and rose up in me like marble. I had everything once more, and I went up to the bow and arranged myself into my shooting position again.

The needles were filling slowly with the beginnings of daylight, and the tree began to glow softly, shining the frail light held by the needles inward on me, and I felt as though I were giving it back outward. I kept looking down the tunnel, now not a massed darkness; there were greens. I opened my mouth so that my breathing would be more silent; so that a nostril would not whistle, or drag with phlegm.

I could see plainly now: the needled and rocky space just beneath the tree, and out from that to the sandy shelf, maybe ten feet wide, with its fringe of tall ragged grass, and beyond that down into space, the eye falling like a body, not dying, but coming to rest on the river. Bobby should be starting now. In a few minutes it would all be over; I would have been either wrong or right, and we would be dead or alive.

Or maybe he had already started, and slipped by me while I was looking for the arrow. There was no way to tell, and I cringed among the branches, waiting to hear a rifle shot from another place, a location I couldn't have guessed or known about.

None came, though. The light strengthened. My sense of utter concealment began to die out of me, and out of the tree. At the right angle, someone standing on the sandy shelf could look right up my tunnel of pine branches at me, and this could be either deliberate or by chance. A lot was hanging on chance.

I moved cautiously, as much as I could like a creature who lived in a tree, craning my neck and leaning out from the trunk to see a foot or two more of the cliff edge, to see if I could make out the canoe.

Something caught the tail of my left eye, and my stomach ach froze. I didn't turn my head at once, but slowly. I knew, though. I knew, and knew.

A rock clicked on another, and a man was walking forward onto the sand with a rifle. He had one hand in his right pocket.

This is it, I thought, but my first hope, one I could not keep off me, was that I could stay in the tree until he went away. My climb up the cliff had left me; all I wanted was my life. Everything in me was shaking; I could not even have nocked the arrow. Then I looked downward and saw my hands holding the bow, with the broadhead's two colors, sharpened and unsharpened, separating from each other. This steadied me, and I began to believe, once more, that I would do what I had come to do, in this kind of deadly charade. If he lay down with his back to me, I would shoot. I squeezed the first and middle fingers around the arrow nock, took a slow open-mouthed breath, and leaned back tense and still.

He was looking up the river and standing now with both hands on the gun, but with the attitude of holding it at his waist without necessarily thinking of raising it to his shoulder. There was something relaxed and enjoying in his body position, something primally graceful; I had never seen a more beautiful or convincing element of a design. I wanted to kill him just like that, and I prayed for Bobby to come into sight at that instant, but I could see nothing on the river, and he apparently couldn't either. He shifted around for some reason, with half of him framed by my tunnel of needles. Wait till he lies down, I said far back in my throat, and then hit him dead center of the back. Make it a problem. Try to break his back, so that even if you don't hit the spine you'll still hit something vital.

But he was still standing there, not indecisively or decisively; just standing, part of his body clear for a shot, but his head and the other part, not. I had better try now; he may move out of my line of fire. I tensed my arm to see if the muscles would work. The string took on a small angle. I looked right at him, and he gave a little more of himself to the hole in the needles. He was sideways to me, but if his face came into view, he had only to raise it a little to be looking directly at me. I knew that my next battle would be with hysteria, the wild hysteria of full draw, of wanting to let the arrow go and get the tension of holding the bow out of the body: in my head the whole delicate routine of making a good archery shot, all the time aware that the most perfect form goes for nothing if the release doesn't happen right; the fingers of the right hand must be relaxed, and above all the bow arm must not move.

He seemed puzzled. He kept looking back from the river down

163

at his feet, at the ground there, half sand and half rock, and every time his head inclined and his hidden face bent down he looked at a place farther from the river and nearer to where I was.

I closed my eyes, took a slow three-quarter breath, held it and leveled the bow inch by inch. When it was approximately in the position I wanted, I went to my muscles and drew. My back spread broader, drawing strength from the tree. The broadhead came back to the bow face along the arrow rest, the unborn calf. It chattered there with the unnatural tension of my body and a sound that was a sound only to the nerves in the palm of my left hand. I pulled the barb of the arrow firmly against the bow, and began checking things in the bow and the arrow and in my hands and arms and body, like a countdown.

He was just out of the frame of thread on the string; my peep sight. I had only to move the bow slightly for him to come into the peep sight and the right-left problem, except possibly for the release, was solved. Martha's orange and the target were now threaded and framed. That left only elevation, always the main problem when shooting downward, and the release. The tip of the arrow appeared, in my secondary vision as I looked at him, to be about six inches under his feet, and I brought it down another inch or so until, as I judged, it looked to me as though I were trying to shoot him through the stomach; looking through the string down the shaft and out the cave of needles, I could see the arrow as being in a plane extending through the middle of him.

We were closed together, and the feeling of a peculiar kind of intimacy increased, for he was shut within a frame within a frame, all of my making: the peep sight and the alleyway of needles, and I knew then that I had him, if my right hand just relaxed and let the arrow tear itself away, and if my left arm did not move, but just took up the shock of the vibrating bow.

164

Everything was right; it could not have been better. My anchor was good and firm, and the broadhead seemed almost rock-steady. I was full of the transfiguring power of full draw, the draw-hysteria that is the ruination of some archers and the making of others, who can conquer it and make it work for them.

I was down to my last two points, and he was still right there, stooping a little but now facing me just a shade more than he had been. Then he moved, slightly but quickly, and I fought to hold on to the arrow. He stirred the ground once with his foot, and I saw his face – saw that he had a face – for the first time. The whole careful structure of my shot began to come apart, and I struggled in my muscles and guts and heart to hold it together. His eyes were moving over the sand and rock, faster and faster. They were coming. When they began to rise from the ground they triggered my release. I never saw the arrow in the air, and I don't believe he did either, though he surely must have heard the bow twang. I had been at full draw so long that even in the instant of release I believed that I would no more have been able to move my left arm than a statue would. I was afraid that my concentration had blown apart under the recognition that he knew where I was, and some of it had; but not all. The shot had been lined up correctly; if the left arm had held, he was hit.

What happened next I was not sure about, and still am not. The tree thrummed like an ax had struck it, and the woods, so long quiet around me, were full of unbelievable sound. The next thing I knew there was no tree with me anymore, nor any bow. A limb caught my leg and tried to tear it off me, and I was going down the trunk backwards and upside down with many things touching and hitting upward at me with live weight, like arms. To this day I will contend that I spent part of the fall checking the fingers of my right hand to see if they were relaxed, had been relaxed when the shot went, and they were.

I tried also to turn in the air so as not to strike on the back of my head, and was beginning to turn, I think, when I hit. Something went through me from behind, and I heard a rip like tearing a bedsheet. Another thing buckled and snapped under me, and I was out of breath on the ground, hurt badly somewhere as the gun went off again, and I could not get to my feet but clawed backward, dragging something. The gun boomed again, then again and again; a branch whipsawed in the tree, but higher than my head would've been if I'd been standing. There was something odd about the shooting; I could tell that even as I was, and I got to one knee and then to my feet from that, and crouched and crow-hopped toward, to, and finally behind some rocks on the upriver side of the tree. I stayed low; the gun went off again. Then I slowly lifted my head over the rock.

He was staggering toward the tree, still ten or fifteen feet from it, trying to get the gun up as though it were something too long, or too limber to raise, like a hose. He fired again, but only a yard in front of his feet. The top of his chest was another color, and as he melted forward and down I saw the arrow hanging down his back just below the neck; it was painted entirely red, and was just hanging by the nock and flipping stiffly and softly. He got carefully down to his knees; blood poured when his mouth opened and seemed to splash up out of the ground, to have the force of something coming out of the earth, a spring revealed when the right stone was moved. Die, I thought, my God, die, die.

I slid down on my right side on the back of the rock and laid my cheek to the stone. What is wrong with me? I asked, as the rock seriously and gravely began to turn, as though it might rise. I looked down at my other side and an arrow, the crooked one from the bow quiver, was sticking through it, and the broken bow was still hanging to it by the power part of the clip.

I put my head down, and was gone. Where? I went comfortably into the distance, and I had a dim image in my head of myself turning around, disappearing into mist, waving good-bye.

Nothing.

More nothing, another kind, and out of this I looked up, amazed. In front of me a man was down on his hands and knees giving up his blood like a man vomiting in the home of a friend, careful to get his head down or into the toilet bowl. I put my head back and went away again.

The hardness of the rock against my breath woke me; it was too difficult to get air, in the place where I had been. I lifted my head and my eyes again, but there was no man there to see with them. I would have lain there forever but for that, but because of the mystery I slowly struggled back into doing something.

I propped up and looked at myself. The arrow had gone through about an inch of flesh in my side, the flesh that age and inactivity were beginning to load on me. I would either have to cut it out of my side or pull the shaft through. As carefully as I could, but with the pain of every move making my soul shrivel and beg for help, I stripped the feathers off the arrow, and then set my teeth and started to work it through and out. It came slowly, and I thought of the arrow paint I was leaving inside the wound, but there was no way to get away from it. I licked my hand and put saliva on the shaft, hoping the lubrication would help. It did at first, and then it didn't; the arrow stuck solidly, and I could not move it at all without coming very close to passing out. I would have to cut.

I took the knife from my belt, sliced away the nylon I was wearing from around it, and looked. Just looked, and that was more terrifying than trying to work the arrow out with my eyes closed. The broadhead had torn my side open, as it was designed to do, and if it had not gone quite as deep it would have just made a bad flesh wound, but that was not the case, and it was in me. In me. The flesh around the metal moved pitifully, like a mouth, when I moved the shaft. I put the knife against the flesh above the wound. Just cut right down, I said aloud. Cut down and cut it loose, and you'll be able to clean the wound out in the river. It will be a lot better that way, boy.

I cut. My stomach heaved at the pain, and I cut inside the cut I had made. The woods and air were dizzy as with birds flying from all the trees straight into my face. I took the knife and turned it so the curved part of the blade was in the wound, and drove it down with both hands. I felt it grate on the shaft. This will have to be it, I said. I'm not going to cut myself any more even if I have to grab the shaft and tear it loose, and tear myself in half with it. The side of the rock was covered with blood, and I felt in my side to see if the shaft was more or less clear of flesh. The knife fell and rang on the stone. The shaft would come; I moved it through me a little more, and the wound changed. The bloody shaft was in my hands, and my side was oozing and pouring down the rock. I went down after it, the arrow still in my hands, and stood up.

There had never been a freedom like it. The pain itself was freedom, and the blood. I picked up the knife and cut one of the nylon sleeves off, the whole thing at the shoulder, and stuffed it in the wound, and then cut a long strip out of my right pants' leg and tied it around my waist. I was thinking like a driven creature, but also like a singing one. Could I walk? What else could I do?

Walking was odd and one-sided but not impossible. I went to the edge of the gorge, which was almost straight up and down.

There was no sign of the canoe, and I reckoned it had already gone by. Well, too bad. I'd wait for a while, try to find the man I had shot and bury him or get rid of him in whatever way I could, and then try to walk out.

I went back over to the rock where I had bled and threw a lot of sand and dirt on the blood, so that at least it didn't shine. That was all the blood I planned to leave in the woods; the rest would have to be somebody else's.

I went over to where the man had been. There was blood on a good many pebbles, and a concentration of it where he had been vomiting. I looked into the forest, and recalled what little I knew about the procedures of deer hunting: after hitting the deer with the arrow, you are supposed to wait half an hour and then follow it by its blood trail. I had no idea of how long ago it had been since I had shot, but from what I had seen I believed he could not be far away; maybe just a few yards. I got down on my hands and knees to try to find a direction for the blood.

Wherever it had been dropped on loose sand it had sunk, and so immediately I knew that the story, if I could figure it out, would be told by rocks. He had moved toward the woods, as he would have to have done. But when I saw his blood confirming this, my confidence rose; I followed where it went, stone by stone.

At the edge of the woods I found the rifle, flat and long and out of place on the pine needles. I left it there, and drew the knife. I was on my knees, bleeding wherever I looked for his blood. Once I had to go back and try to pick up the trail again, for I could not tell which was my blood and which was his. My side had pretty much soaked the middle part of my outfit, and there was some oozing through the cloth. But I did not feel weak at all. I wondered how the blood would clot, with so much of the wound open, but a kind of numbness had set in on that side, and in the time since I'd cut the arrow out I had developed a hugging-with-my-elbow way of standing and walking that already seemed second nature; I felt I could hold myself together for a while, and didn't think any further forward than the next pebble I didn't think I had bled on yet.

There was no path into the woods where I was going. It was dark there, but I could see blood, and when I couldn't see it I could feel it, and, in some cases, smell it. I tried one last time to think like the man I had shot. He was center-shot; it had looked like he was hit just under the throat, though it might have been right through the lower part of the neck. He was dying, he had no weapon, his jugular was probably cut in half. The only thing about him that concerned me was that he was trying to get somewhere he knew about: to some place, or even more pertinent, to someone. I didn't believe this was true, but I didn't know that it wasn't.

And I had to find him. If I didn't, somebody else might, and that would be the end of us, in one way or another, or at least it would be the beginning of explanations, trials, lawyers and all the other things we had tried to prevent when Lewis persuaded us to bury the first man under the ferns.

It was too dark to see from a standing position; I had to get closer to the blood. I went to all fours with my head down like a dog and the knife between my teeth, going through bush limbs one by one until I came out into an empty clearing about fifty yards wide. I could hardly hear the river now; it was only a distant, down-and-far murmur; every leaf I put between it and me diminished it.

But I had lost all contact with the blood. My head would not come up, and I felt faint without feeling particularly weak. The main trouble was that I could not think clearly. But I knew I had to do something about finding his blood again, or everything was gone.

I got up and walked out into the middle of the clearing. A badly hurt man is not going to want to fight through bushes. If he was trying to reach a definite objective, he would have used the open space. He would probably have used it even if he wasn't. He was not in the clearing, so he had gone through it. Straight across? How straight could he have gone? I went across to the other edge, ready to look at every leaf on every bush, and began to work slowly around the border. Shafts of early sunlight were everywhere, sensitive and needled, directed at certain places for no reason, moving slightly on the ground with the wind stirring in the tops of the trees. When I was about halfway around the perimeter one of the rays moved and gave back something. It was a reddish-brown rock about the size of a tennis ball that looked exactly as though it had been hastily painted, and I had to wait a minute, my head heavying even more, before I knew what it meant. This time I knew it was not my blood. You haven't been here yet, I kept saying to myself through the knife; you haven't been here. I went to the rock.

It was the place where he must have given up the last of the blood that had enabled him to move. A few steps farther on into the woods I found blood on a low leaf; crawling, maybe. I thought of getting down on my hands and knees and smelling for blood like an animal again, but the possibility that he was crawling made me want to stand, and I did, though crouching and leaning over the arm that held my own blood in.

I raised my eyes along the ground over the rocks and leaves and pine needles, and twenty yards away it bunched at the foot of a dead tree. It could have been a bush or a stone, but I knew when I first saw it that it was neither. It was not moving, but the light was playing over it and it seemed not entirely inert, but alive in the same way that most of the things in the woods were alive. I walked over to it, and it was a man lying face-down, holding on to one of the roots of the dead tree. He had long thin dirty fingers, and his back was soaking with blood.

Before there was everything to do there was nothing to do. His brain and mine unlocked and fell apart, and in a way I was sorry to see it go. I never had thought with another man's mind on matters of life and death, and would never think that way again. I just stood there looking down, breathing with the knife. Then I took it out of my face.

There was nothing in common, in the way he was lying, with any of the positions I had seen him in while he was alive, until I remembered the pose by the river in which I had most wanted to kill him. He now had that same relaxed, enjoying look of belonging anywhere he happened to be, and particularly in the woods.

I turned him over with a foot, and his hand moved around palm-up, still with the shape of the root. His face came clear.

I fell down; the knife fell away. My heart moved into my bad side and beat there, trying to throw my blood away any way it could. I put my hands over my face and went wild with terror; I could not look again. His mouth was open, and full of yellow teeth.

But was it? I crawled over to him and picked up the knife. I put it in his mouth and pried at the gums, and a partial upper plate began to come out. Did that make the difference? Did that make *enough* difference? I shoved the teeth back in with the handle of the knife, and took a good look. He was dressed like the toothless man in the clearing; whether *exactly* like him I truthfully couldn't say, but very much like. He was about the same size, and he was thin and repulsive-looking. And, though my time close to him in the clearing was burned in my mind, I had still seen him under those circumstances, which were a lot different from these; I believe that if I could have seen him move I would have known, one way or the other. But I didn't, and I don't.

I took the knife in my fist. What? Anything. This, also, is not going to be seen. It is not ever going to be known; you can do what you want to; nothing is too terrible. I can cut off the genitals he was going to use on me. Or I can cut off his head, looking straight into his open eyes. Or I can eat him. I can do anything I have a wish to do, and I waited carefully for some wish to come; I would do what it said.

It did not come, but the ultimate horror circled me and played over the knife. I began to sing. It was a current popular favorite, a folk-rock tune. I finished, and I was withdrawn from. I straightened as well as I could. There he is, I said to him.

The problems came back, one by one, in sequence. I would rather drag him than carry him, but I knew I could make better time if I carried him, so I put the knife back in the case, dropped down on one knee and wrestled him across my shoulders in the fireman's carry from boy scout days. I got up with nearly double my weight and started back toward the clearing. I went around the rock of blood that had led me there, stumbled through the bushes I had crawled in, and tried for the river with my side oozing me wet and the top of my left leg wet and drying and moistening again. The man's body held me to the ground, and I had the feeling that when I got him off my shoulders, I would fly. Blundering through the bushes, I had no idea whether I would make it back to the river. The woods burst slowly open in front of me, across my eyes, and twenty yards ahead dropped off into still, sun-filled space from which the old noise of eternity came back.

I put him down in almost the exact place where I had shot him, and stepped to the edge of the bluff. I looked downriver first, for I was afraid to look upriver and see that unchanging emptiness, but

173

even looking downriver I could tell that the emptiness upstream was not complete, that there was something there like a mote, and I turned to it to be able to face it and make sure. Lewis' canoe shone there, flashing frankly in the sun, riding grayly like a trout, coming out of the rapids. I looked at the dead man. You're dead, Lewis, I said to him. You and Bobby are dead. You didn't start on time; you did everything wrong. I ought to take this rifle and shoot the hell out of you, Bobby, you incompetent asshole, you soft city country-club man. You'd have been dead, you should've been dead, right about exactly now. You're right in line, you're going slow, you're going slow, you're just sitting there. If I hadn't come up here and did what I did, you'd've been floating along now with no brains and no blood, and so would Lewis.

I walked back and picked up the gun, and my craziness increased when I touched it. I sighted down the barrel and put the bead right in the middle of Bobby's chest. Do it, the dead man said. Do it; he's right there. But I got around the feeling just by opening my fingers, and letting the gun fall to the ground. I did think momentarily of firing straight up to attract Bobby's attention, but turned loose of the notion because the sound of a shot might have frightened him into ditching the canoe. Besides, I didn't want to put the thing to my shoulder again; it had been close; very close.

I took the gun by the barrel, wheeled it once around my head and slung it as far out over the river as I could, where it went from a heavy spinning sail into outright falling, turning slower and slower sideways until it hit the water about fifty yards in front of the canoe. I hoped that Bobby had seen it long enough to know what it was, and that it meant we were safe; a gun falling out of the sky.

After it hit, Bobby pulled his paddle out of the river, but did not look up. I put my thumb and forefinger in my mouth and whistled as loud as I could, a high cutting whistle that nearly deafened me, but I had an idea it failed somewhere in the sound of the banks. I climbed the biggest rock at the edge and stood there. Then I figured I ought to put some motion into myself, and I went into the sidestraddle hop from my old PT class in high school; it had more arm and leg movement in it than anything else I could think of. It almost tore me apart, but I danced away while I could. Bobby looked up, finally, and the blank of his tiny face stayed uptilted, looking more. I did a bloody clog step, my tennis shoes silent on the rock and my side tearing but in joy, then pointed down under me. He pulled up his paddle and dug slowly in on his right to turn the canoe in to the cliff.

I went back to the man on the ground, flopped on his side with one leg drawn up, and rolled him onto his back. He looked lazily straight up into the sky. One open eye had been poked into by a branch or a twig, and was cloudy, but the other was clear blue, delicately veined in a curious, uneyelike pattern; I saw myself there, a tiny figure bent over him, growing.

After carrying him I had no trouble touching him, or going through his pockets. Though I had no real interest in who he was anymore, I thought I had better make some effort to find out, for I might need the information in some way later on. I reached into one pocket and turned it inside out. There was nothing in it; one of his inside buttons made a quick cold place in my hand. In the other pocket were five rifle shells – big ones, and I thought of Drew's head – and there was also a card of some sort that I had to straighten up and hold to the light in order to read. His name was Stovall, and he was an honorary deputy sheriff of Helms County, which was, I suppose, where we now were. This worried me some, but not too much, for Lewis had once told me that everybody in the hills, or just about everybody, was an honorary deputy sheriff. The main worry in connection with this was that if someone thought enough of him to give him the card, he might conceivably be a person well known, as they say, in the community – whatever that was in Helms County – and consequently might be searched for. I looked at him, though, and it seemed obvious that he was so nondescript, even for Helms County, that he would probably not be missed by more than a few people, and probably not much by them, either. I balled the card up and unballed it again, tore it up, then packed the pieces into another ball and threw it out over the river, where it came apart in a current of air, suspending its pieces incredibly before it moved wanderingly in many directions, all down. I went and got the death-arrow and threw it like a spear into the river, then picked up the arrow covered with my own blood and threw it over too. Then I pitched out my old broken catapult of a bow. I hated to turn it loose. I thought maybe the handle section might be salvaged, and I wanted very much to have it with me for the rest of my life, but in the end I threw it, and threw it hard.

I uncoiled the rope from my belt. I had a lot of it. I didn't believe I had enough to let the body all the way down to the river, but I could let it down some of the way and after that I was sure I could think of something. I dragged the body to the edge of the cliff and put the rope around it and made it as fast as I could, tying square knot after square knot – the only kind I knew, as it is the only kind that most people know – under the armpits. The head lolled and jerked as I tied, and this irritated me more than anything had in a long time; irritated me more than the set of Thad's secretary's – Wilma's – mouth and her tiresome, hectoring personality posing as duty. The wound in the man's throat was not painful-looking, particularly – it was nothing like as gruesome as the hacked-at hole in my side – for it had closed over and clotted, and now looked like nothing more than a deep scrátch, almost like a bad shaving cut; it was hard to believe that it went all the way through him and out the back, and that it had killed him; that it was his death itself.

I tied the other end of the rope to the tree closest to the edge, and went over and tried to call down to Bobby, but the sound of my voice falling into the abyss frightened me; I knew it would never reach bottom; I could feel the strength and meaning fade from it in the sun that filled the emptiness. There was a kind of crack or fault in the rock, turning green with bushes near the water, and Bobby's face came up through it. There may also have been a little voice with it, something added to the sound of the river and coming up, but if it was there I couldn't make out what it said.

I might as well; it was a thing I had prepared. I shoved the body over the edge with my feet, kicking it and rolling it and holding the rope in both hands. Just after it went over it seemed to hitch in the air to get its feet down, and then settled into a long, hard, unsure pull against me. I worked along the line back to the tree and braced against it, paying the invisible weight out hand over hand down the wall. It was hard going; I kept having to take turns of the thin nylon around one wrist and then the other, and then both, oftener and oftener. The coil at my feet wore away as I sweated, and the red rings around my wrists cut deeper, nearing the blood. I began to wish I had taken a turn of rope around the tree before I started, but I had to hold: there was something about just turning loose of the rope and letting the man fall free and then bring up and dangle, that was shocking to me; I would not do that, no matter what. I sweated and braced, and tried to imagine what Bobby was now thinking, seeing a man come down like this, inch by inch; a man who had held a gun on him while another one corn-holed him, and would have killed him in an instant. I tried also to imagine, from the different tensions on the rope, what the body was doing and how it was doing it, all under a kind of control, undignified and protected by the red rings on my wrists and my pain and work, kneeling on and then falling away from outcroppings, rocks and projections, dangling, sliding, rolling, but even so not falling and bursting apart on the river-rocks like a sack of jellied sticks.

I gave up the last yard of rope I had and stepped back, letting the tree hold the body effortlessly. I had trouble undoing my hands; I tried to undo them as I went back to the edge of the cliff; they still wanted to be holding a rope desperately. As it was, I looked down the green strand going over the sandy edge and over a projecting, dangerously sharp rock on down out of sight, then reappearing, straining in space, catching on something, swaying again, where an invisible body was hanging. Once more I wondered what Bobby could be thinking. I walked back to the tree and checked the knots, then came back to where the rope bent to go down and tried to put my bloody handkerchief under the rope at the edge to keep it from chafing on the stone, but I didn't have the strength to lift it.

Well, all right, I said. The name of the game is trust; you've got to trust things. I looked inland and got down on my knees, took hold of the rope with one hand above and one below the cliff edge, slid my feet over and started down.

It was luxury to know that I knew what to hold on to, and not have to feel around for it, for something that might not be there, something that had never been there or ever would be there. But my hands and arms were almost strengthless; the only way I knew I was still holding, besides the pain in my hands, was that I didn't fall. I talked to my hands continually, and to every stone I came to, for they were all standing out in my face with beautiful clarity, things never looked at – never witnessed or beheld – so closely before. I had to stop in a couple of places, near death and looking deeply at sand grains, and hung out over the river in its high, flowing space, concentrating on seizing it in the mind so deeply that it would always be with me as it was just then: always, night and day and maybe after death too. I braced and panted with the cliff, inbreathing the rock-dust that my outbreathing had stirred up.

The last place I rested was a kind of saw-toothed ledge about six inches wide where I was on it; holding to the rope with both hands, I could almost sit comfortably there. I could see the corpse below me turning with my grip on the rope, terribly heavy-looking and full of dead weight, his head on his chest in midair, pensive and reposeful.

I could also see Bobby, though neither of us had tried to speak yet. He had the canoe in an eddying pocket of water against the bluff face, and was just holding it there gently with a few slight pressures on the river. I started down again, anxious to get rid of my weight. The corpse appeared to be about thirty-five feet above the shore-rocks, and I had no clear idea of what to do when the rope gave out. Both of us would still have a good way to go. I supposed I would have to cut him loose and then leap for the river, myself, but I reckoned I would find out about that when I got down to him.

I was almost on top of the corpse, holding on and bracing out from the cliff with a foot and a knee, trying to figure out a way to get around him or clear of him without having to clamber all over him like Harold Lloyd in an old movie.

The rope broke, and we were gone. Suddenly there was no weight, and nothing to plan for. The plan of the night before saved me though; I got a good kick against the cliff with the foot I had braced there and a kneeshove with the other leg, and this moved me out a few feet from the wall. The rocks were coming, and so was I. When my head came around I could see I was clear, and that was all that mattered, at all.

I had no further control, though. There was an instant of sunny nothing, and of drifting and turning. Where was the river? There was green and blue, in some kind of essential relation, and then the river went into my right ear like an ice pick. I yelled, a tremendous, walled-in yell, and then I felt the current thread through me, first through my head from one ear and out the other and then complicatedly through my body, up my rectum and out my mouth and also in at the side where I was hurt.

I realized that I was in something I knew, in the slow unhurried pull of current. Then the water took to the wound, and nearly took it from me. It had been so many years since I had been really hurt that the feeling was almost luxurious, though I knew when I tried to climb the water to the surface that I had been weakened more than I had thought. Unconsciousness went through me. I was in a room of varying shades of green beautifully graduated from light to dark, and I went toward the palest color, though it seemed that this was to one side of me rather than above. An instant before I broke water I saw the sun, liquid and transformed, and then it exploded in my face.

I was hurt in a couple of new ways, especially in the hands, but after trying my arms and legs against the water I knew I was not hurt so badly that I could not function. I lay forward in the current, thinking vaguely of how to swim, and the thought made me move, for I was doing it.

I came out at the side of the canoe, and pulled up as carefully as I could. My face was no more than eight inches from Lewis'. His eyes were closed, and he looked both resting and dead, but his head turned. His eyes opened. He gave me a long serious glance, closed his eyes again tiredly and settled farther down on his back. His part of the canoe particularly around his head, was full of vomit, the chunks of steak and all the stuff we had brought from the city. I worked around the canoe to land, and faced Bobby.

'Is this what you call first light?'

'Listen,' he said, 'Lewis has been having a bad time. Once I thought he died. He's awful bad hurt.'

'You would have died, yourself. He was waiting for you up there. You didn't do what I told you, and you would have died. He could have shot you fifty times, because you did what you did, and because you didn't do what you should've done. You better look up here at this light, baby. You better look at your own hands and feet, because you liked not to have had them anymore.'

'Listen,' he said again. 'Please listen. I couldn't get him in the canoe at all until I had enough light to see what I was doing. He blacked out two or three times before I ever got him in. I'll tell you, I wouldn't want to spend another night like that. I would've rather been trying to climb up, with you.'

'Fine. Next time, maybe.'

'How did you do it? I never thought you could do it; I never thought I'd see you again. If it'd been me I don't know but what I'd've just taken off, if I'd'a been able to get to the top.'

'I thought about that,' I said. 'But I didn't.'

'You did exactly what you said you'd do,' he said. 'But it's not possible. I don't believe it. I *can't* believe it. I really can't, Ed. This is not happening to us.'

'Well, we've got to make it unhappen. Question is, how?'

'I don't know,' Bobby said. 'Do you really think we can? I mean, *really*?'

'I do really,' I said. 'With all this bad luck, luck is running with us.'

'And you killed him? You *killed* him?'

'I killed him, and I'd kill him again, only better.'

'Did you ambush him?'

'In a way. I set the problem up the way it seemed best to do. And he came right to me.'

We walked over to the shattered body on the rocks, with two or three parts of the denture plate beside the head; he had hit the rocks right on his face. We turned him over; the face was unbelievable; more unbelievable than anything else. I could hear Bobby catch his breath. Then I heard the breath speak.

'It looks like you shot him from the front. How . . . ?'

'I did,' I said. 'I shot straight into him. I was in a tree.'

'A tree?'

'Yes, there are a lot of them around when you're in the woods, you know. Really quite a lot.'

'But . . . ?'

'He didn't see me until he was hit, and maybe not even then. I think he was just getting on to where I was when the arrow hit him. He shot a good many times. Did you hear anything?'

'Maybe once; I'm not sure. Probably not; it was just that I was listening so hard. But, no, I didn't hear anything.'

'There he is,' I said. 'Another one.'

He looked at my side. 'But he shot you, didn't he?'

His voice was full of the best stuff I had ever heard in it. 'Let me look,' he said.

I unzipped, and the flying suit fell away. My shorts were soaked and dried with blood, with more coming.

'Boy,' he said. 'Something really gored you.'

'I fell out of the tree onto the other arrow,' I said. 'I wonder if it would've made any difference if I hadn't sharpened it so well before we left home? And I'm sure glad I don't use four-bladed heads.'

'I tell you,' he said. 'It's unbelievable. That arrow-head is meant to open you up.'

'That's just what it's meant for. And it opened me up. But I think it's a clean wound, and there ain't many of them. I think the river got most of the paint out of me.'

I looked down at my hurt. The climb down and the fall had torn it all the way open, from the half healing and clotting that it had been trying to do in the woods. I was coming out of me, but not as fast as I might have been. I took off my shorts and stood there bleeding and naked, and took the bloody sleeve I had already cut off and used it to hold the shorts into the wound. Then I put what was left of the suit back on. 'Let's finish up and get going,' I said.

We were standing with the corpse, and it was ready. The rope was piled on and off the body, and the frayed part that had broken was giving off glassy hairs where the thing had happened, high up above.

'Are you sure . . . ?' Bobby asked.

I faced into him, into his open mouth and bloodshot eyes. 'No,' I said. 'I would say it was, but I'm not that sure. Maybe if we could get him to hold a gun on you, you could tell me. Or maybe if we could give him back his face, we could tell that way. But I don't know. The only thing I know is that we're here, like we are right now. Let's get him in the river. Let's get him in good.'

We went up and down the bank looking for rocks the right size, going back and forth across each other, dreaming. With both hands I took up part of the river and tried to wash the main rock where his face had smashed and there was a lot of blood. On both knees I washed it, and the blood came. It was on the sand and going into the sand, and there was no more of it. I went back to rock-hunting with Bobby, and we piled up five or six mean-looking stones next to the body. I cut the rope into sections and tied the rocks onto the man with the biggest one around his neck, squeezing the arrow-wound together and almost out of sight.

'Not here,' I said. 'Out in the middle of the river, where it's hardest to get to.'

We struggled with him and with each other, and he and the rocks made it, finally, into the canoe with Lewis, who shifted slightly as if to make room for somebody who belonged there, pretty much as a person would shift to let a familiar body get back in bed with him in the middle of the night.

The canoe moved very badly, with all the weight. We left the bank and for a moment were just going down-stream, too tired to do anything else. The sound of rapids was somewhere in front of us, carrying terror once more, amongst so much other terror. Bobby steadied the canoe while I got to my knees among the blood, vomit and rocks and lifted two of the rocks clear and shoved them over the side. The canoe yawed and I braced back to equalize the weights. The body was straining to get out, but hung on the gunwale. I lifted out another rock and it pulled one of his legs over the side but he was still with us. I picked up the last rock, the one around his neck, and heaved it out with the last energy of all. The wound of his neck tore open bloodlessly – I thought the head had come off – and he was gone. He was gone so completely into the river that he seemed never to have had anything to do with it, or it with him. He had never been in the world at all. I dipped my hand in the stream and left his blood with him.

We were by ourselves, moving.

We turned a long corner. The river freshened before us and around us, and I drove in the paddle, exerting no strength but digging in anyway. We went through some small rapids without much trouble, and I thought of fun. The canoe just followed the channel of its own accord.

On each side the cliffs began to fall; to fall away. They fell and then got back up again almost as they had been, but their authority was leaving them. Every time they rose it was not quite as high.

The sun was behind us, and the pressure on my back shoved us forward. I was glad for it; gladder than it is possible to be. But I could not keep my head up. My side was stiff and sobbing with blood, and my chin kept ending up on my chest and my eyes were blurring into the bottom of the canoe where Lewis lay with one hand over his eyes. I put a hand on my forehead and tried to pull up my eyelids by lifting the skin of my forehead and keeping it lifted, but I was still asleep, looking at the world as though my eyes were closed. I've got to lie down somewhere, I thought; if I don't I will fall back into the river.

That seemed not such a bad prospect, to tell the truth. It would have been wonderful to give all my weight to the water one more time, maybe for good. This was too hard; this was just too hard. It was, and I knew it. Anyone would have known it.

We went over some little rapids that shook us and picked up our speed a little, but not much. They were deep and powerful, but the channels were clear and we rode through them without much maneuvering. I was sure we didn't have much farther to go. Where would we come out? What was there to see, that men had made, that would tell us? What would we see when we got off the river forever?

Lewis lay quietly on the floor with his pants unbuttoned and belt undone; he looked like some great broken thing. I could see the huge muscles of his thigh around the break; they were turning blue. With his free hand, the one that had nothing to do with his face, he was bracing up under the inside of the gunwale, and I thought that perhaps this was a new system, a way to make his leg go to sleep and keep it asleep by putting pressure on it in a special manner; his bracing arm was rigid; the tricep muscle quivered continually with the river, and in it you could see every rock.

The whole stream now was running fast, without rapids. It was deep, and deep green. It was easy going, the easiest of all, and whenever I could get my head up I superimposed a picture of a highway bridge over the river; but I could never match them up; the bridge would hover and disappear.

Far off there was what looked like a stretch of rapids with a few big rocks – the sound was low-throated and pleasant rather than frightening – and beyond that, another wooded turn. We were moving toward the white, light water and were very close to it when I saw Drew's body backed up between the rocks and looking straight at us.

I told Bobby, but he could not get his head up to look. He could not, and I knew he could not, and I didn't blame him. But somebody had to look, had to do something, and it would be better if both of us tried.

'Listen,' I heard myself say. 'Wake up and help me.'

I headed for Drew, for his place in the rocks, pulling hard against the current that wanted to take us past him. I turned the canoe as broadside as I could and asked the rocks to catch us, to help us. They did. We stopped, we lodged lightly, and I got out onto the sandy soil blowing with underwater. I walked up the canoe on two exhausting steps drawn through the river and hit Bobby hard on the side of the shoulder; as hard as I could, but not hard enough for the situation. To help I put the other hand on the knife.

'Did you hear me?' I said, not loudly. 'You help me with this or I'll kill you, just as you sit there on your useless ass. Now come on. We've got to finish it.'

He got slowly out into the water, swaying with the current, his eyes looking at everything but me.

Drew was sitting up, facing upstream, in a kind of rough natural chair made of two stones where part of the river ran through, split off from the main current by a flat rock. Though he was sitting, it was a very easy, careless – even carefree – position, partly on the base of his spine. Water ran up and fell back from the top part of his chest, and a thin continuous spray of it went into his open mouth, making a quivering sensitive silver bell around his lips where one gold filling glinted. His eyelids were also kept propped open by the current, seeming to see out of the open water back up into the mountains, around all the curves of the river, infinitely. The pull of the water on his mouth gave him a cretinous, loose-lipped look, but the eyes had nothing to do with that; they were blue and all-seeing and clear.

I stumbled forward to him like meeting him in a drunken bar. I tried to pull him out of his seat by the straps of his life jacket, but for a moment he wouldn't come. He seemed to settle deeper into the rocks. Then he rose with no muscles into my arms, against the current. Bobby came around to the other side of him, and the three of us trudged through two worlds, water and air, toward the canoe, tripping over the whole river, the undercurrent tangling our feet with his and with each other's. I had not realized he was so big. All three of us fell and he got away eddying with his head back, turning slowly from the waist in his jacket, his crushed face as placid and washed and blank as the sky.

I went after him, stepped in a hole under him, finally wrestled and floated him back to the rock nearest the canoe and laid him over it on his stomach. I looked at his head. Something had hit him awfully hard there, all right. But whether it was a gunshot wound I didn't know; I had never seen a gunshot wound. The only comparison I had to go by were the descriptions of President Kennedy's assassination, the details afforded by eyewitnesses, doctors and autopsy reports which I had read in newspapers and magazines like most other Americans had, at the time. I remembered that part of Kennedy's head had been blown away. There was nothing like that here, though. There was a long raw place under the hair just over his left ear, and the head there seemed oddly pushed in, dented. But there was no brain matter showing, nothing blown away.

'Bobby, come here,' I said. 'There's something we've got to decide about.'

I pointed at the place on Drew's head. Bobby peered, his eyes reddened more, and he leaned away. We hung on the rock, panting.

'Is this a gunshot wound?'

'Ed, you know I wouldn't know. But it sure doesn't look like it to me.'

'Look here, though.'

I showed him the scratch under the hair. 'Knowing what we know, it looks to me like he might have been shot and just grazed. But whether this place *killed* him or not, I don't know.'

'Or whether it was made by a rock, after he'd gone in,' Bobby said.

'If we work this right, we'll never have to explain to anybody but ourselves,' I said. 'But I'd like to *know*. I think we ought to know?'

'How *can* we know?'

'Lewis would come nearer knowing than we would. Let's take Drew over to him and give him a good look.'

We picked Drew up again and dragged him to the canoe. We sank down with him until the back of his head was level with the gunwale and was leaning on it.

'Lewis,' I said quietly.

He didn't answer; his eyes were closed and he was breathing hard.

'Lewis. Give us just a second. It's important. It's very important.'

He turned his head and opened his eyes. Bobby and I held Drew with three hands, and I turned Drew's head and went under his hair to the place I wanted Lewis to see.

'Lewis, was he shot? Did a bullet make this?'

A flicker of the old interest crossed his eyes. He raised his head as much as he could and stared into Drew's hair.

'Well, was he shot? *Was* he? Was he, Lewis?'

He shifted, very slowly, over the center of the stream, his eyes to mine. My brain flinched; I did not know what was coming. He nodded, hardly a motion at all, and then sank back. 'Grazed,' he said.

'Are you sure? Are you *sure*?'

He nodded again, and retched weakly, almost in the same movement. He kept on nodding, and Bobby and I looked at each other. We peered at Drew's wound again.

'Maybe,' Bobby said.

'Maybe, is it,' I said. 'It'll have to be. But we can't have anybody examining him. We can't tell, but there are those who can, and if we have to explain a man with a gunshot wound the whole thing'll come out.'

'Are we going to get out of this? I don't see how we can. I really don't.'

'We're almost out of it now,' I said.

'What are we to do with Drew?'

189

'We're going to sink him in this river,' I said, 'forever.'

'O Lord. O Lord.'

'Listen; it's exactly like I just said. *Exactly*. We *can't* afford for somebody who knows about these things to examine him. If we go back without him, we just had some bad luck. We're a fucking bunch of amateurs, anyway. And let 'em try to disprove *that!* We came up here to run this river without knowing what we were getting into, which is also the God's truth. We did all right for a while, then we spilled. We lost the other canoe. Lewis broke his leg in the rapids, and Drew drowned. Anybody'd believe that. But we can't explain somebody killed with a rifle.'

'If he was.'

'That's right: if he was.'

A faint light came through Bobby's eyes, then either darkened or died. 'There's no end to it,' he said. 'No end.'

'Yes there is,' I said. 'This is the end. This is all we have to do, but we've got to do it right. Everything depends on it. The whole works.'

I fumbled around in my lower leg pocket and got out the extra bowstring. I tied it around a good-sized rock and then around Drew's belt, square-knot on square-knot. We put the rock in the canoe, and I took Drew's body in the kapok jacket and laid it back in the water, wading forward with him past the rapids, hauling and bullying him gently along.

When the water deepened, Bobby stepped into the canoe and picked up the paddle. Drew and I moved off the end of the rapids and I took slow flight in my life preserver. I looked at Drew's hand floating palm-up with the guitar calluses puckered and white and his college class ring on it, and I wondered if his wife might not like to have the ring. But no; I couldn't even do that; it would mean having to explain. I touched the callus on the middle finger of his left hand, and my eyes blinded with tears. I lay with him in my arms for a moment weeping river-water, going with him. I could have cried as long as the river ran, but there was no time. 'You were the best of us, Drew,' I said loud enough for Bobby to hear; I wanted him to hear. 'The only decent one; the only sane one.'

I undid his life belt and let him fall away under me. On his knees beside Lewis in the canoe, Bobby heaved the stone overboard. One of Drew's feet flew up and touched my calf, and we were free and in hell.

I stayed in the water behind the canoe, holding the jacket in one hand. Made weightless, my legs hurt twice as bad. I wanted to sleep, to sink, not have to breathe. I lay and moved with the river, with all nightmares and night sweats to come, but not here, not on me yet. When we came to another shallow place, I got up from the gravel and the crawfish, took up my full weight and half again more, and got into the rear seat with the sun hot and heavy-wet on my shoulders and back, as though packed there in layers.

For a long time nothing happened but fatigue and heat. Insects danced over the canoe between Bobby and me, a singing haze I was not sure wasn't inside my head. But the walls were dropping steadily on both sides. In a few more miles the cliffs gave out on the right, and there was only a low fence of rock on the other side. Then it too slanted to the river, and we were level with the woods again. I knew I must have misjudged the distance we had to go, for there seemed to be no end to it. Bobby's head was down; the most I could hope for from him was to keep steady in the canoe and not fall and tip us over. If we spilled in deep water or rapids now it would be a real problem to get back in, and we would never get Lewis in.

I had put on Drew's life jacket over mine. It was awfully hot that way, but the extra collar came up higher on the back of my neck and kept the sun off it, and I was grateful for that. My mind danced for minutes on end like gnats around the image of the long, tumbling voyage down the rapids the jacket had taken, trying to keep Drew from drowning when he was already dead, probably, from something else.

I could feel my lips swelling with the sun. I was coming slowly up against an absolute limit, but I did not know where it was, or where we would be on the river when I got to it, or what I would do when I did. Was there anything I could say to myself, or even to Bobby, that would help?

'Bobby,' I said suddenly, 'hang on. If we can stay with it for ten miles we'll be out. I know we will. We've come an awful goddamned long way, and it can't be much longer.'

He tried to nod, and partly did.

'Don't rock us, baby. And if you see anything I can't see, tell me. If we hit any rapids, call the rocks for me. If you can't do that, get down with Lewis and pray, but try to help us stay level.'

There was a low new tone in the river: an old one, something I recognized.

'God,' I said. 'Do something for us.'

We went toward it, but when we came around the next turn there was nothing but another turn about a half mile ahead. The sound came from there, or through there.

'I think I hear some rapids, Bobby. I know I do. If we can walk the canoe through, let's do it. We can do it. But if we can't, we'll have to run them.'

We went down, picking up speed, and the step-up in sound, like a dial being tuned, brought up the old terror, but also excitement: the sensation Lewis was always describing; I felt it, tired as I was.

192

We went into the next turn, and I knew, with the sound I was hearing, that if the rapids were on the turn or even within sight when we straightened out, they would not be as bad as some we had been through. But we came off the turn moving still faster, without falls or rapids, with no white water and none in sight, and I knew they would be bad. It was more likely that I was listening to a falls, and I got ready to die again. The sound jumped higher all at once; there was a foaming seethe in it, a hoarse desperation. We turned again. The land to the left broke away, and I looked down a set of rapids steeper – a lot steeper – than any we had been through, and longer, all stepped down toward a funnel that disappeared between two huge boulders that turned the air between them white.

The water glassed out for fifty yards ahead of us and went through an almost formal-looking series of steep little cascades, changing to a lighter color to go faster, and then into an even faster half-white half-green color, then through a short hook to the left where it shot between the big rocks. I couldn't see any farther than that; it was as though the river were being fed into fog. We might have made it to the bank, but I didn't have the strength for it. The current had us; we were going there.

'We can't walk,' I yelled. 'Get you ass down as low as you can.'

He didn't look back, but moved rearward and down and held to the gunwales, letting his knees break over the front seat. Our center of gravity was as low as we could get it, though I also hunched forward myself; I could not control the canoe if I had been any lower than I was, and we were going hard down the water all drawn together like threads running into a loom. The main roar came back in our faces, and then from the sides, and we were in it, hitting the little jolting ripples before the first drop-off. We went over; the nose tipped, the canoe grated under my tailbone, and we went down another, shorter step, a rough shove up through the spine that knocked me up off the seat and drove the canoe partway over on its side. Our speed righted us, and I made an all-out plunge – one stroke with all I had left – on the right to keep us straight with the current. We swung and ran over two more stepdowns, hard shocks at the base of the brain, and in the midst of this I heard a faint, then a quick loud shout or singing or call from somewhere and thought it might be Lewis screaming. Then we were down on level rushing water. We had lost a little speed to the rocks but we picked it up again immediately, then picked up more than that, and were going for the spray and the dark white of the passage. I dug in hard, then tried to backwater on the other side, saw it was useless, dug in on the right again as hard as I could to turn the bow, and we swung, swung and jumped shooting into the hole.

For a second I couldn't see anything at all, and rode like I was standing still with aerated water filling my mouth and little fluttering bumps coming up through the canoe shell. With nothing to see go past, motion died. It was like being in a strange room in a cold building or a shaking cave filled with cold steam. I was wet clear through before I could think: the sun was killed on my shoulders in an instant. I lanced out again to the right with the paddle, mainly because that was the last place I had taken a stroke, and if it was right then it might be right now. I was sure that we had to turn, keep turning left if we could; the right felt like death, and if I couldn't keep it away from us we would spin broadside and the whole river and all the mountains it came from would fall on us, would pour into the canoe ton after ton, never-ending. I dug again, but couldn't tell what I had made us do. Something snatched at the paddle and I pulled it out and dug again, and again. The river showed in front in a blinking leap, and we came shooting forward as though launched to take off into the air. We were going faster than I had ever been in anything without an engine. The force of water around the paddle blade was stupendous; I felt as though I had dipped into some supernatural source of primal energy.

It was like riding on a river of air. The rocks flickered around and under us, then sand, then rocks, changing colors into each other as we streamed through. I half rose out of my seat; nothing else could be said to me but this, in this way. It was unkillableness: the triumph of an illusion when events bear it out. I looked to see what was coming to me next. 'Hold on, baby,' I hollered. 'We're going home.'

Ahead was a tilted flange of rock with water sculpted over it in a long, curling forelocked curve that broke at us and then away from us past the rock, and then a low wall of rocks that looked like they shallowed out on both sides. I dug for the rock to go straight over, to have the thing whole.

We went up, like the beginning of an incline; the nose lifted; a powerful surge caught up with us from the rear. We lost weight completely. We rolled out over the top of the rock in one unstoppable motion. I closed my eyes and screamed with Lewis, mixing my voice with his bestial scream, blasting my lungs out where we hung six feet over the river for an instant and then began to fall. I waited for the upward revengeful smash of the river, but the nose rode down with an odd softness and into the back-scrolled smashed water at the foot of the rock, quivered straight back through the spine of the canoe into mine and into my brain, where I saw a vision of burning jackstraws or needles, and we were back down onto the bedded river in two almost simultaneous stepdowns. I listened for my cry hanging in the wet air above the blue-and-white flag colors of the rock – and I still listen for it – and we were down and slowing forward,

195

back on green water, solid and heavy on it, and it solid and heavy under us.

The bed-rocks fell away; another curve, one without rapids, began to open in front of us a hundred yards farther on. I looked at Bobby. He was still hanging back from his seat, but struggling to sit on it again. He turned half around back to me, and opened the eye on that side. He started to say something but didn't, and I started to and didn't.

Now, in calm water, I began to collect everything we needed to make the future with.

'Right back there is where it all happened,' I said.

He looked at me without any understanding at all.

'Somebody is going to ask us things. When that happens tell him that right back there was where Drew fell out – we all fell out. That was where Lewis broke his leg and we lost the other canoe.'

'OK,' he said, without conviction.

'Look around,' I said. 'Let's pick out some things we can agree were here. All this is so they don't go looking for Drew farther upstream. So look. *Look*.'

He looked dully from side to side, from bank to bank, but I could tell that nothing was registering.

'See that big yellow tree,' I said. 'That's going to be the main thing. That, and the rapids, and that big rock we went over. We can put them together, and that'll be all we need to do.'

I concentrated on the tree, looking at it from all the angles the river gave us as we went by, making it blot out everything else in my mind and leave a deep, recoverable image there. It was about half-dead, with the bark scaled off one side in a jagged pattern. It must have been struck by lightning at one time; the fire had ripped it deep. That was the kind of image I wanted in my mind: like that, the whole tree.

196

'Listen, Bobby,' I said. 'Listen good. We've got to make this right. Drew was drowned back there. I'd say – I'm going to say – that the best place to look for his body is about where we are now. There's no way for him to get down here from where he really is. There are no roads back in to the river where he is, and nobody'll go up there looking for him if we don't give them a reason to.'

'He's here,' Bobby said, putting his hand over his eyes and then raising the outer edge of it to make an eyeshade. 'He's here, down under us. I can say that. I can say it, OK.'

It was exactly what I wanted. Lewis didn't say anything; either he was out or it would have been too much of an effort to answer.

'We spilled at that bad place we just came through,' I said. 'We can even tell them that we spilled going through all that spray between the rocks. We spilled, and Drew was drowned. Since our watches have stopped, we won't be able to say exactly when it was. But we can say where. Where is at that yellow tree.'

Bobby looked a little less tired.

I said, 'There's not anything unbelievable about the story, if we remember the way we want it to go. There's nobody – *nobody* – but us left. Nobody saw, nobody knows. If we don't mess up on the details, we're all right. We're as all right as we're ever going to be, but at least nobody will be messing with us: no police, no investigation, no nothing. Nothing but us.'

'I hope not.'

'So do I. But as Lewis would say, we've got to do more than hope. Control, baby. It can be controlled. So give me back the story.'

He did, and he was accurate. I was pleased; I began to feel safer, for I was dreading going back to men and their questions and systems; I had been dreading it without knowing it.

I was heavy-bodied but light-minded, and felt, as I hadn't for the last few hours, that I could go on for a while. More and more I just let us drift, paddling only enough to keep the nose downriver. The land on both sides was wooded, but it was not the wild, tangled woods of the gorge, nor the dark, still growth before it. We were not far from men. I expected to see something human at every bend we cleared.

There it was. A cow was lying under a tree at the edge of the river. It swung its head, and came to be gazing at us over the flow. We drifted toward it.

'It's a farm, Bobby,' I said. 'We're here. We can turn in anytime.' But I didn't want to have to walk a long way over pastures and fields, looking for a farmhouse. I decided to go downriver for a little while yet, where there was a bridge or a road.

The cows increased, vivid white and dead, living black, lying along the watercourse and up its banks, chewing, drinking, lifting themselves off the river with a heavy toss of horns, eternally stupid, huge, and useless to themselves. One more curve, I was sure, and we would be back.

We went around the same turn – I could not have told you how they differed – eight or ten more times. After about another hour, which would have made it, from the heat and the height of the sun, about noon or early afternoon, we came around another turn like the others, but across the river was a plank bridge set in a steel frame. Just beyond it was a gentle spillway; a man and a boy were fishing with cane poles below it.

We muscled the canoe laboriously cross-river to land. When we touched the bank, Bobby got to his feet in the canoe and swayed for a minute, then stepped out into the kudzu. I got into the slime and waded out of the river, and never touched it again with my feet or legs. We beached the canoe and took off our life preservers.

Lewis lay there beyond us, with his hands crossed over him. He was terrifically sunburned; flakes of skin came off his lips when he moved them.

'Lewis,' I said from land. 'Do you hear me?'

'I hear you,' he said calmly and strongly, but with his eyes closed. 'I hear you and I've been hearing you. You've got it figured; we can get out of this. They won't ask me anything, and if they do I've got the word, same as you gave Bobby. You're doing it exactly right; you're doing it better than I could do. Hang in there.'

'Do you feel anything in your leg?'

'No, but I haven't moved it or fooled with it or thought about it for a long time. I kept trying to put it to sleep, back yonder, and now I can't wake it up. It doesn't matter, though. I'm all right.'

'I'm going to get somebody,' I said. 'Can you hold out a little longer?'

'Sure,' he said. 'My God, those falls must have been something, back there.'

'They were something. We could have done a lot better if we'd'a had you, buddy.'

'You had me,' he said.

'You should have seen the water between those rocks.'

'I don't know,' he said, getting faint again. 'I had it another way. I felt it in my leg, and I tell you, I know something I didn't know before.'

There was a good smile on his face. He tried to get his head up from the dried vomit, then sank back in it.

'Are you sure about Drew?' he asked. 'They can't find him?'

'They won't find him,' I said. 'Not if I have anything to say about it.'

'That's it, then, I guess,' he said. 'Go and get somebody.

199

Anybody. I want to get out of this goddamned roasting oven. I want to get out of my own coffin, this fucking piece of tin junk.'

'Lie still. We're home free. Lie still and don't worry.'

I told Bobby to stay with the canoe and climbed up the kudzu of the bank to the road that ran across the bridge. It was a thin blacktop state highway, and about a half a mile along it was a country gas station, a store with two stark yellow pumps, probably Shell. I stood, wondering how I could get there without killing myself, and also waiting for the road to unfreeze and begin to flow around me. The stillness underfoot was disturbing, but it stayed, and from it I looked back down at the river. It was beautiful, and I was sure I would feel all my life the particular pull of it at different places, the weight and depth and speed of it; they had been given to me.

I was heavy in the air now, and floundered a little, walking. My side was caked shut, and the part of the flying suit I had tied around me had clotted into the wound; I could not have gotten it out without fainting, so I let it stay, holding it in with an elbow and leaning over it a little, away from the road. I went toward the station, crossing the bridge over the spillway. The station moved off in the sun and shimmered like an oil slick, and I went after it as best I could. My side hurt badly, but it seemed to have moved off from me a little bit; the rags seemed to go around it instead of through it, so that it was like carrying a painful package or ball under my arm. I had a quick dry period between the time when the river water dried off my legs and the close nylon began to flap with sweat; by the time I got to the station I was striped with my own darkness.

A country teen-ager was sitting on the backless bottom of a kitchen chair just inside the screen door, which was shifting and tapping with flies. Though he had probably been watching me come, he could not believe me at close range. He got up and opened the door.

'Is there a phone here?' I asked.

He looked as though he didn't know whether there was or not.

'I've got to get an ambulance out here,' I said. 'And I've got to get to the highway patrol. People are hurting, and one's dead.'

I let him make the calls, because I didn't know where on earth the station was. 'Just tell them there's been an accident on the river,' I said. 'And tell them where to come, but tell them to come quick. I don't think I can last, and there's another man hurt worse than I am.'

He hung up, finally, and said there'd be somebody along toreckly.

I sat down and tilted back in a chair and was perfectly still, getting my story together one more time, the most important time. But back of the story was the reason for the story, and the woods and the river, and all that had happened. There must be some way for me to get used to the idea that I had buried three men in two days, and that I had killed one of them. I had never seen a dead man in my life, except a brief glance at my father in his coffin. It was strange to be a murderer, especially sitting where I was sitting, but I was too tired to be worried, and didn't worry, except about Bobby's ability to remember what I had told him.

A car or two went by, and I waited to hear one slow down. My side hurt, but the pain was in repose, and lay there under my arm, a part of me that I had made, and could live with. I wondered if I should tell whatever doctor dressed it that I had gored myself on my own arrow, or that I had cut myself on the canoe when we turned over, since there were several places on it where the banging around it had taken on the rocks had forced the metal apart and made flanges and projections that might conceivably cut. I decided to go with the arrow, for there might still be some paint in the wound, and some parts of the wound were clean-cut by the razor-head, and the jagged aluminum wouldn't have done that.

I began to take on so much weight that I could not get up, and then I could not even get my head up. I could feel my still body still trying to make paddling movements. I thought I was stiff, but I must not have been, for when someone touched my bare arm at the shoulder where I had cut off the sleeve the muscles jumped tight again. It was a Negro ambulance driver.

'Have you got a doctor with you?'

'We got one,' he said. 'We got a good one; he young and good. What in this world happened to you, man? What in this world? Somebody shoot you?'

'The river,' I said. 'The river happened to me. But I'm not the one; I'm just the only one who can move. We've got a man back down across the bridge who's bad hurt, and the other fellow had to stay with him. Also one was killed, or I guess he was. We couldn't find him.'

'You want to come show us where your man is at?'

'I'll come if I can get up. If I sit in this chair much longer I'm going to fall out of it.'

He went to my good side and I rose like a mountain into the air of fan belts, where a few cheap cockeyed pairs of dark glasses formed on a piece of yellow cardboard.

'Hold on to me, man,' he said.

He was slight and steady, and I put my good arm around his shoulders, but my knees were going; the world was going.

'You can't make it,' he said. 'You sit right back down.'

'I can make it,' I said, as the glasses focused again.

I told the boy at the store to tell the police where we were going, and the driver and I walked out into the sun where the little white country ambulance sat. The doctor was in the front seat writing something. He looked up and got out all in the same motion.

He opened the back doors. 'Bring him around here and let him lie down.'

I crawled onto the stretcher and turned on my back. It was hard to do; I didn't want to turn loose the driver. He not only felt good to me, but he felt like a good person, and I needed one bad; just that contact was what I needed most. I didn't need myself anymore; I had had too much of that for too long.

The young doctor, sandy haired and pale, crouched beside me.

'No, no,' I said. 'It's not me. I can wait. Go back across the bridge. There's a man in a canoe who's got a bad fracture. It may have hemorrhaged in some way. Let's get him looked after first.'

We drove down the highway – a land-motion of machines, and peculiar – to the bridge, and I got out one more time. I probably didn't have to, but I thought it would be best.

Lewis was still in the canoe, stretched out and sweating, his shirt half-dark and his arm over his eyes, and Bobby was talking to the man and boy who had been fishing. I knew Bobby must have been testing his story out on them, and I hoped he had made good use of the time to get it straight; the others looked as though they believed him. It is hard to disbelieve injured, exhausted men, and that was a great advantage.

The driver and the doctor helped Lewis out of the canoe and onto the stretcher. The County Hospital was in Aintry, about seven miles off. We got ready to go, but while we were standing around the ambulance the highway patrol drove up, the siren droning faintly. A short fellow stepped out, and then a rough-looking blond boy. I got ready.

'What's going on?' the blond officer said.

'We've had a bad accident,' I said, swaying a little more than I was actually swaying. I cut that out; acting might ruin the whole thing. 'One of our party drowned in the river about ten miles upstream.'

He looked at me. '*Drownded*?'

'Yes,' I said. I believed I had got past the first of it, like the first of a bad set of rapids. But there was no way out except to keep on.

'How do you know he drownded?'

'Well, we capsized in the rapids, and it was just every man for himself. I don't know what happened to him. He may have hit his head on a rock. But I don't know. We just couldn't find him, and I don't see how he could not be drowned. I hope he's not, but I'm afraid he is; he has to be.'

While I was talking I looked him in the eyes, which was surprisingly easy to do; they were sharp but sympathetic. As I went through some of the story that Bobby and I had rehearsed on the river, I made it a point to try to visualize the things I was saying as though they had really happened. I could see us searching for Drew, though we never had. I saw these things happen at the place near the yellow tree, and for me they were happening as I talked; it was hard to realize that they had not taken place in the actual world; as I saw him taking them into account, they became part of a world, the believed world, the world of recorded events, of history.

'Well,' he said, 'we'll have to drag the river. Can you show us 'bout where it was?'

'I think so,' I said, not wanting to appear too sure, but fairly sure. 'I don't know if there's a road in there, but I believe I'd know the place if I could get to it. We've got a hurt man, though. We've got to get him to a hospital.'

204

'OK,' he said, a little reluctant to have the situation pass from his jurisdiction to the doctor's. 'We'll check in on you at the hospital later.'

'Fine,' I said, and crawled back into the ambulance beside Lewis.

We rode, and this kind of riding, though it wasn't what I had got used to, was never better. The tires crunched at last, and we stopped. I sat up, a little at a time. We were off in a field, and alongside us was a long flat building that looked like a rural high school. A warm wind was blowing over it. The doctor opened my vision wide, a door in each hand. 'This is it, buddy,' he said. 'Take it easy; we'll get your friend out. Just go along with Cornelius.'

I took hold of the driver again, and we went through some glass doors, up a ramp, into a long hall that appeared to run out of sight, ending in a window the size of microfilm, way off and across.

'Second door to the right,' the driver said, and we went there. I sagged down on a white, tight table, the sheets straining under me. In a minute or two they brought Lewis, but didn't bring him into the room. They put him on a table outside the door, and then noiselessly rolled him on, toward the faraway window. I lay and held my old friend, my side.

The doctor came back on soft feet. 'Let's see now, buddy,' he said. 'Can you raise up just a little bit? Does this zipper still work?'

'I think so,' I mumbled. I tried to sit up, and made it easily, and even zipped the zipper down with my good hand. He took off my tennis shoes and I slithered out of the remains of the flying suit. My shorts were stuck into the wound like the nylon I had bound up in it, but he put something painless out of a bottle in the whole mass of cloth and flesh, and the shorts began

205

to come away. He threw what I had been wearing into a corner, and started working on my side.

Things were dissolving there. Piece after piece of cloth, or of me, softened, softened, and came away, and he kept throwing them down below me, in the bare room. My side was breathing like a mouth, and it did not feel at all bad anymore, only stranger and more open.

'Good Lord, fellow,' he said. 'What's been chopping on you? Looks like somebody hit you in the side with an ax.'

'Does?'

Then more professionally, 'How'd you do this?'

'We were trying to do a little illegal bowhunting up and down the banks of the river,' I said. 'It's not such a good thing to be doing, but we were doing it. We were going to miss the regular season, and we wanted to try it this way.'

'How in hell did you manage to shoot yourself with an arrow? I didn't think it could be done.'

He was working and looking into my blood all the time, very busy and talking calmly.

I talked calmly. 'I had the bow and arrows in the canoe with me when we dumped. I tried to hold on to the bow because I didn't want to be in the woods without any weapon at all, and it sliced up my hands.' I held up the hand the arrows *had* sliced up, just as I said, 'and the next thing I knew I had tangled with a rock and something was going through my side and the bow was gone. I don't have any idea where it went. Downriver; that's all I know.'

'Well, it made a good clean cut,' he said, 'that got ragged. Part of it is real clean, and part of it is hacked up and looks sawed. You've got some kind of foreign matter in here, that I'm going to have to get out.'

'There was some camouflage paint on the arrows,' I said.

206

'That's what it is. But there might be something else in there, too. God knows what's in there.'

'We'll get it out,' he said. 'Then we'll sew you up like a quilt. You want a shot?'

'Yeah,' I said. 'Scotch.'

'You can have another kind, before you get the Scotch,' he said. 'You might have to wait awhile for the Scotch; this is a dry country.'

'You mean you don't have any moonshine in this here hospital? And you way off in the country like this? What the hell is north Georgia coming to?'

'No white lightning,' he said. 'We advise against it. Contains lead salts, most of it.'

He gave me a shot in the hip, and started working again. I looked out the window at the closing green of the day. There was nothing to see but the changes of green.

'You want to stay here with us tonight? There's plenty of room. We've got a whole hospital. And you'll never get another chance like this one; I can tell you. It's peaceful here. No shotgunned farmers. Nobody who tangled with a tractor. Nobody on glucose from a drunk smashup. Nobody but you and your buddy, and a little boy, a snakebite case. And he'll be gone tomorrow. Copperhead poison is not such hot poison.'

'No thanks,' I said, though I would have stayed with Lewis if I thought there was any use in it. 'Get me sewed up and tell me where there's a rooming house I can stay in. I'd like to call my wife, and I'd like to be by myself. I wouldn't like sleeping in a ward, if I can help it, or in a hospital room if I don't absolutely have to.'

'You've lost some blood,' he said. 'You'll be pretty weak.'

'I've been weak for days,' I said. 'Give me whatever you need to give me, and I'll get going.'

'I sent your friend, the other fellow at the canoe, to Biddiford's, down in town. They'll treat you OK. But if I were you I'd stay out here tonight.'

'No thanks,' I said. 'I'll be all right. Tell the police where I am. Just drive me over there and take care of Lewis.'

'The other doctor's working on him. It looks like a complicated situation, with him. He'll be lucky if there's not some gangrene building up around that place. That's a hell of a break.'

'We're lucky we've got you,' I said.

'You're fucking aye,' he said. 'Hands of an angel.'

He drove me in his own car down through town, and in the main filling station were sitting Lewis' station wagon and Drew's Olds. I went in, up tight in my side but not having to hold it together anymore, and talked to the owner, and got the addresses of the Griner brothers so that we could send them the rest of the money. Lewis had arranged it all, and I had to have the owner of the station give back to me what I was supposed to do. I didn't have enough money, but I could either get it from Lewis or mail it in when I got back to the city. The main thing was that the keys were there. I said goodbye to the doctor, told him I'd come out to the hospital the next day. Then I called Martha and told her something bad had happened, that Drew had drowned and Lewis had broken a leg. I asked her to call Lewis' wife and say he was in the hospital up here and would be for some time, but that he was going to be OK. If Mrs. Ballinger called on Lewis' wife they were just to say that we'd be back in a couple of days. I wanted to tell Mrs. Ballinger about Drew's death myself. I said I thought I'd be home about the middle of the week.

I drove Drew's car down to Biddiford's, a big frame house booming and knocking with people and light. Everybody was at supper around a long swaybacked pine table with strips of flypaper hanging down to within a foot of it. Bobby was there with his face working around a mouthful of food, and I winked at him and sat down. They made a place for us – farmers, woodsawyers and small merchants – and I lost interest in everything but eating. Fried chicken came around me – came at me from every angle – again and again, and potato salad, and heavy coarse biscuits and gravy and butter and collards and lima beans and big hominy and turnip greens and cherry pie. It was good; it was all good.

Afterwards a woman showed me upstairs to a room with a big double bed, which was all they had left; Bobby was somewhere else. But for some reason I was too dry; my mouth was dry, and my skin. So I went down and took a shower in the basement, in the blue-green country night, where I stood with the river-water pouring over my head, making my tight new bandage grow like a heavy side pack, making it bleed a little with the warm water. I nearly went to sleep there, but woke up as the water gradually turned cold. Then I went upstairs, my hair and side wet, and got in bed. It was over. I lay awake all night in brilliant sleep.

After

W HEN I woke up I was holding onto my side again, a tight, glowing package. I came awake fairly fast, because the midmorning sun, or so it looked and felt, was beginning to sting my eyelids. I was in a big country room with loud reddish curtains and a huge mirror on the wall opposite me, a little bathroom behind me, a dresser with all the knobs missing on one side, and a hooked rug on the floor under the bed and all around.

I lay and thought. I wanted to see Bobby first, and then Lewis. I got up, naked except for the bandage, which felt very much like clothes of some sort, and picked up what was left of my flying suit from the floor, clotted, armless and ragged. I sure didn't want to put it back on, but I did, and felt for some money. I had a couple of bills that appeared to have been made and issued by the river, but they were still money, and we needed it. I left the knife and belt in the room, and started to go after Bobby. There, in the mirror, I was the survivor of some kind of explosion, with a shirt-sleeve ripped off and a pants' leg blown open, bearded and red eyed, not able to speak. Out of this I smiled, very whitely, splitting the beard.

When I found out from the lady clearing away breakfast where Bobby was, I went up to his room and knocked on the door. He was still asleep, but it would be better to settle the new things I had been thinking about with him now than later. I kept knocking, and after a time he came.

I sat down in a rocking chair and he sat on the bed.

'First of all,' I said, 'I need some clothes. You probably ought to have some too, if we've got enough money. Your clothes are in better shape than mine, so you go out and get me some pants – blue jeans are all right – and a shirt. Get yourself whatever you need, and, if you've got anything left, buy me some shoes. Brogans.'

'OK. There ought to be a hardware store right around here. In this town, everything is right around here.'

'Now listen, one more time. We're all right so far; we're golden. Lewis is getting taken care of, and our stories – or maybe I should say our story – is going over. I didn't see a flicker of doubt in anybody's eye. Did you?'

'I don't think so, but I'm not as sure as you are. Did that one guy ask you about the canoes?'

'No. What guy? What about the canoes?'

'The little old guy who's some sort of local lawman. He asked me about the other canoe: where was it, when did we lose it, what was in it.'

'What did you tell him?'

'I told him what we agreed to tell him: that we lost it in that last bad place.'

'Did he say anything else?'

'No, I don't have any idea what he was getting at.'

'I do,' I said, 'at least I think I do, and it could be trouble; maybe not real trouble, but trouble.'

'Why, for the Lord's sake?'

'Because we lost the green canoe the day before yesterday and it, or part of it, might even have been found before we got to the place where we said we lost it.'

'Jesus!'

'We'll have to try to patch it up, then. It's likely that this little guy is going to get the word around to the state police that something doesn't jibe in our story, and then they'll be asking all of us questions. Remember your movies; police like to separate suspects and try to get them to contradict each other. So we've just got to sit here right now and become contradict-proof.'

'Can we do it?'

'We have to try. I think we can. Let's go back. We lost the other canoe when Drew was really killed, right?'

'Right. There's nobody who can argue with that. But if we take them up there, or if they go up there . . .'

'Now wait a minute. We'll say we spilled first a long ways upriver and that's where we lost the green canoe and Lewis was hurt. But we all survived and tried to make it downriver in Lewis' canoe. We were overloaded and taking chances trying to get Lewis out and just couldn't control the canoe when we hit the bad rapids. That last half-mile of falls got us, and Drew didn't make it. Now stay with that. Stay with it. If we do we'll make it home tomorrow night, or maybe even tonight.'

'Suppose they don't believe us? What am I going to say when that little rat-faced bastard faces me up to telling him where I said we lost the canoe?'

'Tell him – and anybody else around – that he misread you. Was there anybody else listening to you when he was talking to you yesterday?'

'No, I don't believe so.'

'That's good. And I don't think I let it slip to that first trooper. Anyway, it's more likely than not that he won't ask you, but will come around and ask me. When he does, I'll let him have it. I'm ready for him. I'm sure glad you told me about him. I sure am.'

'Is that all we have to change?'

'As far as I can tell,' I said.

'Again, Ed, what if they don't believe us? What if there's just enough doubt so that they go looking farther up?'

'Then, like I said, we may be in some trouble. But I don't think they will. Look, there are an awful lot of falls and rapids we came down day before yesterday. It could have happened anywhere up there. And the place where Drew was killed – and the part where we sunk that other guy – was right where the banks of the gorge are the highest and steepest. The only three ways to get there are upriver, which would make the whole search party have to fight rapids after rapids for hour after hour and probably day after day, searching the river in the rapids and between them foot by foot, and they're not going to want to take that on, just because one local guy disbelieves a survivor's story. An outboard wouldn't stand a chance in that stuff, and anything else'd be too heavy for the shallows. The other way is downstream, and if they came that way they'd have to run the same rapids we did, and you know what they're like. How'd you like to have to do that again? They'd be risking their lives, and it just wouldn't be worth it. Besides, how could they be doing that and searching too?'

'They could search in the calm places, and that's where Drew is.'

'Right; in *one* of them. But which one?'

'All right,' he said. 'I guess all right, anyway.'

'The only other way in is to come down the cliff. But they'd have to go down and come up it time after time, and they wouldn't do much of that, I can tell you. They might start out doing it, but they wouldn't keep on.'

'What if they went that far back and found the broken rope?'

'Chances are they wouldn't. The rope broke at the very top

and there's a lot of cliff. Anyway, there's not a damn thing we can do about it.'

'Is that all, now?'

'Yes; all but one thing. We didn't see anybody on the river. Not since we left Oree have we seen another human being. That's awfully important, and we can't vary from it.'

'I'm not going to vary from it, I can clue you. We haven't seen anybody. I wish we hadn't.'

'We didn't. The only other thing is whether somebody was reported missing in that area, and people knew more or less where the person was going. That bothers me a little, but not so much as some of the other problems. Those were awful-looking men; who'd care where they were?'

'Somebody might.'

'That's right. Somebody might. But whether the person would know where they went, or the area or direction they went in, we just can't have any idea. That one is beyond us. That's where we've got to ride on luck. And I feel lucky; the odds is good.'

Bobby laughed, and some of it was really laughter. 'Do you reckon this room is bugged? Or that someone could be listening?'

'It's not bugged,' I said. 'but that sure is a thoughty notion of yours, cousin.'

I slid off my tennis shoes and went to the door sock-footed, and listened. 'Keep talking,' I whispered back to Bobby. 'Keep talking, and give me time to listen, too.'

I listened; I listened for the nose-whistle of breath, and maybe it was there. But then you always can hear breath, anywhere, when you want to. I couldn't hear enough, though, for it really to be breath. Or at least I didn't think I could. I took hold of the knob and jerked the door inward. Nothing. Was there any sound going down the stairs? No. I was sure. No.

I turned back to Bobby and held up a circle of fingers.

'I'll be in my room,' I said. 'Go get us those clothes and then we'll hustle our asses over to the hospital. Lewis'll still be knocked out, I bet, and I doubt they'll pump him too hard anyway, but we better try and get the change in story across to him or see what he remembers of the first one.'

I went back to my room, shucked off the nylon and lay thinking again. I was looking forward to the encounter with the local sheriff, or whatever he was; I was looking forward to his local species of entrapment.

The sun came up more, and I pushed back the covers and lay in it. I was still tired, but the main tiredness had pulled back from me, and the bright light held it off me. It was very good, lying there wounded and stronger. Not so badly wounded now – the stitches were pulling me together – and a lot stronger. Yes indeed.

Bobby came back with the clothes, and I pulled on dry blue jeans, a work shirt, white socks and a pair of clod-hopping brogans that linked me to the earth with every step. But I was not that tired anymore, and I enjoyed lifting them just enough.

I wadded up the nylon in my hand, and we went downstairs together, both in farm clothes. It was exhilarating, now, to be so dry.

The woman who owned the place was dusting.

'Would you get rid of these for me?' I asked her, holding out the nylon outfit full of my blood.

She looked at me. 'Be glad to,' she said. 'Ain't but one thing to do with them.'

'I can't think of anything more to do with them,' I said, 'except to burn them.'

'That's what I mean,' she said. 'Can't use them for rags.'

She smiled; we smiled.

Bobby and I got into Drew's car and drove out to the hospital. There were two highway patrol cars there. 'Here we go,' I said. 'Hold on.'

We went in, and a fellow in white showed us to the ward where Lewis was. There were three highway patrol officers there, talking quietly among themselves with toothpicks in their mouths, and Lewis was lying either asleep or under sedation in a corner of the empty ward with a sheet medically levitated over his legs. The sandy-haired doctor was beside him, inclining his head and writing something again. He turned as he heard my heavy new steps.

'Hello, killer,' he said. 'How'd you sleep?'

'Good. Better than the riverbank.'

'Stitches holding?'

'You know it; holding me together, like you said. There ain't *nothing* getting in or out.'

'Good,' he said, in his way of going serious I liked.

Lewis came to us before I had a chance to say anything else. He moved a little, up from the waist; he came like a muscular act; the veins of his biceps jumped clear, clear as anatomy, and he opened eyes.

I turned to the patrolmen. 'Have you been talking to him?' I asked.

'No,' one of them said. 'We've been waiting for him to come around.'

'He's around, I expect,' I said. 'Or he will be soon. Give him a minute.'

He was looking straight at me. 'Hello, Tarzan,' I said. 'How's the world of the Great White Doctor?'

'White,' he said.

'What've they been trying to do to you?'

'You tell me,' he said. 'I've got a heavy leg, and there's some pain in there rambling around. But we got clean sheets, and there ain't that grating sound when I move. So I guess it's all right.'

I got in between Lewis and the nearest patrolman – got in close, almost head to head – and winked. He winked back, though anybody who didn't know it was a wink, wouldn't have. 'Just don't let's get on that last stretch of water again, buddy,' he said. 'Not today, anyway.'

He had given it to me without knowing it; I took it hoping that it had been loud enough.

'Everything went,' I said. 'Drew was killed; you remember me telling you?'

'I think so,' he said. 'I don't remember him in the canoe, after that. I don't remember.'

'You remember all that spray?' I asked.

'I remember, sort of,' he said. 'Was that where it was?'

'That's where it was for Drew,' I said slowly. 'You and Steinhauser's tub bought it in the first spill, *up*-river.'

'I couldn't see anything,' he said. 'Looking straight up, I couldn't even see the sky.'

'No sky,' I said.

'No sky at all.'

I rounded my hurt side, back to the patrolman. 'Wait'll you see it,' I said. 'You'll understand what the man's talking about.'

'Y'all want to wait, on down here a ways?' one of the policemen, a new one, said to us. We pulled back, down along the corridor. But Lewis had got the message; I was sure he had, and not too soon.

Bobby and I walked along in our new clothes. Neither of us had had a chance to shave, and we were pretty grubby, but clean. A shave would have made me a completely new person, but I was half-new anyway, and half-new was very good; it is better to come back easily.

After about fifteen minutes the new officer walked ordinarily along to us. 'Why'ont we go on back into town?' he said.

'All right,' I told him. 'Whatever you say.'

I got into the front seat of the patrol car with him, and we started back. I didn't say anything and he didn't either. When we reached town he went into a cafe and made a couple of calls. It frightened me some to watch him talk through the tripled glass – windshield, plate glass and phone booth glass – for it made me feel caught in the whole vast, inexorable web of modern communications. I was not sure that this was not the beginning of the enormous, unfathomable apparatus of crime detection, from which no one is entirely free: I could imagine stupendous filing systems, IBM machines tirelessly sorting punch cards, one thing being checked against another: I was not sure he was not talking to J. Edgar Hoover. Our story could not stand up against that, I was sure. And yet it might, even so.

The patrolman came back and sat with me, with his door open. In a little while two more patrol cars showed up. A small crowd started to drift together; a head turned toward us, and another: eventually, all heads looked at us at least once, and most of them more than once. I sat still, in my clothes of the country. I could prove where I had bought them. My hurt was good in the midst of the general unhurt.

One of the police from another car was talking to a local fellow about roads going up the river. A few minutes after this, we all got ready to start out. I looked for Bobby; he was in one of the new highway patrol cars. As we left, another police car, very local-looking, drove up and by, and I saw my man, an old fellow, rusty and quiet. There was going to be a meeting, somewhere up-river. My beard tingled at the roots, and I started to calculate, yet once again.

We turned off the highway and drove down a little road that swung through a farmer's yard and then through his chicken yard. A woman was feeding chickens, muffled up against the sun as though against cold.

We moved on, slower and slower. Nothing had happened yet; nothing had happened to any of us yet. There had been no accusations made, nothing discovered. My lies seemed better, more and more like truth; the bodies in the woods and in the river did not move.

We were the lead car. We took off through some glaring cornfields and then into poor-looking woods, second-growth pines like turpentine trees. I listened for the river, but saw it before I heard it. The road got worse and worse the nearer we got; it figured. At the river's edge we were crawling.

'This about where it was?' the cop asked me.

'No,' I said, waking from a half-sleep I didn't know I was in. 'It was farther up. We wouldn't have come down here all the way from Oree if we wanted to turn the canoe over in calm water.'

He looked at me oddly, or I suppose he did, for I was watching straight ahead for the yellow tree, and listening – one more time – for the falls; it seemed curious to be going toward them from this direction.

It was an hour of slow going, over gullies and washouts with just enough track for regular cars – if it had got any worse it would have been jeep or Land Rover country – before we saw the tree. I saw the color and then the lightning jag, and my heart jumped like a whole being, inside me and nearly out. The rapids were roaring, upstream about a quarter of a mile; I could see some of them now, and they were a lot worse, even, than I remembered.

220

The falloff was a good six feet, and the only place where a canoe could get through was a funnel of water into which the whole river cramped and shot, blizzarding through the stones and beating and fuming like some enormous force chained to the spot.

The policeman pointed. 'He'd be right in here?'

'I'd say so,' I said. 'He may be downstream farther, though. Or he may be caught in the rocks. But we probably ought to start here.'

We all got out and moved toward each other. I watched Bobby over the hoods and backs of cars. He was not moving among the men. They were wandering rather freely around him, and his stillness in the midst of them suggested that he was not able to move as freely as they, or at all. I don't think anyone noticed this but me, or put this interpretation on it, but it made me nervous; he already looked like a prisoner; for an instant I actually thought he was in leg shackles. I started toward him, but the police from the three cars always came between us, which must have been intentional, though they managed to give the impression it wasn't. Then Bobby moved like everybody else, toward the river.

Meanwhile other cars were creeping up to us, and pretty soon they filled up the bank all the way out of sight downriver. The men who got out of them were farmers, mostly, and small merchants, or so I supposed. Some of them brought long ropes with hooks – grapples – on them, and I understood the full horror of the phrase I was always seeing in the newspapers, especially in the summer: 'drag the river for the body.' Drag was right.

'This the place?' the patrolman asked me again.

'It's the best I can do,' I said. 'As far as I'm concerned, this is it.'

The men began to deploy with their ropes and hooks. The

221

stream was not deep at this point, about up to their waists or lower chests. The river ran through them easily. I watched the chains and ropes and wire cables come up from the water empty, in a certain rhythm. They always seemed to have grasped something when the hooks were underwater, and just to have let it go when they were pulled back up. I sat under a bush with the patrolman who had driven me out, watching each of the men in waders do what he was doing at the moment, and remembered the ring on Drew's finger and the dead guitar calluses on his hand as he fell from my arms.

Someone was coming, casually but deliberately. I turned to say something to the patrolman, so that I would seem unaware of the other person's approach.

'Say, buddy,' the new man said. 'Can I talk to you for a minute?'

'Sure,' I said. 'Sit down.'

He did. We shook hands. He was an old seam-faced light-bodied man with hazel eyes. He wore his hat at the prescribed country tilt, which always amused me wherever I saw it. I almost smiled, but instead took a cigarette he offered and lit up.

'You sure this is the place?'

I repeated, 'Not all *that* sure. But I can't do any better. He's either in those rocks up there, or here, or downstream. How far downstream I don't know.'

'You say you'us coming down this-yere river in a canoe?'

'Two canoes, we started with.'

'How come?'

'How come what?'

'How come you to be doing this, in the fust place?'

'Oh,' I said, hesitating and not really knowing the answer, even now. 'I guess we just wanted to get out a little. All of us work in the city, and it gets pretty tiresome, just sitting in

222

an office all the time. The fellow who broke his leg's been up here before, fishing. He said we ought to see it before they dam the river and make a public park out of it. That's all. No really good reason, I suppose. Just boredom.'

'I kin understand that,' he said after a little while. 'You didn't know what you'uz agettin' into, did you?'

'No indeed, we didn't,' I said. 'We sure didn't know it would be anything like this.'

He thought this over. 'You see these big old wide rocks yonder? How come you didn't get out and drag your canoe over 'em, 'stead of trying to come through that-there bad place? How come you to try to ride on through?'

'The river's running awful fast, up above here. These are just the very last of the rapids. We had too much speed by then. And this part didn't look as bad as it is; we couldn't see the drop-off until we were right on top of it and going too fast to do anything but go over it. And when it fell off, we fell out.'

'Then your buddy couldn't be back up yonder in them other rocks, now, could he?'

'No,' I said. 'That's why I suggested that y'all start looking for him right here. He wouldn't be in the upstream rocks, but he could be hung up under a rock someplace under the drop-off.'

'Wouldn't be much of him left, would there?'

'I guess not.'

'You say you started out day before yesterday?'

'We started Friday, at about four o'clock in the afternoon.'

'In two canoes.'

'Right.'

'And you lost one of them right here?'

'No, a long ways upstream. When we came through here, we were all in one canoe.'

This was the silence now. It went on for at least a minute. 'Your buddy says different.'

'I'll be damned if he does,' I said. 'Go ask him.'

'I already done asked him.'

'Ask him again, or the one in the hospital.'

'No; no. You done had a chance to talk to 'em.'

'Your hearing must not be any too good.'

'It's good enough. We ain't going to find no body right in here. We're going to find it farther up.'

'What the hell are you driving at?' I said, and the indignation was real; he was assaulting my story, which had cost me so much time and energy, and, yes, blood.

I leaned to the state policeman. 'Look, do I have to put up with this? I'll be goddamned if I will, I can tell you. Is he authorized to do this?'

'Maybe you better answer a few more questions. Then he can handle it however he wants to.'

'We found that other canoe – or half of it – before you say you even got down in this part of the river.'

'So what? I told you we lost the other one farther up. Back up in a gorge. If you want to try to go up in there, I can take you and show you where it was.'

'You know we can't get back up in there.'

'That's your problem. What the hell is all this about, anyway? We've been through a goddamned bad time, and I'm damned if I want to put up with this kind of shit. Listen: are you the sheriff here?'

'Depitty.'

'Is the sheriff around here?'

'He's right over yonder.'

'Well, go get him. I want to talk to him.'

He got up and went over to a beefy, Texas-y farmer with a

badge, and they came back together. I shook hands with the sheriff, whose name was Bullard.

'Sheriff, I don't know what this man has in mind, because he won't tell me. But from what I can gather he thinks we threw one of our party in the river, or something.'

'Maybe you did,' the old man said.

'For Christ's sake, for what reason?'

'How would I know that? I know you can't get your stories straight, and there ain't no good reason for you to be lyin'.'

'Easy, Mr. Queen,' the sheriff said. Then to me, 'What about this?'

'What do you *mean*, what about it? Look, if you can find one person, and I mean *one*, who'll back up what he says, I'll be perfectly happy to do anything you want me to do – go back up in the woods with you, wade up the river, join your crew out there dragging – anything you say. But this man is just confused. He's got some kind of personal stake in this, he doesn't like city people, he's trying to create interest in himself, God knows what. What's the matter, Mr. Queen? People feel like you're not earning your money?'

'I'll tell you what's the matter, you city son of a bitch,' Queen said, in that country-murderous tone that always bled me white. 'My sister called me yesterday and told me her husband had been out hunting and hadn't come back. They ain't nobody off in them woods up yonder. I'll just goddamned well guarantee y'all met up with him somewhere. And I'm on prove it.'

'Fine, prove it.'

'What's wrong with you, Mr. Queen?' the sheriff asked. 'Why jump on these fellows about something in your family? Just 'cause they're from the city? Maybe your brother-in-law fell down and got hurt.'

'No, he wudna.'

225

'Why are you so damned sure that anything happened to him?' I said.

'I just got a feeling,' Queen said. 'And I ain't ever wrong about that.'

'Well, you're wrong this time,' I said. 'Now stop bothering me. Go and do whatever you've got a mind to do. But get off my back. I've had it with this river, with the woods, with the whole fucking business up here and most especially with you. Unless you've got something to accuse us of, and have got some evidence to support what you're saying – whatever it is – you can goddamned well let me alone.'

He backed off, muttering, and I went over to the patrolman I had been sitting beside. Queen didn't have a thing on us, and he wouldn't get anything. I wondered if one of the two men we had killed had really been his brother-in-law, and I tried to think of a way to find out his name, but decided I had better let it go There was no real reason I needed to know his name, except for my own satisfaction, and I doubted that it would be much satisfaction, either way.

The men in the river were working downstream. Every now and then one of the hooks would snag a rock, and everybody would converge on it. I could see the light in their eyes change, some dreading, some anticipating, some happy. My blood quickened and my side hurt within its hurt when this happened, but it was always for nothing. All day, almost, the wound leapt and subsided, and in all that time the searchers made only about two hundred yards.

Sheriff Bullard came over. 'Looks like that's goin' to haf to wind it up tonight,' he said. 'Gettin' too dark.'

I nodded and got up.

'You boys be staying in Aintry this evenin'?'

'I guess so,' I said. 'We're still pretty tired and beatup. And I want to see how Lewis is doing, in the hospital. He has a bad break in his leg.'

'Is bad,' the sheriff said. 'Doctor said he's never seen a worst un.'

'We're at Biddiford's,' I said. 'But you know that.'

'Yeah, I know it. We'll be coming back out chere tomorrow morning. You can come if you want to, but you don't have to.'

'I don't see any reason for us to come,' I said. 'If the body's not right in here, I don't know where it is. Maybe farther downstream.'

'We're going to try upstream, a little.'

'No use,' I said. 'But do whatever you think's right. If you find any bodies up there, though, they won't be Drew's. This is where he went under, and if you find him it'll be downstream.'

'Maybe we'll split up, and some work up and some work down.'

'OK. Fine. But this is the place; I'd bet my life on it. I marked it with that big yellow tree, and I kept looking at it all the time we were trying to find him. He's downriver; there's not but one way he can go.'

'Right,' said the sheriff. 'Not but one way. We'll let you know if we find him, and I'll come by to see y'all sometime tomorrow afternoon. Much obliged to you, for your trouble.'

Bobby and I ate another big dinner, and went up to bed. There was no need to talk anymore; all the talking had been done. Now was the time for the finding or the not finding.

The next day we went out to see Lewis, who was much better. His leg was raised in pulleys, and he was reading the county paper, which had a story about Drew's disappearance, and an account of dragging the river for him, with a picture in which I could recognize myself and Deputy Queen. He had his fist up at my face, and I knew that the picture had been taken during the last part of the time we had been talking. I looked like I was being tolerant, just barely listening out of courtesy. Everything helped; this too.

There were no policemen with Lewis, but he was not alone in the ward anymore, for the night before they had brought in a farmer whose foot had been run over by a tractor. He was at the other end, and asleep. I told Lewis what had happened, and told him that Bobby would drive his car back down to the city and his wife or somebody could come after him whenever he was ready to move. That was all right with him.

Bobby and I walked over to say good-bye to Lewis. He was eased back in the pillows.

'I ought to be out of here in a week or two, myself,' he said.

'Sure,' I said. 'Lie back and enjoy yourself. This is not such a bad town.'

Bobby and I drove back to Biddiford's to wait for the sheriff.

He came at five-thirty, and evil little Queen was with him. The sheriff took out a piece of paper. 'You can use this for a statement,' he said. 'See if it says what you told us.'

I read it through. 'It's all right,' I said. 'But I don't know these place names. Is this the right name of the rapids where I said we capsized?'

'Yeah,' he said. 'That's the name: Griffin's Shoot.'

'OK,' I said, and signed it.

'You're sure, now,' Sheriff Bullard asked.

'You better believe I'm sure.'

'He ain't sure,' Deputy Queen said, a lot louder than any of us. 'He's lyin'. He's lyin' thu his teeth. He's done somethin', up yonder. He's done kilt my brother-in-law.'

228

'Listen, you little bastard,' I said, and my voice was really quivering. 'Maybe your brother-in-law killed somebody. Why are you bringing in all this talk of killing? The river did all the killing we saw. If you don't think it'll kill you, get your stupid ass on it and see for yourself.'

'Now, Mr. Gentry,' the sheriff said. 'Don't talk like that. Ain't no call for it.'

'Well, this'll do till there is,' I said.

'He's lyin', Sheriff; don't let him go. Don't let the son of a bitch go.'

'We got nothing to hold him for, Arthel,' the sheriff said. 'Nothing. These boys've been through a lot. They want to get back home.'

'Don't let him go, I'm telling you. Listen, my sister called up last night, and she was just a-crying. Benson ain't come home yet. She knows he's dead. She just knows it. He ain't never been gone this long before. And these fellers was the only ones up in there, when he was.'

'Now, you don't know that, Arthel,' the sheriff said. 'What you mean is, they was the only city fellows.'

I shook my head as though I couldn't believe such stupidity, which was the case, sure enough.

'Y'all can go any time you want to,' the sheriff said. 'Just leave me your addresses.'

I did and said, 'OK. Let us know if you find anything.'

'Don't worry. You'll be the fust.'

I slept again, as in a place beyond all sleep, around on the other side of death, and came back, floating, when I thought I heard the ringing of the owl on the other birds, in Martha's wind-toy at home. It was early, and we were free. I dressed and went to Bobby's room and woke him. The woman who owned the place

229

was up, and we paid her with the last of our money and drove to the filling station to get Lewis' car. The sheriff was sitting there talking to the owner. We got out.

'Morning,' he said. 'Y'all getting an early start, eh?'

'Thought we would,' I said. 'What can we do for you?'

'Not a thing,' he said. 'Just wanted to make sure you had your keys, and everything you need.'

'We can make it fine,' I said. 'There is one thing, Sheriff, though. We owe some fellows up in Oree for bringing these cars down to us. Would you tell them that we'll send them the money, just as quick as we get back to the city? They'll believe you before they will us, because you live up here; they know who you are.'

'Be glad to,' he said. 'What're their names?'

'Griner. They run a garage up there.'

'I'll get word to 'em. Don't worry about it. And you say they're the last people you saw, before you got down here?'

'The last and only. There was also another man with them. I don't know who he was.'

'Maybe we ought to know who he was. I might even go up there and talk to all of 'em myself. And you kin be sure I'll tell 'em about the money.'

'OK. We're going along now.'

'Take it easy going home,' he said. 'And, buddy, let me tell you one thing. Don't ever do anything like this again. Don't come back up here.'

'You don't have to worry about that,' I said. I grinned, and slowly, so did he. 'Is this your way of telling me to get out of town and not show my face in these-here parts again?'

'You might say that,' he said.

'Aw, now, Sheriff, you know we ain't no hired guns,' I said, like Texas. 'We're all bow-and-arrow men.'

'You listen to me, now, boy.'

'You ought to be in the movies, Sheriff. Or go live in Montana. You could probably find worse bad men than me in either one.'

'I might do that,' he said. 'Not much action here, I can tell you. A few people stealing chickens, and a little moonshining. Not much action.'

'Not till we came.'

'Yeah; we don't want no more of that. Dragging that river's tough.'

'Neither do we; you won't see us again.'

'OK. So long. Have a good trip.'

'So long. And I hope Deputy Queen finds his brother-in-law.'

'Aw, he'll come in drunk. He's a mean bastard anyway. Old Queen's sister'd be better off without him. So would everybody else.'

I started to get in Drew's car.

' 'Fore you go, buddy, let me ask you something and tell you something.'

'Ask me.'

'How come you-all ended up with four life jackets?'

'We had an extra one. In fact we had two. You're liable to find another one downriver. They float, you know. Now what was it you wanted to tell me?'

'You done good.'

'Somebody had to do something,' I said. 'I didn't want to die, either.'

'You'us hurt bad, but if it wudn't for you you'd all be in the river with your other man.'

'Thanks, Sheriff. I'll take that with me.'

'You damned fucking ape,' he said. 'Who on earth was your father, boy?'

231

'Tarzan,' I said.

Bobby settled into Lewis' wagon, and I got a map from the rack at the station and buckled down in the other car.

'Let's go get the canoe,' I hollered over.

'Jesus, no,' he said. 'Leave it. I never want to see it or touch it or smell it again. Leave the goddamned thing.'

'No,' I said. 'We're going to get it. Follow me. It'll just take a minute.'

Some kids were playing in the canoe. And I thought this was a good sign, indicating that Deputy Queen wasn't around. Also, they might have washed out Lewis' vomit, or some of it, anyway. I got the kids out and took a long look at the hull. It was really battered and beat-up, not only along the bottom but on the sides clear up to the gunwales in some places; I felt the rock shocks all over again, just looking at them. There were a couple of holes – small holes – close together in the middle, but it could have stood some more, though maybe not a whole lot.

Before we began to struggle with the boat, I chanced to look up across the river, and there were some men moving among the trees. There was a little cemetery there, so well hidden among the trees and bushes that I would not have seen it at all except for the human forms moving there.

I asked one of the children what was happening. 'Is it a funeral?'

'Naw,' one muddy little girl said. 'They're gonna move them people 'fore they finish the dam. They're diggin' 'em up.'

I had known that it was no funeral; there was too much movement. But I wasn't quite prepared for this. I looked closer, and there were some green coffins stacked together, and a couple of the men were disappearing below the ground and coming back up together, heaving at something.

'Like TVA, I guess,' I said to Bobby.

'I guess,' he said. 'Come on, for God's sake. Let's leave this place.'

We wrestled the canoe through the kudzu and strapped it to the roof of the wagon.

'Go ahead, Bobby,' I said. 'You know where Lewis lives. Tell Mrs. Medlock what happened, and remember to tell it like it was. She'll take care of you. And call Martha when you get in and tell her I'll be right along.'

'I'll remember what to say,' he said. 'How could I forget?'

I went back down to the spillway and stood next to the water for the last time. I stooped and drank from the river.

Going back was easy and pleasant, though I was driving a dead man's car, and everything in it reminded me of him: the good shape the engine was in, the neatness of it, the little decal of the company he worked for on the windshield. The thing to do was to get outside the car into the landscape, and to watch my own world develop from it as I went toward the city. After four hours I passed slowly from the Country of Nine-Fingered People and Prepare to Meet Thy God into the Drive-ins and Motels and Homes of the Whopper, but all I could see was the river. It came at me between rocks – and here the car would involuntarily speed up – it came at me in slow loops and green stillnesses, with trees and cliffs and lifesaving bridges.

And I could not leave off worrying about the details of the story we had told, and what the ramifications of any one of them might be. I was sure about Lewis, as sure of him as I was of myself, but who could be *that* sure of either, of any man? But I was not sure of Bobby. He drank an awful lot, and a person will say, a lot of times, exactly the most perverse and self-incriminating thing he can think of when he is drunk enough, and when he is like Bobby. But what would keep his mouth shut about the truth was himself kneeling over the log with a shotgun at his head, howling and bawling and kicking his feet like a little boy. He wouldn't want anybody to know that, no matter what; no matter how drunk he was. No, he would stay with my version of things.

The version was strong; I had made it and tried it out against the world, and it had held. It had become so strong in my mind that I had trouble getting back through it to the truth. But when I did, the truth was there: the moon shone and pressed down the wild river, the cliff was against my heart, beating back at it with the pulse of stone, and a pine needle went subtly into my ear as I waited in a tree for the light to come.

I was on the final four-lane now; I had eaten in almost every drive-in along here. I had shopped in about half the stores in the shopping center where I was now turning off, and Martha had shopped in them all. I went up the long residential hill, away from the moan of the great trucks and Amoco rigs. I turned off again, and went curving easily home.

It was about two o'clock. I drove into the yard and knocked on the back door. They were going to save me, here. Martha opened the door. We stood for a while feeling each other closely and then went in. I took off my brogans and stood them in the corner and walked around on the wall-to-wall carpeting. I went out to the car and took the knife and belt and slung them off deep into the suburban woods.

'I could use a drink, sugar,' I said.

'Tell me,' she said, looking at my side. 'Tell me. What happened to you? I knew something like this would happen.'

'No you didn't,' I said. 'Not anything like this.'

'Come lie down, baby,' she said. 'Let me have a look.'

I went with her to the bedroom, where she put an old rag-sheet on the bed, and I lay down on it. She pulled off my shirt and looked, with pure, practical love, and then she stepped to the bathroom for three or four bottles. The whole medicine cabinet looked like a small hospital itself, packed into the wall. She came back shaking bottles.

'Give me that drink, love,' I said. 'Then we can get into all this playing doctor.'

'All doctors play doctor,' she said. 'And all nurses play nurse. And all ex-nurses play nurse, especially when they love somebody.'

She brought me the bottle of Wild Turkey, and I turned it up and drank. Then she started soaking through the bandage with some household mystery from the bathroom. It came off me shred by shred, and the inside was bloody indeed. The stitches were slimy with blood and some other bodily matter; whatever I had at that place.

'You're all right,' she said. 'It's a good job. The edges are pulling together.'

'Good news,' I said. 'Can you fix it up again?'

'I can fix it,' she said. 'But what happened to you? These are cut wounds, clean edges, most of them. Did somebody get you with a knife? An awful sharp one?'

'I did,' I said. 'It was me.'

'What kind of an accident . . . ?'

'No accident,' I said . . . 'Look, let me go to see Drew's wife. Then I'm coming back and sleep for a week. Right with you. Right with you.'

She was professional and tender, and tough, what I would have hoped for; what I knew I could have expected; what I had undervalued. She put antibiotic salve all over the place and then several layers of gauze, and then tape, expertly, letting the air come through. When I got up, the wound was not so stiff, and my side had begun to be a part of me again; though it still hurt, and hurt badly, it was not pulling against me at every move.

'Will you follow me over and drive me back?'

She nodded.

At Drew's house his horned little boy in a cub scout uniform opened the door. I went in with the car keys in my hand while Pope went to get Mrs. Ballinger. I stood there, surrounded by Drew's things, the walls full of tape recorders and record cabinets, the sales awards and company citations. The keys in my hand were jangling.

'Mrs. Ballinger,' I said, as she came at me, 'Drew has been killed.' It was as though I had said it to stop her, to keep her from getting at me.

It stopped her. One hand came up slowly, almost dreamingly, from her side and went to her mouth, and the other came over it, to hold it down. Behind her fingers her head shook in a small, intense movement of disbelief.

'He was drowned,' I said. 'Lewis broke his leg. Bobby and I were just lucky. We could have all been killed.'

She held her mouth. The keys jangled and rang.

'I brought the car back.'

'So useless,' she said, her voice filled with fingers. 'So useless.'

'Yes, it was useless,' I said. 'We shouldn't have gone. But we did. We did.'

'Such a goddamned useless way to die.'

'I guess every way is useless,' I said.

'Not this useless.'

'We stayed as long as they needed us up there, looking for the body. They're still looking. I don't think they'll find it, but they're looking.'

'Useless.'

'Drew was the best man we had,' I said. 'I'm so sorry. I'm so goddamned sorry. Is there anything I can do? I mean that. Can I . . .'

'You can get out of here, Mr Gentry. You can get out of here and go find that insane friend of yours, Lewis Medlock, and you can shoot him. That's what you can do.'

'He's pretty badly hurt, himself. And he's just as sorry as I am. Please understand that. It's not his fault. It's the river's fault. It's our fault for going with him.'

'All right,' she said from far off, from the future, from all the years coming up, and from the first night alone in bed. 'All right, Ed. Nobody can do anything. Nobody can ever do anything. It's all so useless. Everything is useless. It always has been.'

I saw she was becoming speechless, but I tried one more thing.

'Can I have Martha come over and stay with you for a couple of days?'

'I don't want Martha. I want Drew.'

She broke, and I started toward her, but she shook her head violently and I backed off, turned, put the keys on the coffee table beside the company history, and went out.

As we drove home I wondered if it would have been any better if I'd been able to tell the truth. Would it be easier for her if I could tell her that Drew was lying in a wild stretch of the Cahulawassee with part of his head bashed in either by a bullet or a rock, sunk down with a stone and a bowstring, eddying a little back and forth, side to side with the motion of the water? I did not see how knowing that would help. The only possibility was that it might spark in her the animal mania for revenge, if he truly had been shot, and nothing more could be done about that than had already been done: no electric chair, no rope or gas chamber could avenge him better, or as well.

Back at home I put an easy chair in front of the picture window and got a blanket and a pillow and sat looking out onto the street with the phone beside me all afternoon. I was shaking. Martha sat on the floor and put her head in my lap and held my hand, and then went and got a bottle of whiskey and a couple of glasses.

'Baby,' she said. 'Tell me what it is. Is somebody after you?'

'I don't know,' I said. 'I don't think so. But I'm not sure. Somebody may be after me. Also, the law may be after me. I've just got to tough it out. If nothing happens for a couple of weeks, I think we'll be all right.'

'Can't you tell me?'

'No, I can't tell you now. Maybe I can't ever tell you.'

'Who cut you, Ed? Who cut my good man?'

'I did it,' I said. 'I fell on one of my arrows, and I had to cut it out with a knife. There was not any other way; I couldn't get us downriver with an arrow sticking through me. So I cut. I'm glad the knife was sharp, or I'd probably still be hacking.'

'Go to sleep, honey. I'll let you know if anything happens. I'm right here with you. There's no more woods and no more river. Go to sleep.'

But I couldn't. We live on a dead-end street, so that any car that comes down it either belongs to the people who live on the street or has some business with them. I watched the few cars I recognized come in, and turn into the various driveways. About ten o'clock one stopped in front of our house. The lights swung slowly around and enveloped us, and Martha closed my mouth with a warm hand as I sat there blinded. Ours was the last driveway, and the driver was just using it to turn around in. He went away, and finally so did I.

* * *

I woke up and Martha was still with me. It was light. The

238

crooked part in her hair was very precious. She was asleep, and gently as I could I got up from under her, put her head in the chair, picked up a glass and the whiskey and went into the bathroom. I turned around and Martha was standing there too. She kissed me, and then sat on the toilet seat and pulled the bandage-tape off my side with quick, surgical rips.

'Better,' she said. 'It's going to be fine. Jesus, you're healthy.'

'I don't feel so healthy, I can tell you. I'm still tired.'

'Well, you rest up.'

'No, I'm going to the office.'

'No you're not; that's the damned silliest idea I ever heard. You're going to bed.'

'Really, I want to go down there. I want to and I need to. For lots of reasons.'

'All right, dum-dum. Go ahead and kill yourself.'

'Not a chance,' I said. 'But if I don't keep busy I'll fall apart. I can't stand any more of this car-watching.'

She re-dressed my side and I went downtown. The main thing was to get back into my life as quickly and as deeply as I could; as if I had never left it. I walked into my office and opened the door wide so that anybody who wanted to look could see me there, shuffling papers and layouts.

At lunch I went out and bought a paper. There was a notice of Drew's death, and an old picture of him from his college annual. That was all. I worked hard the rest of the day, and when I drove the freeway home it was like a miracle of movement and of freedom.

And so it ended, except in my mind, which changed the events more deeply into what they were, into what they meant to me alone. There is still a special small fear in any strange automobile headlights near the house, or any phone call with an unfamiliar voice in it, either at the office or at home, or when Martha calls me at the office. For a long time I went through both daily papers from column to column every day, but only once did the word Cahulawassee come off the page at me, and that was when the dam at Aintry was completed. The governor dedicated it, there was a ceremony with college and high school bands, and the governor was said to have made a very good speech about the benefits, mainly electrical and industrial, that the dam would bring to the area, and touching on the recreational facilities that would be available when the lake filled in. Every night as the water rose higher I slept better, feeling the green, darkening color crawl up the cliff, up the sides of rock, feeling for the handholds I had had, dragging itself up, until finally I slept as deeply as Drew was sleeping. Only a few days after I saw the story in the paper I knew that the grave of the man we had buried in the woods was under water, and from the beginning of the inundation Drew and the other man were going deeper and deeper, piling fathoms and hundreds of tons of pressure and darkness on themselves, falling farther and farther out of sight, farther and farther from any influence on the living.

Another odd thing happened. The river and everything I remembered about it became a possession to me, a personal, private possession, as nothing else in my life ever had. Now it ran nowhere but in my head, but there it ran as though immortally. I could feel it – I can feel it – on different places on my body. It pleases me in some curious way that the river does not exist, and that I have it. In me it still is, and will be until I die, green, rocky, deep, fast, slow, and beautiful beyond reality. I had a friend there who in a way had died for me, and my enemy was there.

The river underlies, in one way or another, everything I do. It is always finding a way to serve me, from my archery to some of my recent ads and to the new collages I have been attempting for my friends. George Holley, my old Braque enthusiast, bought one from me when I hired him back, and it hangs in his cubicle, full of sinuous forms threading among the headlines of war and student strikes. George has become my best friend, next to Lewis, and we do a lot of serious talking about art; more than we should, with the work load the studio has been accumulating.

I saw Bobby only once or twice in the city, just nodding to each other in public places. I couldn't tell from looking at him how he was, but he had returned to the affable, faintly nasty manner he had always had, and I was as glad as not to leave him alone; he would always look like dead weight and like screaming, and that was no good to me. I later heard that he quit the company he was working for and tried to go into business with a partner running a Chicken-in-a-Basket drive-in and carry-out near a local engineering college, but it failed after a year and he moved to another city, and then, I heard, to Hawaii.

Thad and I are getting along much better than before. The studio is still boring, but not as boring as it was. Dean is growing up well, though he is a strangely silent boy. He looks at me sometimes from the sides of his eyes, and seems about to speak in a way he has not spoken before. But that is probably only my imagination; he has never said anything except the things any boy would say to his father. Otherwise he is sturdy and uncomplicated, and beginning to be handsome. Lewis is something of an idol to him; he is lifting weights already.

Because of the associations she had for me, I looked up the girl in the Kitt'n Britches ad and took her out to dinner a couple of times. I still loved the way she looked, but her gold-halved eye had lost its fascination. Its place was in the night river, in the land of impossibility. That's where its magic was for me. I left it there, though I would have liked to see her hold her breast once more, in a small space full of men. I see her every now and then, and the studio uses her. She is a pleasant part of the world, but minor. She is imaginary.

Martha is not. In summer we sit by a lake where we have an A-frame cottage – it is not Lake Cahula, it is over on the other side of the state, but it is also a dammed lake – and look out over the water, maybe drinking a beer in the evening. There is a marina on the other side; we sit and watch the boats go out, and the water skiers leap from the earthside to their long, endless feathery step on the green topsoil of water. Lewis limps over from his cabin now and then and we look at each other with intelligence, feeling the true weight and purpose of all water. He has changed, too, but not in obvious ways. He can die now; he knows that dying is better than immortality. He is a human being, and a good one. Sometimes he refers to me as 'U.C.,' which means – to him and me – 'Unorganized Crime,' and this has become a kind of minor conversation piece at parties, and at lunch in the city with strangers.

Sometimes, too, we shoot archery at the lake, where Lewis has put a bale and a field target in a beautiful downhill shot, about fifty-five yards, between trees. We shoot dozens of aluminum arrows, but I have never put another broadhead in the bow. My side wouldn't allow it; I can feel it cry out at the idea. Besides, there is no need to; the bow I use now is too light for hunting.

Lewis is still a good shot, and it is still a pleasure to watch him. 'I think my release is passing over into Zen,' he said once. 'Those gooks are right. You shouldn't fight it. Better to cooperate with it. Then it'll take you there; take the arrow there.'

Though Lake Cahula hasn't built up like the one we're on, there are indications that people are getting interested in it, as they always do any time a new, nice place opens up in what the real estate people call an unspoiled location. I expect there are still a few deer around Lake Cahula – deer that used to spend most of their time on the high ground at the top of the gorge – but in a few years they will be gone, and perhaps only the unkillable tribe of rabbits will be left. One big marina is already built on the south end of the lake, and my wife's younger brother says that the area is beginning to catch on, especially with the new generation, the one just getting out of high school.

A NOTE ON THE AUTHOR

James Dickey, born in Atlanta, Georgia, in 1923, published his first book of poetry called *Into the Stone* in 1960. In 1966 his *Buckdancer's Choice* won the National Book Award. His first novel, *Deliverance*, was published in 1970. Dickey's magnificent poetry, criticism and fiction rank him among the seminal authors of our time.